Frederic Raphael was born in Chicago in 1931. He was educated at Charterhouse and St John's College, Cambridge, where he was a Major Scholar in Classics. He has written eighteen novels, two biographies (Somerset Maugham and Byron), three volumes of short stories and a number of screenplays, including *Darling,* for which he won an Oscar. For his sequence of television plays, *The Glittering Prizes* he won the Royal Television Society Writer of the Year Award. His series *After the War* was screened to worldwide acclaim in 1989. His other works include translations, notably of Aeschylus and Catullus (with Kenneth McLeish), essays and radio plays. He is a regular contributor to the *Sunday Times* literary and travel pages and is a Fellow of the Royal Society of Literature. Married with three children, Frederic Raphael divides his time between France and England.

The Latin Lover
and other stories

FREDERIC RAPHAEL

PHŒNIX

A PHOENIX PAPERBACK

First published in Great Britain by Orion in 1994
This paperback edition published in 1995 by Phoenix,
a division of Orion Books Ltd,
Orion House, 5 Upper St Martin's Lane, London WC2H 9EA

A CIP catalogue record for this book is available
from the British Library.

ISBN: 1 85799 064 1

Printed and bound in Great Britain by
The Guernsey Press Co. Ltd,
Guernsey, C.I.

For Paul, Sarah and Stephen

Contents

A Fairly Regular Four   1

The Wife of My Friend   11

The Beverly Hills Snowman   21

Jimmy   33

These Things Happen   40

Melanie   50

Eugene   58

Kill or Cure   68

Victor   79

Concerto Grossman   86

When in Rome   95

Merce   105

Costa Christmas   118

In the Other Room   125

We are Members of the Guardia Civil   135

Stolen Property   146

An Old, Old Story   155

The Latin Lover   162

Acknowledgements

A Fairly Regular Four BBC Radio 4 – 26 November 1990. *Best Short Stories 1991*, William Heinemann.

An Old, Old Story London Daily News – 16 March 1987

Kill or Cure Femail

Costa Christmas Sunday Express Magazine, December 1989

The Beverly Hills Snowman Sunday Express Magazine, December 1990

The Wife of My Friend BBC Radio 3 FM – January 1993

In the Other Room BBC Radio 3 FM – January 1993

Stolen Property BBC Radio 3 FM – January 1993

These Things Happen BBC Radio 3 FM – January 1993

When in Rome (as The Latin Lover) BBC Radio 3 FM – January 1993

Concerto Grossman Commissioned by BBC *Music Magazine* and BBC Radio 3 FM and subsequently anthologized in *Best Short Stories 1994*

Jimmy BBC Radio 4 – March 1994 *Regent* magazine, Hong Kong

Eugene BBC Radio 4 – March 1994

Merce (as Bel Air) BBC Radio 4 – March 1994 *Regent* magazine, Hong Kong

Melanie BBC Radio 4 – March 1994

Victor BBC Radio 4 – March 1994

A fairly regular four

It began, like modern history, in the mid-1960s. At first I used only to observe them enviously. Ronnie Trafford and his friends would take over the covered court after I had finished my lesson with old Ralph Prentis. Ralph had been a Davis Cup player, once, for England. He had been given the elbow immediately after his doubles match against France. By the time he accepted me as a pupil, he was bent at the waist like some antique butler, warped by deference. In fact, he called you 'sir' in a tone that promised no further courtesies. He belonged to a school of coaches who did not believe in tempering the wind, especially when the client was no lamb. As his long white trousers indicated, Ralph was a traditionalist. He would have deplored the short back-lift and the top-spin loops of the modern game. The racket, he insisted, should describe a capital D, up and around and through, in order to effect the classical forehand drive.

I did my best to honour his calligraphic instructions. Often, however, I had hardly sharpened my pencil, as it were, before his sliced forehand, with no noticeable back-lift, was thumping against the green skirting at the back of the brick barn, just off the Harrow Road, where I received weekly instruction. He would then murmur 'Pity!' and propose that I advance to the net.

As he gathered the statutory six balls in his left hand (clutching them against the yellowing cable-stitch of his England sweater), Ralph reminded me that the volley was the simplest of shots. 'You are a carpenter,' he declared, 'tapping in a nail.' He clearly had small knowledge of my joinery and the purple thumbs that resulted from it.

1

Simplicity, in my experience, is rarely an easy business. If my net-work proved at all satisfactory, Ralph had a trick to trump my vanity: he could procure a net-cord apparently at will. The ball would then strike the tape and leap over my outstretched weapon. 'Pity!'

How then did I ever become a member of Ronnie Trafford's 'syndicate' (as Jolyon Walters, our Lloyd's man, termed it)? Well, I make up in determination for what I lack in natural aptitude. I may not have much of an eye, but I do have two enthusiastic feet. I will, as the sporting journalists have been known to say, run all day. My service can, on occasion, be so inspired that I begin to wonder whether I shall ever again lose a service game. A nemesis of double-faults usually follows, but my moments are still my moments, and I do have them. There are times when I can appear quite useful, especially to three players without a fourth.

The covered court where Ralph wielded his mild sceptre had a spectator's gallery along one side, under the glassed skylight. At the end of my hour, Ronnie Trafford would appear, double-sweatered like a fast bowler in the deep-field, and watch as the clock jerked towards the end of my lease. He did not like to miss a minute, and he particularly disliked being kept waiting by the others. A defaulter was mercilessly treated. One day, as Ralph allowed one of my smashes to prove too good for him, Ronnie called down that he had a problem. 'Franco della Robbia's mother appears to be ill. We're one short, Ralph. Would you make us up?'

Ralph was rolling several dozen balls towards the corner where his plastic bucket awaited them. 'Short notice,' he said.

'He's let us down at the last second. Come on, Ralph. You can relive past glories.'

'I doubt it,' Ralph said. 'What about Mr Raphael?'

'He's tired,' Ronnie said, with brutal consideration.

'He's young,' Ralph said.

Ronnie Trafford looked at me as if he doubted it. I doubted it myself. 'I've got work to do,' I said.

'I say,' Ronnie said, 'I haven't seen you on the television, have I?'

In those days, I had abundant, longish hair and sometimes displayed it on the box, while I said the sort of thing about other people's films that I hated hearing said about mine. It was already clear twenty years ago that if you wanted to be recognised in the street, it was better to be the TV weatherman than a Nobel prizewinner. *'Et in Arcadia ego,'* I said.

'Come on, Ralph,' Ronnie said, 'be a sport.'

'My wife wouldn't like it.'

'She need never know.' Ronnie winked at me as I began my slow walk to the showers.

'Doctor's orders.'

'Your wife's a doctor? I never knew that.'

Ronnie was coming down the spiral staircase from the gallery as I went into the changing room. He came after me and held out his hand. 'Ronald Trafford. You wouldn't care to make us up, I suppose?'

A flush of excitement rushed blood around my body and rendered my affectations of apathy somewhat breathless. I was, God help me, thrilled. 'I don't mind,' I said.

'Just a friendly four,' Ronnie said.

Friendliness was not, in the event, its only characteristic. Once the 'morning, morning' formalities were concluded, daggers were regularly drawn. A tense ritual of elimination established who should partner whom. If there were two roughs and two smooths at the first twist, that settled it. If not, the three smoothies (or ruffians) spun again, until an odd man emerged to join the waiting fourth. Sometimes, however, if there was a particularly competent guest appearance, Ronnie would pre-empt him. Even in those comparatively modest days, he was the manifest boss. It was he who had secured access to the court, which was privately owned, and it was his secretary (he had only one

3

at that time) who circulated the syndicate for their availability and informed them, in due course, who had been chosen, and who merely called, for the following month's games.

Anyone who had been late or whose form had been responsible, as his partner, for Ronnie's humiliation was liable to find himself ruled out of court.

Trafford was a handsome and affable man. He had begun in modest circumstances, but he was going to change all that. The Jag was already in the driveway and the driveway was in Ealing. So was the estate agency founded by his late father. It had been a small local firm when Ronnie returned from decorated service in the King's Own Scottish Borderers. His energy and contacts soon enlarged it. Ronnie knew his way around; the officers' mess had been his university and the M.C. was his passport. He did not make crude use of his well-placed friends, but he found them useful. Women liked him and he married one with a fair face and a fair amount of scratch. He worked hard and he played hard. Business was business and, thanks to his imaginative accountant, pleasure could often be business too.

Ronnie knew the angles. He had been an officer and had every intention of becoming a gentleman. Good form was important to him. He frowned at Milstein's terrible socks and his failure to change them after a game. Ronnie carried his business suit into the changing room in a plastic sac. His toiletries were arranged on the glass shelf in the ablutions.

If he had a fault, it was that he very much liked to win. Who am I to talk? I must confess, before others accuse me, that I can get quite sulky over tiddlywinks. I curse my luck at French cricket. At tennis, I have been known not merely to fling my racket about but even to toss it over the netting into the shrubbery. A lost ball is one thing but a lost racket is a rarity. Ronnie showed no such embarrassing signs of temperament, but he did sometimes take an eccentric view of where the baseline was. When Oliver Randall and I were deemed to have lost the last point after my partner's smash had clearly whitened the tape at the far end, only to be called 'Unlucky' by a triumphant Ronnie, I shook hands with the rueful elation of one who had, I dared to think, acquitted himself pretty damned well at the higher level. 'Thanks for the game,' I said.

'Are you regularly free of a Tuesday morning?' Ronnie asked, as he gathered his many monogrammed rackets. 'Because we're sometimes short a man.'

'My typewriter calls,' I said, 'but if you ever really need someone . . .'

'My secretary, the invaluable Jane, will be in touch.'

To my flattered surprise, I did indeed receive a roneoed form on which to tick my availability in the coming month. In due course, I was even more flattered to have been selected for two Tuesdays out of four. Oliver, a City journalist, had to go to Washington for a meeting of important scoundrels. Ronnie himself, of course, played every week. Milstein was an infrequent regular who had a way of turning up only just on time. Ronnie looked at him balefully as Louis XIV at a courtier who arrived as the clock was chiming the hour of their appointment. ('J'ai failli attendre,' the king remarked, of which a lame translation might be, 'I have been all but kept waiting.')

As the years swung by I became more and more of a fixture. A film star, who was courting Ronnie's pretty daugher, joined us briefly before departing to shoot it out in series work in the US; an Etonian leader writer, who didn't like my language, gave us a brief demonstration of elegance; a man from the Argentine Embassy was rather too good for us, especially when approached as a partner by Ronnie. 6–0, 6–0, 6–0 is not all that much fun. On the whole, Jolyon and Oliver and Ronnie and I constituted the old guard and had the most conspicuous battle honours.

Ronnie grew prosperous. Her son married well and the lovely Flora even better. He himself moved from Ealing to Chiswick and then to Chiswick Mall, the location of locations. He opened a West End office and then another in Cannes. Having spotted Spain as a growth area ('The California of Europe,' he promised us), he was one of the first to see the potential of the Costa del Sol. The hideous consequences of his foresight remind us why it was not long before the old Jag became the new Roller. A capped chauffeur paraded the sac with the Huntsman suits into the changing rooms.

The Abacus Road quartet celebrated one anniversary after another. Waistlines thickened; hairlines receded; teeth lengthened. But the game went on. Did friendships ripen? Hardly; we saw each other only on court. In the changing room or under the scalding shower, we discussed politics and public scandal, rarely personal matters. Once, I recall, Jolyon's naked back was seen to be covered with a scrawl of red lacerations. Ronnie and I looked at each other and were simultaneously aware that Joylon must be engaged in a passionate romance. Exclusion made a strange, perhaps spurious bond between us. Jolyon dried himself, oblivious of our reticence, and wished us good day without seeming to know that he had given us a glimpse of something his mild manner and rather dry humour had never remotely suggested. Shortly afterwards, he told us that he had got married. We wished him luck, but were not surprised not to have been invited. Tennis was tennis; life was life.

By the early 1970s, Ronnie had the country house (Wilts) and the summer spread on Cap d'Antibes. He took the family to Gstaad immediately after Christmas and they sailed out of Bodrum in the summer. During these brief absences, the syndicate learned what *Hamlet* was like without the player-king. Fewer balls that landed on the line were called out; fewer aces were deemed, belatedly, just to have nicked the net. On the down-side (as people were beginning to say), Milstein was much less punctual than when Ronnie was there to glower. Once, when there was snow, he failed to arrive at all. Ralph was pressed into reluctant action as my partner and I struck him a violent blow on the ear with one of my cannon-balls. He never flinched, but his ear grew bigger and redder. When I went to his office to apologise again, after the match, he was drinking from his usual tin of Heinz Scotch Broth. I suspected that it was now more often Scotch than broth. He looked wizened and tired. I wondered how much longer he would last.

Ronnie returned, bronzed from the slopes, and the old reliables resumed. Oliver and Jolyon and I would sometimes smile at Ronnie's autocratic vanities, but his capacity for bending the rules, and the lines, more amused than exasperated the rest of us. We knew each other's game so well that we inhabited a kind of corporate fantasy in which we could believe that we were forever reaching new heights, enjoying rallies that were longer and more dramatic than ever. If one of us had to be absent, it punctured the dream and we accepted even the Old Etonian with forced tolerance, when he was enrolled as sub. Whatever the weather, or the indulgences of the night before, we took unspoken pride in our promptness.

It was, therefore, against all precedent when, one winter morning, Jolyon failed to show. 'He'll be here,' Oliver said, but he was wrong. Finally, the telephone rang and Jolyon informed us that he was terribly sorry but he had a crisis and he couldn't make it this week. Ralph refused to be cajoled and we played one of those unsatisfactory threesomes which everyone always pretended to have been hugely enjoyable.

Ronnie had a word with Jolyon, who promised that everything was now all right. The following week, Oliver was there ahead of time, so was I. Ronnie's clothes preceded him into the dressing-room. The hour struck. No Jolyon. 'Really!' Ronnie said.

'I like a good knock-up,' I said.

Jolyon arrived ten minutes later. It was no crime, but it was a misdemeanour. I greeted him affably from the far end, where Oliver and I were giving Ronnie the honour of hitting every ball, as he took for granted we would. 'You may as well play with me,' Ronnie said, as Jolyon removed his track-suit.

'You're the boss,' Jolyon said.

It was soon evident that Jolyon's heart was not in the game nor his eye on the ball. He was usually a resourceful and reliable partner, but you would not have guessed it that day. Oliver and I looked covertly at each other as even Ronnie's inventive umpiring failed to stop us winning game after game. If I hoisted a short lob for Jolyon to kill with his usual skill, he tapped it into the net. When he served, the old kick was sadly lame. Ronnie grew baleful. We trooped into the showers without any of the usual *badinage*. All might have been well, or at least endurable, if Ronnie had not said, 'I hope this isn't going to be a regular occurrence, your keeping us waiting.'

Jolyon had always struck me as imperturbable. If he was capable of passion, he was the last person whom one imagined bursting into tears. But that is exactly what he now did. Naked, he cried like a baby. No, he cried like a man; pain shook him like a fever. He looked at us with shameless anguish. She had left him. She had taken his child. He didn't know what he was going to do. Did we have any idea what she meant to him? We sighed and bit our lips. We were truly sorry. Ronnie powdered and anointed himself and tied his tie in the patent knot he favoured. Jolyon stumbled into his clothes, scarcely dry from the shower, indifferent to prudence. Ronnie took the trees from his Lobb shoes and sat down to put them on. 'Is this likely to happen again?' he asked. 'Because if so . . .'

'My wife has walked out on me, you bastard,' Jolyon said.

'So you were saying. Is it going to have permanent consequences on your punctuality, do you think?'

'Christ almighty,' Jolyon said, 'who do you think you are?'

'I think I'm the man who arranges the game, brings the balls three times out of four and decides who is going to play when. Who did you think I was?'

'Has anyone ever told you – ?'

'*Jolyon*,' I said, futilely.

' – what a ludicrous old cheat you are? What a ludicrous, pretentious, ridiculous old cheat you bloody well are?'

Ronnie put his shoe-trees in the pouch of his Gucci sac, filed his Homme toiletries in their plasticated place and prepared to go to lunch via his Mount Street office. ('Laze A' was his usual watering hole.) 'I take it,' he said, 'that you won't be here next week.'

'If only you knew,' Jolyon said, 'how much more enjoyable this occasion is when you're not here to call balls out when they're in and to take two more when yours are out and when we don't have to hear how your titled son-in-law wants you to go shooting with him on papa's estate when everyone knows – '

'That will do.'

' – when everyone knows what a jumped-up poop you are, with your fake accent and your pretentious gear and your grotesque vanity!'

Ronnie stood there. I began almost to look forward to the expected tirade. He would surely blow Jolyon away, as perhaps he deserved, as soon as he had taken a deep breath.

'You may have been an officer – you've certainly said so often enough,' Jolyon went on, 'but you'll never bloody well be a gentleman, never mind who your daughter's managed to marry.'

Ronnie took his sac and his briefcase and looked at me. I was ashamed. How often we had laughed at the Sultan behind his back! I prayed for him to draw his scimitar. The blue eyes were brimming with tears he was determined not to shed. I realised that he could not trust himself to speak. He walked out of the changing room.

The month reached its end without a roneoed form from

9

the lovely Jane. I telephoned Ronnie's office to see what was wrong. Were the postmen playing silly buggers or what? Jane's normally warm voice was chilly. 'Mr Trafford is not in the office,' she said, 'and I don't expect him. It seems that there isn't going to be any more tennis, at least not . . . in the usual fashion.'

When I telephoned the court, for a keep-fit session with Ralph, there was no reply. I drove past a few days later and saw that the place was locked. A board announced that the freehold had been sold. RONALD TRAFFORD ASSOCIATES had handled the sale. I discovered Jolyon's number and, when the weather was better, we played a few times, with Milstein and Oliver, at the courts by the Royal Hospital, in Chelsea. No one called the ball out when it was in; no ace was demoted to a net-cord. There were no chauffeurs or toiletries or tales of famous companions on the slopes or on the yacht. No one glared at you if you were late or assumed that you preferred to serve into the sun, but somehow the game lacked magic.

When Jolyon remarried, his new wife made up a four, which was quite proper but rather dull. He had not been foolish enough to choose a passionate mate twice. Ronnie made a bomb out of the Abacus Road site, so a satirical magazine (prompted by Jolyon?) reported. Certainly he had enough to make a fat contribution to Tory party funds. Might a peerage one day be his reward? I can imagine, with a certain affection, how he will have his racket covers emblazoned with his coat of arms. Jolyon was quite right about him, in a way, but I look back with nostalgia on the court in Abacus Road where the eighteen-storey headquarters of International Pharmaceuticals now stands. When I drive past I hear the ghost of Ralph, Scotch Broth in hand, as it murmurs, 'Pity!'

The wife of my friend

We were told that the steamer left Piraeus in the evening and arrived at three in the morning. In the early spring there were few other passengers. The *Despina* – the Greek word for Mistress – had once been a channel steamer; at the head of the stairs, an embossed steel plate declared its origins on Tyneside. First-class passengers could rent tight, stuffy cabins. Our two children fell asleep innocently enough but, knowing that I should be roused in a few hours, I left Sylvia with them and went on deck. Coastal lights swung up and down as though the horizon were a line strung with tiny lanterns.

I had brought a volume of Sophocles with me, like homework I should have finished years before. I was leaning against the rail, under a lamp, when a man who was neither tall nor short, neither thin nor fat, but both commanding and solid, came out of the saloon and lit a cigarette.

Was I holding my book in order that he could see what a serious Hellenist I was? I know only that I pretended to be surprised when I heard him say, 'Sophoklis!' He might have been recognising me rather than my text. Although it was a relief to discover that Vassili spoke much better English than I ever would Greek, our friendship was stranded from the beginning on an island where neither of us could express ourselves without a certain fear either of being misunderstood or of saying the wrong thing.

Hindsight may have freighted that first meeting with an excess of significance, but even after a quarter of a century I can recall the look which he gave to two army officers as they stepped out of the saloon to go to their cabins, the major with worry beads deferring to the colonel without. They were accompanied on their lurching way by a Greek Orthodox priest, whose hieratic beard and cylindrical hat seemed to have been borrowed from Byzantium.

Vassili said, 'Picturesque, do you think?'

I said, 'The traveller sees as scenery what others experience as power.'

He came closer and stood calmly on the pitching deck. 'How long will you stay?'

'As long as we can afford it.'

'Everyone can afford Greece,' Vassili said. 'Greece is easy to buy. *Sigaretta?*' It sounded more like an order than an offer. Even before he told me that he had been a sea captain, he gave an impression of expecting to be obeyed. 'You don't even have to buy it; you can just shake it sometimes. Greece, I mean.'

'*Then kapneezo.*' I said, glad to prove how diligently I had studied my phrasebook. 'I don't smoke.'

'We always know precisely what we don't do. We never know exactly what we will, or might.'

A beautiful woman with very white teeth and frowning black brows leaned out round the door of the saloon. Because her head alone was visible, with its crown of raven hair, she reminded me of some ancient coin, artfully lit to sharpen its profile. She had gleaming dark eyes and the classic Greek nose so few Greeks have. Her skin was almost chalky, though her lips were brightly reddened. She said, 'Vassili? *To cafe!*'

'*Erchome, erchome.*' He looked at me with the same hint of irony as before. 'You want to have a coffee?'

I said, 'Your wife?'

He said, 'The wife of my friend.'

A few hours later, the steward called the name of the island which had been recommended to us for its unspoiled remoteness. At first there was nothing to be seen, but then the *Despina* rounded a headland and a lighthouse twitched its blind welcome. Stunned with surprise at being woken, our children gazed out as we surged past the bright rocks and seemed to enter a new pit of blackness. After a few moments, I pointed to a fluctuating red glow coming towards the *Despina*'s side. The anchor rattled and fell into the harbour. The raspberry of light came from the cigarette of one of the men rowing out to meet us.

The harbour had no jetty. We were already going down the unsteady ladder when Vassili and the other disembarking passengers came on deck. I watched anxiously as my children and my wife and my typewriter were received into the lurching boat. Vassili allowed the beautiful woman and another, less beautiful, to precede him. He and his friend came last.

Vassili's wife was called Anna. The beautiful woman was introduced to us, as other travellers came down with their luggage, including two goats and some chickens heartlessly immobilised with tightly bound claws. Her name was Elektra. Her husband, Loukas, was a journalist, thin and unsmiling, almost bald, with thick spectacles which required him to tilt his head back in order to bring you into focus. He could give you his attention only by backing away.

Vassili and Anna had a place on the island to which, as we parted, he invited us. 'Ask for Pavlides' house.'

I was anxious to find a cottage, where I should be able to work and where Sylvia and the children could feel at home. At a distance, I had been sure that we should have no problem. Now, marooned on the island, I felt like Sisyphus, doomed forever to roll the stone of family responsibility. Having told myself that I should not seek Vassili's help, I soon went to the turreted house overlooking the harbour and explained the problem. Vassili knew of a little cottage in the *campo* with two rooms and a kitchen. It was owned by a peasant who would think he was cheating us for two pounds a week. There was a well, but no electricity. The lavatory was a hut on the edge of a field with a hole in the floor. A grape vine covered the terrace. There was a table for the typewriter. The children had portable beds we had brought from England; Niko could offer only a rusty bed-frame and a straw mattress which rested on planks. What more could one want?

Vassili asked us to eat with them on the evening before they went back to Athens. Their maid, Flora, came to listen for the children. Vassili's wife, Anna, cooked lobster and we drank jugs of harsh *retsina*. Loukas talked politics. His jargon was more savage than his tone; his contempt for the royal family and for the 'classic right-wing' was uttered almost tenderly. He thought the boy-king, whom he called 'the yachtsman', a fool who had been dominated by his German mother. While the beautiful Elektra helped to prepare the dinner, she told Sylvia that she and Loukas had two children, who were staying in Athens with her mother. Vassili and Anna, who owned two carpet shops on Ermou Street, had three daughters. Our new friends' lives were not as neat as envy would wish.

A year later, the Colonels' tanks clanked into Athens. Loukas was soon arrested; his articles had goaded them with unforgivable satires. Advised to go into hiding, he elected to wait in open scorn for their vengeance. In the Sixties, fortunes changed very swiftly. The book I wrote on the island, watched by our landlord, Niko, who had never before seen a typewriter, was sold to the movies. I was hired to write the screenplay and we were able to buy a house in Chelsea. Loukas was in jail.

In the early months of the Colonels' régime, the new tyrants were torn between ruthlessness at home and making a good impression abroad. One day the telephone rang in Seymour Walk. It was Vassili. 'A friend of mine will come to your house in a few days. Please give him whatever he asks. I will repay it when I see you.'

The friend was Loukas. He was alone in London. The Colonels had expelled him from Greece, but they had refused exit visas to Elektra and their children. 'I am muzzled, you see: I am forbidden to write and I am forbidden to speak. Otherwise, I am free!' His voice carried something of Vassili's accusing wryness. 'I need five hundred pounds.'

As we walked to the bank, I asked how his wife and children would cope. He smiled, as if it were the natural response to pain. 'Vassili will look after them. Vassili is very fond of Elektra.' Did he scan me for the reaction I was careful not to have? I had never forgotten how Elektra had looked at Vassili, and he at her, when I first met them. It was not by chance that I had assumed her his wife. How could the dumpy, competent Anna satisfy a beached corsair like Vassili?

During that busy, inane time in London when I wrote movies and grew my hair and appeared on television and tried, as it were, to eat ten meals a day (most of them at Franco and Mario's), I also took Greek lessons from Loukas. I hoped for news from the Athens underground, perhaps even to be enrolled in its courier service, but I discovered Loukas to be a dry teacher. When he gave me grammatical rules to learn and homework to do, I proved a more reliable paymaster than I was student. I admired Loukas and I was sorry for him in his loneliness, but I could not warm to him.

When Vassili rang me to ask when we were coming to Greece, I said that my friends thought that we should boycott the Fascist régime. He said, 'Come. Show your contempt for them. They have hijacked Greece. Besides – ' and now I can imagine the curl of his lip, the grey humour in his eyes ' – besides, you have credit here.'

We did not go until the following summer. We had dinner with Vassili and Anna in Kifissia. We went to their elegant shop and admired the hand-woven carpets from Volos. He repaid the money I had advanced to Loukas. When I thanked him, he said, 'Why do you thank me? Did you not expect to see it again?'

I asked after Elektra. 'You will see her,' he said. 'She is on the island. I am coming next week.'

Aware that Anna was watching me, I said, 'How is she managing?'

'She has a job. She is also quite clever, you know.' The way he said 'also' was the only allusion I ever heard him make to the beauty of the woman I assumed him to love.

Elektra had the capacity, shared by many beautiful women, to behave modestly, as if no one was looking at her. On the island, she wore no make-up, a black skirt and a collarless cotton shirt, of the kind they called 'choriatiko', as made in the village. While we were at the cottage, our children played with hers, but not often, and not easily: little Pavlo was a ruffian.

When Vassili came from Athens, he brought us two rugs which we had admired. With English squeamishness, I had not cared to ask their price. I tried to refuse what was now a gift. 'Among Greeks,' Vassili said, 'we accept what our friends give us.'

Did I somehow convey my feeling that it was not right that he should be with the wife of a man who was in exile? I took refuge in work. Sylvia spent the mornings on the beach, while I filled the quota required to satisfy my statistical muse. Vassili and Elektra would sometimes join her, with Dmitra and the meaty little Pavlo.

When the boat came in, with fresh vegetables from Naxos, I went up to the village to do some shopping and saw Vassili in Kosta's cafe. He was reading one of the newspapers which were still allowed to publish. He held the folded front page towards me, indicating where I should read. I frowned at the text as I once did at Green Unseen examination papers. The gist was that the Colonels' Greece was regarded as a much more reliable ally by the Americans and the English. 'And you are the friends of liberty,' Vassili said. 'The countrymen of Lord Byron!'

'They kicked Byron out like your people did Loukas,' I said.

'My people? Do you call that scum mine?' He had turned so that his words would carry across the square, to where the village priest and the police chief could hear him. 'Your wife doesn't approve of me. She thinks me . . . sarcastic.'

'She's extremely grateful to you,' I said. 'Me too. The carpets are wonderful. Just what the cottage needed.'

'I want no gratitude for carpets. She thinks I have no shame. Why are you red in the face?'

'Because it's hot.'

He said, 'What do you think of Elektra and me?'

'I don't think anything.'

'A writer who does not think,' Vassili said, 'can only be English!'

'All right then, I think she's very beautiful and that you are a man who does what he wants to do.'

'And sells carpets? You insult me! I gave up the sea for my wife. I carry a fan now, like Lord Byron. Do you think I am sleeping with Elektra? What will you say to Loukas? What will you *not* say? The only interesting thing about Englishmen is what they hide. For your information, I have not *touched* Elektra – I have literally not touched Elektra – since Loukas was arrested. Do you believe me?'

'Yes. I believe you.'

'Why? Because I tell you to?'

'Because it combines honour and perversity.'

'Thank you,' Vassili said. 'For your first intelligent words.'

After we flew back to England, I wrote to thank him for the carpets, one of which we took back to Chelsea. Loukas smiled when he saw it; his smile, like Vassili's, was more expressive than any English smile because it made no pretence of amusement. When I told Loukas how well his wife looked and how nicely his children had played with ours, he did not press for details, but began an analysis of the king's latest ineptitude. He seemed more intimately concerned with public than with private events. He had found a job in a Greek bookshop and had a busier social life. I continued to give him money, but our regular lessons ceased.

The next time we went to the island, Vassili's home was shuttered and empty. Sylvia was not sorry; I said that I wasn't. In Athens, on the way home, I went to the big shop, but to my disappointed relief he was not there. Anna looked fatter and she was suddenly grey; I suppose she has ceased to dye her hair. I asked how Vassili was and she said, 'How is he? He is a man who does what he chooses to do. Now he wants to buy a ship.'

Whenever I saw Loukas, which was rarely, since I had a film shooting in France, I expected to hear that Vassili had been arrested, but nothing like that happened. What did happen was more prosaic: the next time we were in Athens, I went to Ermou Street and found that the big shop was closed and padlocked. Vassili was in the smaller one, which was mostly basement. 'Ah,' he said, 'the occasional tourist.'

I had the impression that things were not good, but his pride was, if anything, more obvious. I told him that Loukas now had a job and that I wanted to regard the additional money he had had from me as a bonus for his teaching me Greek.

Vassili said, 'If he is that good, why are we speaking English? Let us speak Greek.' He began to do so, at speed. His flattery of my linguistic competence made a fool of me. However, I could understand very well that he was full of scorn for people of his own generation, who were relying on the students at Athens University to show the courage they lacked. And what about England? England, I said, was full of strikes, economic crises and loud social confrontations. 'That sounds wonderful. Because listen.' Vassili indicated the street. 'What do you hear?'

I said, 'It sounds very quiet.'

'It *is* very quiet. Athens is very quiet. Aristophanes is banned and no one says anything! That is the one joke they have left us.'

Elektra was not on the island. We stayed a couple of weeks in the cottage, but things were changing in the

18

Cyclades. Some Americans, who were terribly friendly, were building a house between us and the sea. They were bringing in electricity and, of course, running water. The next year we went to France. We promised ourselves we would go to Greece again after the Colonels fell, if they ever did. Our absences from London meant that I had received the last of my Greek lessons and lost contact with Loukas.

Then the Colonels did fall. I went to a rally to celebrate the recall of Constantine Karamanlis to Athens. In the crowd, I saw Loukas. He was balder and scrawnier and greyer and more myopic than ever. 'At last!' I said. 'This is a happy day.'

'It could have been happier.'

'When are you going back?'

'I may go to America,' Loukas said. 'There is a danger of a right-wing backlash, funded – of course – by the CIA. There are things that have to be said, even if they are not popular.'

'What about Elektra and the children? Will they go with you?'

He looked at me as if I had all but vanished over his horizon. 'I have told Elektra that she should not wait for me. I have told her that I have changed. One must be a man about certain things.'

'I don't know if I ought to say this, Loukas, but I happen to know that what you think happened never happened. Never. I would stake my life on it. You can trust Vassili absolutely.'

He puffed his lips slightly, as if it was hardly worth wasting further words trying to educate me. 'I *do* trust Vassili,' he said. He turned and was looking in the crowd. His attention and mine was caught by a woman in a red anorak, with unruly dyed blonde hair, who was addressing a Labour politician in a very caustic manner over his government's complicity with the fallen Colonels.

'She could go fifteen rounds with Mohammed Ali,' I said, 'that one.'

He said, 'Evgenia is the woman I intend to make my new life with.'

'*What?*'

'Are you shocked? You are shocked.'

I said, 'But . . . but how *can* you? Vassili . . . Elektra . . . they . . . he . . . she . . . And all this time . . .'

'There is no comparison.'

'Of course there's a bloody comparison.'

He put an arm round the brassy blonde in the anorak. 'Not at all,' he said. 'Evgenia is not the wife of my friend.'

'I don't understand.'

'You don't understand because you never will be a Greek. *Poté, poté, poté!* Never, never, never.'

The Beverly Hills snowman

I first met Harry Brackett in London in the Sixties. He had not come to swing; he came because the dollar was strong and it was cheaper to produce movies in Europe than in California. Swinging could wait; Harry preferred the roundabouts. Almost to his surprise, he discovered that he favoured the English style altogether; Huntsman suits and Huntingdonshire (he had to have a weekend place) and even Huntley and Palmer's biscuits appealed to him. He might have ridden to hounds if his wife had liked horses, or disliked foxes, enough. As it was, he hunted only for subjects to make into movies and, to start with, for writers to script them.

I had been warned against Hollywood by a thousand cautionary tales. Did we not know what had happened to Aldous and to Christopher and, of course, to Scott? If I was eager to be involved in Cinema, which was a Cause, I was never going to go into the Movies, which were a Business. When Harry Brackett called to say that he had seen a television play I had done and that he thought there might be a full-blown movie in it, I was properly dubious. He suggested that we lunch and talk about it. Did I know Les Ambassadeurs? Would that be all right?

I took the opportunity to tell him that I had no appetite for the kind of candified crap with which, as I indicated with clumsy candour, I associated his name. I had read Lindsay Anderson and I had learnt to advertise my contempt for Big Stars and routine capitalist apologetics. 'Listen,' Harry said, 'tell me something you want to do and let's see if we can't do that.'

Strictly on those terms, I went along with plovers' eggs

21

and fresh salmon stuffed with Beluga, but I ate them in a sceptical style; I am sure that Harry sensed the hint of satire in my attitude to the Dom Perignon. He could hardly have failed to see that I was a leather-jacketed, no-tie man who was not there to be taught the meaning of the word compromise. As for Harry, the charcoal-silk suit, the Sulka tie, the off-pink Turnbull and Asser shirt (did it have double-buttoned cuffs in 1969?) and the Lobb shoes announced the naturalised Londoner for whose lapses of style I waited with disappointed duplicity. Harry was really very nice and he talked a lot of sense. If I hoped for a legendary Californian monster who puffed Romeo y Julieta smoke in my face and wanted to make a happy-ending musical out of *Crime and Punishment*, I was lunching with the wrong man. Harry, it seemed, approached intellectuals with respect as well as with money. There are more unpleasant conditions.

He told me about his early life as if it were a comedy. He had struggled, but he had had a great time in the late Thirties and early Forties; they hadn't had too much of a war in New York City. Broadway could be a place of heartbreak, sure, but also of crazy opportunities. Before he was twenty, Harry was a stage-manager; then he became a producer, thanks to a writer friend of his. First time around, he lost a bunch of money he didn't have (his backer, unfortunately, insisted on marrying him after the show had folded), but then he got lucky. One hit led to another and suddenly California was calling: Darryl wanted to buy the new play. Harry didn't want to sell. Darryl called back; he was sore but he was accommodating and Harry went to work at Fox. He was there right through the war (frankly, he rented an ulcer to keep him out of the service) and by 1945 he was seriously established. He was known as a producer who did elegant movies and ran a tight ship, but being a bastard was never his style. 'You can only be what you are,' he told me.

'Bleak news,' I said.

He looked at me with wistful admiration. 'Not if you're young and talented.'

'You don't look too old to me,' I said.

'When are you going to say something about talented? And what are we going to do together?'

I was scornful when he suggested (only because it had been suggested to him) a musical version of *It Happened One Night*, but when I proposed something – based on one of my own stories – which I said I *knew* he would never *dream* of doing, Harry said, 'OK, let's do that.' How do you get out of a situation like that?

Business and pleasure, wise men had warned me, should always be kept distinct, like friends and associates. In The Industry, however, it is not always easy to separate them. I tried, at first, to regard Harry Brackett as a Mythical Figure, but he was not keen to remain Olympian. He seemed to like me and, although I should never have told Lindsay Anderson as much, I found that I liked him. When we started to work together, on the second draft of the screenplay, he would often arrange for us to lunch in his Hyde Park Gardens flat; it was quiet and the food was tactful to the ulcer which he now, unfortunately, had for real.

The apartment had been styled by David Hicks. The living room featured porphyry-streaked Renaissance busts on each side of the Adams mantelpiece. A French walnut table was big enough for more Regency snuff-boxes than a regiment of bucks could have needed. A rare Gobelins tapestry (of a *fête champêtre*) was braced above the three-seater brocaded Chesterfield which faced its twin across a coffee table where two little Henry Moore figures lounged together. I tried, of course, to find such tasteful opulence despicable, but it had a certain charm. I particularly liked the Haddon Hall plates on which the smoked salmon and the fresh asparagus were so regularly served, in silent competence, by the Spanish maid and butler. The apartment promised that there were certain compensations for being rich and successful, but it always seemed a little lonely. Somehow, and for no good reason, Harry's spruce cheerfulness made me feel sorry for him. Although he took his various medicines with a smile, I wanted to make him feel better.

One evening, at the White Elephant, a once blacklisted writer-producer, who was now again a Force, came up to where Sylvia and I were dining. Carl was wearing a new Douggie Hayward suit – the flattering waist and racy slope of the pockets were as good as Douggie's signature – and the serious glasses which reminded you that he had a radical past, with which he had by no means entirely broken. Carl was behind one of the most successful World War II pictures ever made, but he had taken outspoken positions against the Vietnam involvement. 'Outspeaking always was one of Carl's favourite art-forms,' an old friend of his, now an executive at Columbia, had told me. 'He seriously opposes all wars that don't make money at the box office.'

'So,' Carl said, 'you're working with Harry Brackett. How's it going?'

'We have Audrey in a negotiation,' I said. 'Not that I would ever boast to you of such a thing.'

'Send a gun-boat,' he said. 'That little angel makes an Armenian look like a push-over. Have you met *her* yet?'

'She only just got the script.'

'Not her; *her*: the legendary Lola. Alias Mrs Brackett.'

'Isn't she still in the States? Her mother – '

'If she isn't one devoted family gal! She doesn't hurry back, does she? At least not for Harry. How are you, Sylvia?'

'Oh, am I here?' my wife said. 'Hullo, Carl.'

'I like your suit,' I said.

'You don't think it's a little bit eminent?'

'A little. Aren't you going to say anything about mine?'

Carl felt my new, narrow lapels. 'Why pay more?' he said.

The morning Audrey agreed to do our picture, Harry

24

Brackett looked like a new man; she might have been the cure for his ulcer. His sallowness was purged; the blood showed in his cheeks. I heard him call to Pat to book a table at the Mirabelle, for three. He and I were already in our napkinned places when Lola walked in. She was wearing a Jean Muir number and no jewellery except for her eyes. A movie star sitting between Spiegel and Preminger looked at the newcomer as though she were the messenger in a tragedy: all the light in the room seemed concentrated on her. Preminger had to get up and kiss her on the hand. 'Oh Otto,' she said, 'please don't behave!'

Lola may have been a beauty, but she was also very charming; she congratulated me on Audrey, saying that it was all due to the fabulous script, and she apologised for intruding on our celebrations. I forgave her; I should have forgiven her for a recital of Serbian folk-songs. At that first meeting, she was like a goddess on her day off. What had Harry done to deserve her?

We had to wait some months before we could actually shoot the movie. It was a time of luxurious frustration; I bought a set of Haddon Hall china for Sylvia and I tried to resume work on a novel which now seemed rather provincial in its obsession with English snobberies. I hated to admit it, even to myself, but I cared more about whom we were going to find to play opposite Audrey than whether – without making this my overt subject, of course – my fictional couple could convincingly stand for the reconciliation of liberty with the need for Socialism.

Now that Lola was back in London, she and Harry had a busy social life. Sylvia and I were soon recruited to be part of it; the apartment in Hyde Park Gardens was now as crowded as it had earlier seemed barren. Lola's dinner parties were brilliant and entertaining; the only bores were millionaires. Yet despite the frequent presence of Warren and Leslie and David and Carl and Sophia and Peter, Harry Brackett always welcomed Sylvia and me as if we were the only people he really wanted to see, even though he appeared to have as many friends as the finest weather could procure.

Could I have been a little jealous of the famous people who commanded a share of Harry's time? Perhaps I was only being clever, but one evening I said, 'How about we do a musical of *Timon of Athens*? We can do the whole show right here in the barn.' I indicated the revamped living room, where the snuff-boxes had yielded to Hindu sculptures and the Gobelins tapestry had been replaced by three Hockneys. The Moores were still in the room, but the alabaster coffee table sported a collection of Warhol's latest Campbell tin cans. Benny Bligh said that you could tell they were art, because the soup came separately. 'We can always give *Timon* a happy ending, if we have to.'

Harry said, 'Happy? *Here?*'

I laughed; in the Sixties, we laughed at everything except napalm and socialism. Yes, I laughed, but was I amused? Harry might have been alone in the world and something in that crowded solitude of his sounded an alarm in my head which seemed to ring and ring. It had been so convenient to see Harry as a father-figure, the evidence that happiness could be a function of money, that I had been determined to believe him and Lola to be as contented as our children insisted that Sylvia and I were. Now Harry's guard slipped, or I had pulled it aside, and I could not rid myself of that brief sight of the lonely truth about him.

The next day, when we were due to talk about the list of changes which Paul wanted in the script before he would agree to team up with Audrey, I approached Harry's office in the hope that my silly remarks, and his bitter response, would have no place in the edited version of the previous night's party. I found him on the telephone to a duke. His Grace would not, it seemed, be available to dine on a certain day. Harry was begging him to rearrange his diary; he begged like a rich and successful man, but the tone of supplication was unmistakable. I looked at the trades and wished that he did not sound so desperate. When, finally, he achieved what he wanted, the face he turned to me was neither smiling nor triumphant. 'See what I mean?' he said. 'About happy?'

I said, 'About these changes.'

'Why not?'

'I don't go along with them, not all of them.'

'Then don't do them. I don't want to do what people want. But I do it. You're lucky; you don't have to.'

'Then why am I here?' I said.

Harry Brackett responded with a look of such anguish that I almost felt like the shit I was pretending to be. 'Do you mean that?'

'If I meant it,' I said, 'would I be saying it?'

'England!' he said. 'You think you understand it, but do you? Ever?'

'Let me buy you lunch today, Harry, will you? Spoil me.'

I took him to Scott's; they were still in their old Edwardian premises in Coventry Street. The staircase rising from the centre of the entranceway seemed to promise that heaven too would be a place of courteous recognitions where someone would take you to a reserved place without even pausing to check your name.

Harry said, 'Freddie, you're happy, aren't you, in your marriage? You're lucky.'

'We both are,' I said.

'You and Sylvia? I'll say.'

'I was thinking of you and me.'

'Oh don't do that,' he said. 'She doesn't love me, Freddie; she never did.'

'Then why did she marry you?'

'I asked her,' he said. 'A lot.'

'Lola could marry anybody she wanted to.'

'She never wanted anybody. Being wanted is what she wants. Believe me, I know all there is to know about long-stem roses and Cartier watches. And getting what she wants. Did I tell you about our honeymoon?'

I said, 'I didn't know people even had those any more.'

'She wanted to go to Klosters. It was Christmas. The planes were jammed. The hotels too. I said, "How about Wengen? Wengen is nice." She said it wasn't; everyone was going to be at Klosters. I said, "I'll be at Wengen, if you will." "Klosters," she said, "fix it." I had to call a banker in Zurich just to get on to the plane, but the best hotel he couldn't help me with and only the best hotel would do. Finally I found a room, but a suite was impossible. "Fix it," she said. I pulled strings till my hands were raw. Finally I bought a raft of shares in the hotel's holding company; a week before Christmas! She got her suite, and we had a honeymoon surrounded by more people than'll ever come to my funeral. I don't feel like we were alone for more than ten minutes and then she was getting ready for something or other that certainly wasn't me. Lola is a beautiful, beautiful woman, so long as she gets everything she wants. I just don't happen to be on the list. She likes you. A lot.'

'Don't fix it,' I said.

The dinner parties at Hyde Park Gardens went on for a season and then, in early December, they stopped; Lola's mother, in Little Rock, had taken a turn for the worse and she flew out to be with her. We were in pre-production by then and Harry had the usual budget problems, but nothing took precedence over Lola. Her absence was omnipresent: he often called her and he often waited for calls from her. One day, the telephone rang and I heard the operator say, 'Mr Brackett? Mrs Brackett is calling from the United States. Will you pay for the call?'

Harry said, 'Of course.' And then he said, 'Darling?' And then his voice changed and he said, *'Mother!'* Lola had actually called Harry's mother to get her to tell him that she could not be back in time for Christmas. That was how I came to invite Harry to spend it with us in the country.

Sylvia was afraid that he would find it primitive. If he did, he also seemed to like it. He bought presents for our children (our grand-daughter still has the rocking-horse Harry gave Sarah) and he was generous enough to seem genuinely glad to be with us. When it snowed on Christmas Eve, he rolled the biggest snowball the kids had ever seen and turned it into a snowman to remember. He took pictures of the children on its shoulders, just to prove how big it was (oh, and how big they were too!). All the time, he was waiting for Lola to call, but the lines must have been very busy. When he tried to call her, there was no answer: she must have been taking her mother for a drive, didn't we agree? Of course we did.

Just as we were assuming that she was about to put Harry out of his humiliating agony, Lola came back to England; her mother had recovered sufficiently for Harry to have her taken care of at a place in Fort Lauderdale. As for Lola herself, she had lost her zeal for London life; she spent her time at the cottage where the neighbours had less money, she said, but more sincerity. There were no new adjustments to the décor at Hyde Park Gardens. We finally got our movie made, but despite Audrey's perfect performance, Benny Bligh gave it the thumbs down (it is now regularly 'taught' in film school, at least in California). When the Seventies began, and the Beatles proved nothing lasts, Harry decided that he had to return to Los Angeles. 'Go with the money is the oldest rule in the movies,' he told me. We asked him and Lola to dinner for a last farewell to the Sixties, but we had, it seemed, already said goodbye to them. Lola wanted to spend every minute she could in Huntingdonshire; she was not taking the move back to the States in good part, but there were things that not even Harry could fix.

In due course, I wrote a new screenplay, from a novel Columbia had bought for Harry, for six figures, and we had to fly out to California to discuss the changes to the changes. It was almost Christmas, but we told the children that it would be a change to have it in the sun. Why not? Harry's new place on Chevy Chase had a guest wing almost as big as the Ritz and we could pick our own oranges. As far as we were concerned, Lola was as nice as she could be, and she could be very nice. If I knew she had to be a prize bitch, I kept liking her, at least until Harry was unguarded enough to bring out the pictures of the white Christmas he had spent with us in Suffolk.

'That's what I'd like to have,' she said. 'A white Christmas. Right here in Beverly Hills.'

'They don't make them, angel.'

'I want to make a snowman.'

'You want Christmas in Alaska?'

'I want to make one here, in the garden.'

I looked at Sylvia and then I looked up. The clear sky meant trouble; I could see it coming.

Harry said, 'We'll just have to settle for the new palm trees.' They were twice as tall as basket-ball players and they had arrived on a truck that morning. 'Unless it snows.'

Lola said, 'Fix it.'

'Why don't you ask to go skating on the swimming pool too, while you're at it?'

I recognised the sound of a worm who had half-decided to turn.

'OK,' she said, 'if you're such a big-shot. Why not? I'd like to go skating on the swimming pool.'

'You never swam in the damn thing and now you want to skate on it?'

'Nobody swims in Beverly Hills.'

'You want ice, you want a snowman; anything else you want?'

'If there's anything else,' she said, 'I'll ask Santa.'

We were relieved to go back to our separate quarters and choose between eighteen channels of junk on the TV. Harry and I had a series of conferences with the director who had an agenda of problems he needed to have us address. While Stu and I talked, Harry made some calls. He had this friend who had built a winter sports complex and another who owned this ice hockey team. He refused to worry about what it was going to cost; he was determined to give Lola exactly what she wanted.

30

Early on Christmas morning, dead-heating with Santa himself, a very big truck pulled up in Chevy Chase. Some very large and very loud and very ingenious machinery came down the ramp. Not longer afterwards, a bunch of guys on double overtime came in with some more machinery, this time from the ice hockey rink. I was not there to see how they did it, but by sun-up the new palm trees were up to their knees in authentic Hollywood snow. By breakfast-time, the swimming pool was rimed with greeny-white ice.

Lola had just one present under the eight-foot spruce under the cathedral-ceilinged living room: a pair of championship quality skates. She took one look and said, 'Harry, I haven't skated in years; you know that.'

'You made a deal,' Harry said. 'Honour it.'

'I don't think you should talk to me that way.'

'Now.'

We and the children were outside, playing with the truly generous things from F. A. O. Schwarz which Harry had given them, when Lola came out and sat on the diving board and – with hatred in those exquisite green eyes of hers – laced up her skates. Harry took her hand, with all the tenderness of an implacably tactful executioner, and helped her onto the ice.

'Skate,' he said. 'Like you promised Santa you would.'

She skated. She started tentatively – who could blame her? – but then she got better. She began to enjoy herself; she swooped and she spun. Hatred gave her wings; she flew. The blades scored and scorched the ice; cold sparks salted the morning. If she had started reluctantly, it seemed that she was never going to stop. The sun steepened in the Californian sky, but Lola was untiring. And then, all of a sudden, it seemed, with infinite and predictable slowness, the ice first creaked and then cracked. It folded in like Monsieur Hulot's famous canvas canoe and, quite abruptly now, Lola was no longer skating. She was in the deep end and the blades of her skates were pedalling silver fish.

31

There was no tragedy, but comedy too can end in tears. We hauled her out, shaking with shock and rage, quite as if Harry's malice, not her own obstinacy, had kept her on the ice until it could no longer support her. She swore that she had caught pneumonia. She wrapped herself in yards of towel and then she got into her Mercedes and said she was going straight to Merce Sugarwater's house to talk about a divorce and there was nothing anybody in the world could do about it.

We had retreated, with cowardly courtesy, to the guest house before the final slam of the car door, the yells and the problem with the electronic gate (it would not respond to Lola's bleeper), and I thought it prudent to do nothing for as long as possible. However, the moment came when I felt I had to go over to the main house.

As I approached the French windows, I heard a terrible sound. Imagine discovering your father-figure in tears. Harry Brackett was sitting in a genuine colonial rocking chair, of the best period, and his hands were pressed on his wet cheeks, as if he were afraid that his eyes were going to fall out. Choking noises broke from his chest in husky convulsions. Should I go in? I went in. I stood in front of him and I coughed. Then I said, 'Harry, I'm . . . I'm so sorry.'

He removed his hands and looked up and I saw that he was not a father-figure at all, but a naughty boy.

'*Harry!*' I said. 'Don't tell me . . .'

He nodded. 'I fixed it,' he said.

'Well,' I said, 'I guess it was about time.'

'It sure was,' he said. 'Now let's go make that snowman.'

We did; and it was just as good as the Suffolk one had been. Sarah thought it was possibly even better. But it didn't last, of course. In Beverly Hills, what does?

Jimmy

It is remarkable how, in every generation, a commonplace Christian name can come to be associated with a single individual. In the Twenties, anyone who mentioned Scott could be referring only to Scott Fitzgerald, just as in the Thirties Ernest could only be Hemingway; in the Forties Larry was always Olivier and in the Fifties Sophia was unquestionably Miss Loren. Today, to whom else can Jimmy refer other than to Jimmy Cameron, the only man over sixty of whom young girls speak with clocked longing to their therapists?

I first came across Jimmy in 1955. Sylvia and I were living in a basement on Chelsea Embankment, where the direct light of day never shone. I was writing my second novel, which was always said to be (and proved) extremely difficult. Owing to a brief season of undergraduate fame, I had acquired a showbiz agent who had once been a drummer in provincial variety theatres, where immobile girls, wearing only nether garments technically known as 'fleshings', used to display their breasts between low comedy acts.

I had agreed to be represented by Jock Friedman after he saw me capering in the Cambridge Footlights revue in which I impersonated a band-leader for whose double, he assured me, he had worked for several years. 'Freddie,' he said, 'you made me laugh and you made Fritzi laugh' (Fritzi, I was to discover, was his usually unsmiling wife) 'and you also made Jimmy laugh. I took Jimmy to see your show and you made Jimmy laugh. You made him hoot.'

I said, 'Jimmy hooted? I like him. Who is he?'

'Jimmy Cameron. He's about to make his first picture out

at Pinewood. He's going to be up there with your Larry Olivers and your Garry Grants and people like that.'

If Jock had any inkling of his limitations, he refused to be inhibited by them. He would call important film producers, winking at me as he did so, and tell them how they ought to do themselves a favour and meet young Rayfel. Although I had no cinematic experience, he procured me friendly, and fruitless, meetings with Danny and Raymond and George and Alfred, in a series of offices lined with dated playbills and decked with silver-framed photographs of stars professing undying love, x x x, for whoever was sitting behind the big desk and telling me how difficult things were just at the moment.

Pinewood Studios, where Jock sent me to meet Gino Amadei, had the unthreatening air of a suburban golf club. The panelled refectory was full of convivial Nazis from the *Graf Spee*, sharing grey roast beef, salty cabbage and leathered roast potatoes with the crews of His Majesty's ships *Exeter*, *Ajax* and *Achilles*. When the bell rang, all hands returned with admirable phlegm to the afternoon session of the Battle of the River Plate.

Gino was the producer assigned to *Bust Up!*, a comedy-thriller project which was intended to make Jimmy Cameron into a star at least as big as Michael Craig or Tony Wright, who currently had the beefiest reputation on the lot. Gino endured his office with twinkling melancholy. 'This film, the *Bust Up*, it's a comedy-thriller but I have to say it's not particularly comic and it doesn't thrill me. What is your favourite film, Fred, if I may ask?'

I said, '*Citizen Kane*, of course.'

'In that case, my advice to you is to get out of here as fast as you can. If you want to have a coffee first, have a coffee first.'

'What we've got to do,' I said, 'is make them change their ideas. I really want to make films that have something to say.'

'Don't wait for the coffee,' Gino said. 'Go now. I call you a taxi. Alternatively, will you at least read the script? It could do with a few touches of wit and humour. If we have to be honest, it could to with a lot.'

I should like to believe that he was exaggerating, but Gino recently promised me that when I went to see him in his Oakwood Mansions flat, after reading the multi-coloured script, my first, immodest words were, 'What do you want to make this piece of shit for?'

My haughtiness abated after Jock negotiated for me to do three weeks' work at a hundred and fifty pounds a week. It was a fortune. I abandoned my fictional indictment of small-minded suburbia and steeled myself to the task of beefing up *Bust Up!* Before I started, Gino said, 'Fred, I must tell you one thing. Whatever you do to the script, don't change the scene numbers. Nothing is sacred in the film business, except the scene numbers.'

When I had delivered, Jimmy telephoned and asked whether he could come round to discuss a few things. He arrived wearing a light blue cashmere sweater and matching Daks slacks. He had plenty of hair in those days and was forever running his hand through it, as if to make sure that it was still there. When Sylvia came in from buying biscuits for tea, Jimmy stood up, like someone who had been told that he should, and said, 'Hello there.'

When we got down to cases, he pointed out weaknesses in my work without jeering at them and without threatening my confidence. After we had finished scribbling through the script, Sylvia asked if he wanted some supper. He said, 'Love to, only I've got my Pegs waiting for me at home. We've got this lamb chop all bought and paid for!' What a nice, unspoiled chap he was!

I walked him to his car. It turned out to be a brand new Ford Consul, with a radio. 'Don't you worry, Frederic,' he said, 'I'm going to have a much better barouche than this before I hang up my boots.' I was reminded that he had once had a trial, as a goalkeeper, for Celtic. 'And so are you, laddie.'

I cannot say that I was a regular presence on the floor during the shooting of *Bust Up!*, but I did go several times to watch John Russell Noakes directing. His skill seemed to consist in saying 'Cut', putting his arms round people and then calling out, 'Try one more, Jimmy, shall we?' Jimmy would wink at me and say, 'You do crack the whip, Mr Noakes, but I'll go as often as you say.'

'An infinite capacity for giving pains,' Noakes said, 'that's the secret of my success, cockie! One more then. We want Earl to be happy, don't we?'

In the event, Earl – who was Head of Production – was not happy at all. Jimmy had done his virile best to give Bluey Mackintosh the cool humour of Garry Grant and the mordant panache of Larry Oliver, but he came across, in the rough cut, as a nice young stevedore who had been briefly to drama school. During our many post mortems, all kinds of resurrective remedies were mooted. In the middle of one of them, Gino was bidden to lunch in the executive dining room. His contract was about to expire; the issue of its renewal was bound to feature on the menu.

No sooner had Gino arrived, and been dosed with an anaesthetic thimble of sweet sherry, than the accountant who ran the studio told him that, to avoid indigestion, he might as well know that he had some bad news for him. Towards the end of the boiled beef, Gino looked at his watch and said that he was sorry but he had some work to do and therefore he would like to know what the bad news was. The Head of the Studio frowned and said, 'I thought you'd realised, Gino: we're not going to renew your contract.'

'Yes, I gathered that,' Gino said, 'but what is the bad news?'

Gino's departure coincided with the decision to shelve *Bust Up!* The studio charlady test (if Mrs Mop likes it, *they*'ll like it) had proved it to be too bad even for the Rank muscleman to bong his gong for. I did not expect to hear from Jimmy Cameron again nor, I confess, did I give him much of a thought. As the flatulent Fifties ended and the sexy Sixties swung into the calendar, I had fresher fish to fry. I noticed only that, after some fallow years, Jimmy surfaced as a co-star in a cheapo ATV series about the Gorbals in the Thirties; if he looked good as a plain-clothes sergeant in a cloth cap, he seemed unlikely to rise to a higher rank.

When Philip Geary's thriller, *A Bit of Spare*, made his hero, Randy O'Toole, into a best-selling troubleshooter who, in the dismissive, often quoted words of the *New Statesman* reviewer, 'made James Bond seem like a sensitive character out of Henry James', everyone wondered who would play him in the inevitable film. Jimmy made the short list, but that is only another way of saying that he had failed to get the part. I happened to bump into him in Curzon Street and admired his lack of bitterness: 'Rich is a better actor than I am,' he said, 'and he's got a more expensive wife, so good luck to him.' We went into the White Elephant and I bought him a couple of drinks. He was as nice as pie. One thing everyone says for Jimmy: he is the nicest man in the world who never stood his round.

Of course, everyone also knows very well that, after the producers were a couple of zeros short of Mr Burton's price, Jimmy did, after all, play Randy O'Toole. No one gave the film a hope of success. *A Bit of Spare* was cheap; it was vulgar; it was all tits and innuendo and *double entrendres*; it was violent and escapist and without the smallest tincture of art or subtlety. On reflection, how could anyone have imagined for a second that it would fail to be a record-breaking smash-hit?

Jimmy was instantly famous and soon rich. I saw him in a brand new Roller riding down Park Lane; he waved, but he did not offer me a lift. The girl beside him was not his wife and shortly afterwards neither was his wife. He could now afford one as expensive as Mr Burton's. If Jimmy's new wealth did not go to his head, nor did it go to entertain his friends. However, he was generous with everything except his own money; you could always rely on him to signal you over to join somebody else's party. When, at one of them, he met and was soon expertly induced to marry Cosima Campoamor, then at the height of her modelling fame (she really wanted to act, of course), he was quickly persuaded that he and the love of his life should live somewhere beautiful and with a less taxing climate.

The Finca Antoñita was sumptuous, in the Moorish style; its hanging gardens overlooked a private bay at the north end of the Costa Brava. It also had the necessary pool for those who preferred unsalted swimming. Since its owner had died, at sea, of a strangulated hernia, while wrestling with a marlin heavier than he was, the property was knocked down at a price which any millionaire could afford and which, to Mr Box Office, was hardly more than a heap of negligible beans.

The villa's only displeasing feature, in Cosima's fastidious eyes, was the loudly polychrome swimming pool. Since Jimmy was about to leave in order to make *Call for Randy* and *Randy Does It Again*, back to back, for ten million dollars on account of fifteen percent of the gross, and since she was the love of his life, he gave Cosima *carte blanche* to rip out the gaudy tiles and put in something which would appeal to the smart friends who would be coming to the housewarming party as soon as Jimmy had persuaded his producer to fund it.

Sylvia and I were not embarrassed with an invitation. It was only through the Oscar-winning director of Jimmy's next film, a version of *Macbeth* set in the Gorbals, in which Cosima was daringly slated to star as the first Lady Macbeth with a Spanish accent, that we learned precisely what happened on that superstar-studded night. The PR people had only spoken with candid reticence of 'irreconcilable differences' between a couple who had, a press release or two earlier, been billed as Mr and Mrs Inseparable.

John told us that it all began with happy fireworks as the guests were limousined or choppered in. 'I can only tell you,' he said, 'that Cosima looked like Botticelli's Venus, but better dressed, and Jimmy was drooling all over her. He took me over the whole place and I had to agree, the girl had put his money where it showed to best advantage. Being Jimmy, he had to tell me that it wasn't just beautiful, it was also an investment. Who was I to argue, dear? Nothing seemed less likely that what finally happened.'

'Presumably someone told her about the floozies?'

'Wait for it, dear,' John said, 'because it's coming, I promise you. Jimmy was playing the happy householder as if to the *finca* born and he was particularly pleased when some Catalan duchess arrived in a horse-drawn tiara. The old biddy said how dingy the previous occupants had made the place and how happy she was that he had turned a white elephant into a dream house. "All the credit goes to Cosima," he said. That was when the duchess said, "I do so want to see the swimming pool again." "I don't know about again," Jimmy said, "but we'd be glad to show you what we've done to it." They go down the steps and through the yew hedge and the duchess takes one look at Cosima's exquisitely tasteful Talavera tiles and the under-water lighting and she positively freaks, dear. "What have you done?" she says, "Tell me it's a joke!"

'Cosima gave her a patient look that could kill and said, "Joke? The old pool was a joke, if you like, with all those garish tiles and that hideously obscene minotaur writhing about on the bottom." "It may have been obscene, my dear," says madame, "but it was one of Pablo's most original efforts." I was there, dear, and I heard Jimmy say, "Pablo? Pablo who exactly?" As if there was more than one Pablo!

'When the duchess told them how Picasso had stayed there in 1935 and what the current value was of what Cosima had destroyed, well, dear, that was when our mutual chum shoved three and a half thousand quids' worth of Balenciaga's best sequins into the pool and went to call his lawyer. On the double.'

'That's Jimmy,' I said.

These things happen

Doctor Archambaud was recommended to us when I had to take our kitten to be castrated. If you have a farmhouse in the Périgord, a cat is essential, unless you want to come back to find that large numbers of mice have become your tenants. However, when our neighbours gave us a ginger kitten, they advised us to have it attended to, unless we wanted to find that large numbers of mice had been displaced by large numbers of cats. Doctor Archambaud, the local vet, would take care of the matter in a few seconds. He lived on the edge of Caillac, the little town which serves as our metropolis. It was not easy to understand why a man of manifest substance – the house was large and had a considerable garden – should choose a characterless villa, made of dun-coloured stone, when the Périgord is full of antique buildings of weathered charm and individuality. Perhaps, as a man of science, Archambaud liked the aseptic functionalism of 'Leonora', which was the name that dangled on a gantry next to the gate. When I accused him of being a Beethoven fan, he told me that his name was Léon and his wife's Nora.

As he prepared our ginger kitten for the treatment which logic recommended and sentiment abhorred, Archambaud confessed that he was indeed a music-lover, but that he preferred Italian opera to orchestral works. His size and the volume of his own sonorous phrasing suggested that the larger-than-life world of Puccini or Verdi might indeed be congenial to him. While he handled Minou with implacable gentleness, he proclaimed the cultural deficiencies of the Périgord. He swore that he could tell me stories of the peasants and their morals to keep my hair on end for weeks. Doctor Archambaud clearly prided himself on his plain, and loud, speech. Since he performed invaluable services, the peasants endured, and were assumed to relish, his dictatorial manner. He saved their cows when they were giving birth; he vaccinated their sheep; he repaired their dogs when they had been shot by jealous neighbours who swore that they looked just like the fox which had been after the hens for the last month. In short, he was granted the respect born of necessity.

The castration of Minou was not a complicated operation, but while the inoffensive animal was being rendered even more helpless, by being enclosed in a wooden box which left its rear end accessible to the vet's neutering scissors, the door of the surgery opened and a rather striking woman entered. 'I present to you my wife,' Archambaud said.

Madame Archambaud was tall and – how shall I say? – sinuously statuesque. The businesslike white *tablier*, in which she served in the office of theatre-sister, did not flaunt but nor did it conceal her proud figure. She had a mass of coppery hair which set off her pale green eyes. A twitch of the sumptuous lips suggested complacent amusement at the pride she excited in her large husband. As he prepared Minou for his irrevocable stroke, the defenceless-ness of those two little bulbs, covered with white fuzz, filled me with remorseful nausea. 'Tell me,' Archambaud said, 'is it true that English girls are the easiest in Europe?'

In the mock-pompous style which comes easily to expatriates, I said, 'My dear doctor, you're talking to a married man.'

'An English girl, they tell me, will do anything for a roof over her head. True or false?'

Madame Archambaud's fine eyes were on me as she held out the plastic bag into which Minou's minuscule testicles were to be dropped. If only Archambaud would do quickly what I had come to pay him for! I said, 'My impression is that English girls these days do what they want and not

41

what men want them to do. Are French women any different? I doubt it. Perhaps we were born a little too early. It all seems a lot more healthy these days. Women are much freer.'

Did Madame Archambaud's face shiver in veiled appreciation of my answer? As she smiled, those fine green eyes slid sideways to glance at Archambaud. 'And that you find healthy, do you?' Minou's testicles fell into the green plastic bag as lightly as, yes, catkins. Archambaud went, with an air of achieved dexterity, to wash his hands. 'Ah, *monsieur*,' he said, 'we are not favoured in this *région*, do you agree?'

'I think we are,' I said. 'I regard it as one of the most beautiful in the world.'

'You've travelled widely. I should like to travel, so would my wife, would you not? She wants to go to China. You've been to China?'

I said that I had not.

'You should,' he said. 'But be careful. Be very careful. Are you aware of the main form of fertiliser employed in China? Human excrement. Human excrement, *monsieur*.' I had the feeling that he expected me to make a note of it. 'On no account eat raw vegetables in China. The bacteria enter directly into the vegetation and cholera is only one of the endemic menaces.' His voice had swollen in volume so that those in the waiting room might profit from his expertise when they next had occasion to visit the Orient. 'When I say that our region is not favoured, I refer to female pulchritude.'

I said, 'Oh, I see quite a few beautiful women here.'

'My wife,' he said, 'is of Scandinavian provenance. I found her in Toulon. She had just abandoned a Swede who was almost twice her height.'

I looked at Madame Archambaud. 'You're *Swedish*?'

She shook her head. 'I have a Danish grandmother. He thinks that makes me Scandinavian.'

'The hair, *monsieur*! The hair, have you ever seen hair like that on a Frenchwoman?'

42

Madame Archambaud said, 'I get my hair in Bergerac, once a fortnight, but he doesn't believe me.'

I could hear the yapping of dogs and the alarmed piping of some bird or other through the waiting-room wall. When I had gathered Minou and covered him with apologetic caresses, Madame Archambaud accompanied me into the office where she put on spectacles to draw up the account. Archambaud appeared in the doorway with a labrador in his huge arms. 'English girls changed,' he said, 'in the Sixties – that's when they discovered what they were supposed to put in their little purses, am I right? *And* how nice it was to keep it there?'

'So we've all been told.'

'And yet, of course, a very high percentage of English men are – if I dare say it – very little interested in women.' He was holding his wife by the upper arm. His thick fingers were long enough to encircle it. 'They lack the Latin potency. Porridge and pudding are bad for the blood. I am not a moralist. I judge no one. I am a humanist; nothing human is alien to me. But facts are facts. Englishwomen are badly served in their own country. One has evidence. Montaigne, do you remember? *Nihil alienum* . . .'

'I remember,' I said.

Madame Archambaud said, 'One hundred and ten francs.'

I drove from Archambaud's surgery to the Mayor's house. I left Minou in his basket on the back seat where he wailed with a rhythmic regularity which, in my petty guilt, I associated with having turned him into a sort of female. I had to visit Jean-François Carrier because he occupied himself with insurance; I wanted to take out a policy to protect me in cases of *'responsabilités civiles'*, which cover such things as starting fires by mistake or having the *femme de ménage* fall off a ladder while reaching for a cobweb. The simple life is full of complications.

The Mayor was a young man who sat behind his desk in a tracksuit. He had taken over both his office and his profession from his father, whose fine town house, with its corbelled Renaissance windows and circular tower, dominated the *place du marché*. There was something incongruous in the severely furnished grandeur of the *hôtel particulier* and the sportive agility of young Carrier, whose father was now relegated to elder statesmanship but whose tastes continued to inform the house. Jean-François and I sometimes played tennis together at the little club behind the municipal swimming pool, but I would hesitate to call him a friend. Courtesies between natives and foreigners are not uncommon in our region, but confidences are rare. How can I ever know for certain whether he tolerated my fluctuating forehand because he liked me or because he wanted my business. As I filled in forms, I mentioned that I had come from castrating the cat.

Jean-François said, 'Did Archambaud talk your head off?'

'My head and my cat's . . . masculinity.'

'He'll be the loudest voice at his own funeral, that one. I don't know how she stands it.'

'She seems to like him,' I said.

'You think?'

As I went back to the car, I saw Jean-François' wife, Marité, unloading some rose bushes, in plastic pots, from the back of her red Citröen *deux-chevaux*. She was a school-teacher at the *collège* and, on the tennis court, an opponent who watched the ball very closely. I smiled and waved and called out *'Bonjour'* without having any disposition to prolong the conversation. I always wondered why Jean-François did not find himself someone who knew how to smile. He was full of energy, but there was something rueful in his tirelessness.

We lead a rather hermetic life in the Périgord. Our house is several kilometres from Caillac and we are happy to close our gates on the expatriate community, whose appetite for whisky and gossip, as early in the morning as possible, we do not share. Nor do I find it easy to write and keep my ear to the ground at the same time. As a result, when I took the now accusingly placid Minou up to Caillac for his injections against feline maladies, I was more surprised than I might have been to be met by an entirely silent Archambaud. There was no sign of the garrulous and opinionated practitioner of a few weeks before. I was relieved not to be quizzed about the erotic urgency of the English female and by the speed with which the required *piqûre* was administered to the cat, but the brevity of Archambaud's silent service was an anti-climax.

Was I imagining it, or did his clinical garment hang more gauntly on his still large, but somehow hollower frame? As I gave him the fee which he wrote out on a piece of squared paper, I was tempted by an inner voice to ask him whether the cat had literally got his tongue. Instead, I said, 'How is your wife?'

A look of reproachful desolation doubted the innocence of my question. Those lips which, on my previous visit, had been so prompt with garrulity could only tremble, 'My wife,' he said, 'has betrayed me.'

Caught in my own trap, I tried to be the man of the world he had previously incited me to be. I said, 'That's life, I suppose.'

'No, *monsieur*; it is *my* life. It is not yours. Your wife does not behave as mine has. I am a ruined man. No one has told you?'

'Perhaps no one knows,' I said.

'*Everyone* knows. I am not a man any more. I am, at best, an ox. She has cut them off, *monsieur*. You know what I am talking about. Why am I still here? Because, *monsieur*, if I walk out of this house, I should have nowhere to go. She will change the locks and I will be without resources. Absolutely. What do you suggest? Should I kill him?'

'Kill whom?'

'Ah, *monsieur*, her lover. Who else? Or should I kill her? There are our children to consider. Posterity, not conscience, makes cowards of us all.'

'I shouldn't kill anyone, if I were you. Perhaps she'll come back.'

'How would you define a woman who walks out on her family and goes to live in a shack without running water which belongs to her lover?'

I thought that I should define her as someone with the courage of her passions, but I did not think it wise to say so.

'Never save a woman from destitution and disaster, *monsieur*. Such a good turn is something they can never support. Treachery is their only form of gratitude. *Experto crede*, if you know what I mean. Your cat is very healthy. I've cleaned its ears. Seventy francs.'

I said, 'I hope everything works out.'

Archambaud regarded me with the contempt he felt for himself. 'I shall oppose him,' he said, 'at the next election. Without hope but with dignity. I shall denounce him for a scoundrel and a hypocrite. Have you found that he is slow to pay when you make a claim and that often he does not pay at all?'

'Jean-François?'

'Carrier, the son, none other.'

'You surprise me.'

'Then you are alone in that.'

I had promised to go to the nursery at Le Coux to collect some rose bushes for the corner of our new courtyard. As I drove in, I saw a red *deux-chevaux* which I recognised as that of Marité, Jean-François' wife. I decided to affect the ignorance of her husband's liaison with the vet's wife which had, until an hour earlier, been quite genuine and, if possible, to do no more than wave. Despite my tactful effort, she emerged from the little shop and made a point of coming across to me. I dreaded the embittered expression I expected to see on her joyless face. 'Good morning, good morning,' she said. She taught English, as well as Spanish and German, and spoke it well. 'How are you today?'

She seemed to have put on the weight which Archambaud had lost, not all of it perhaps, but enough to fill her cheeks and lend her a bouncy quality I had not observed before. Could she really be smiling? For a woman whose husband was allegedly conducting a flagrant affair with the vet's wife, she seemed to be taking it like a cure. I said, 'You're looking very well, Marité. Have you been playing a lot of tennis?'

'Tennis? No. Not at present.'

'Well, whatever you're doing,' I said, 'I advise you to continue.'

At that moment, Anton van Leyden, who runs the nursery, came out of the little shop, bare-chested as usual. He is a very tall and very fair young Dutchman who gives excellent advice on horticultural matters. 'Marité,' he said, 'shall we do it?'

'Anton is giving me Dutch lessons.'

I said, 'Why not?'

The next thing I heard was that Archambaud was refusing to go on his rounds. He was unmoved by pregnant cows and indifferent to the bleating of young lambs; Madame Lacombe had held her languishing poodle against his sitting-room window for two hours without moving him from his torpor. When at last she tapped demandingly on the glass, Archambaud did something which shocked her, profoundly: he barked. He barked and he snarled and, when he came to the door, he bared his teeth and caused Madame Lacombe to run for the first time in many years.

'*Monsieur*,' the postman said to me, 'this is no longer a matter of sentiment, it is squarely a matter of the common interest. Enough is enough; do you say that in English?'

'Quite often,' I said, 'but there's rarely much we can do about it.'

'Here in France,' the postman said, 'we know what to do: we move to the political level.'

A deputation of peasants in collars and ties waited on the Mayor. Their spokesman, Fernand Martegoutte, who owned the biggest herds in the region, was as forthright as he was polite: they were not the judge of morals but to earn a healthy living they needed healthy animals. Archambaud would not work unless his wife went back to him, therefore she must be returned, unless the Mayor did not wish to be re-elected, or to have the deputation's insurance policies renewed. Jean-François combined indignation with prudence. He denounced the intrusion into his personal life, but he conceded the practical point. He would do what he could, but Madame Archambaud was a free agent.

'*Monsieur le Maire,*' said Martegoutte, 'her liberty is her right, but this is the time for solidarity, above all amongst men.'

It took a little while, but Madame Archambaud was persuaded, *pro bono publico,* as her husband almost certainly would have put it, to return to the conjugal roof. Archambaud resumed his veterinary activities and the peasants treated him with a facsimile of the respect they had shown before his horns became as obvious as those on the Charolais herds his syringe was required to inseminate. His wife did not resume her activities as theatre-sister however; she shared his hearth and, I daresay, his bed, but she was no longer there with her plastic bag during operations. When I next had occasion to take Minou to the vet, Archambaud seemed to have recovered much of his former confidence, though there was a residue of balefulness in his bombast. As he was about to give Minou his *piqûre,* he called loudly for the appropriate *flacon* to someone in the dispensary. It was brought by a young, somewhat intimidated, woman who was wearing the same white *tablier* which Madame Archambaud had worn during Minou's castration; the poor cat wailed at its appearance.

When Archambaud and I were alone in the office, he said, 'Well, what do you think? Not bad, do you agree? The new nurse.'

'She seems very nice.'

'I'm teaching her. She's learning. She knows almost nothing. She's Belgian. She may one day be my partner. Today, she is strictly my slave.'

'Congratulations.'

'Oh,' he said, 'my dear *monsieur*, if only you could find

me a *petite anglaise*. I am as good a European as you could hope to find, but one can never be a complete man with a Belgian. Ah, no!'

Jean-François is rarely free to play tennis these days. He has been elected a *conseiller régional* and, apart from his insurance work, he has opened a travel agency, in association with Nora Archambaud. There is some talk of them going to China together, on business. I am sure they will be very careful about the vegetables they eat. Marité Carrier now speaks fluent Dutch. Our cat was run over last week. These things happen.

Melanie

I can still remember walking along the beach at Malibu with Melanie White. Despite having worked, intermittently, in the movies for much of my writing life, I have no illusion of belonging to the movie world, nor do I often find myself alone with girls as pretty as Melanie. Although she was then only in her mid-twenties and had the moisturised complexion and exercised figure of a girl, Melanie had already been quite a famous screen actress, though never quite a star, for eight or nine years. Everyone had heard of movies she was in, though few went to one of them only because she was in it.

Her walk along the beach that California December morning was exactly as rehearsed: springy, but not bouncy. She displayed the off-duty modesty of a girl for whom being pretty was more a business than a pleasure. Her auburn hair was tied back with careful carelessness. If her open air expression indicated that she was happy, she refrained from smiling widely enough to wrinkle that uncreased skin. When a girl comes from Council Bluffs, Iowa, and plans never to go back, she learns to take care of herself. Who else is going to do it?

Melanie seemed nervous of me, just as I was of her, though not for similar reasons. I suspected that her nervousness was due to Charlie Lehmann having warned her that I wrote books as well as scripts and that he hoped she would like me. I was working with Charlie; it would be convenient if we all got along. My nervousness derived from a fear that Melanie would find me too English and too unamusing. Despite its Sunday morning casualness, our walk along the beach was a Charles Lehmann production.

We were heading for Von's supermarket in Malibu village to get some charcoal to barbecue the chicken pieces which she and Charlie had brought to his new beach house where they had asked me and Sylvia to lunch. Charlie and my wife were tossing salad and dressing the chicken with oil and herbs. Charlie loved to do without servants, as long as there was nothing much for him to do.

The houses along Malibu beach are often not much more than very fancy beach-huts. Wide plank decks on thick stilts overhang buffers made of old railroad sleepers; the ocean may loll pacifically along the sands most of the year, but in certain seasons, it can surge and crash with splintering violence. Simple-lifers and their halter-topped, barefoot mates looked up from watering their succulents and called, 'hullo' as Melanie and I passed them below. A matelot-style, designer beach bum who was exercising five hundred bucks' work of golden retriever changed direction towards us. 'Hi, Melanie, what's happening?'

Melanie said, 'Spencer, how *are* you?'

'Good,' Spencer said. 'I'm good.'

Melanie saw that he was looking at me. That was when she said, 'Spencer, you know Tom Stone, don't you? Spencer Levitt.'

Spencer looked at me and then, almost immediately, he said, 'How are you, Tom?'

I said, 'Hullo, Spencer. I'm fine.' On Malibu beach, what sense was there in making waves? I may not have been Tom Stone, but I was fine.

After Melanie had told Spencer about this TV special she just might be doing, if Benny Blitzstein could get the script *and* the goddam budget right, and Spencer had told Melanie that right now he was into taking a long, hard look at his life-style, and we had all agreed that it was good seeing each other again, Melanie and I cut up across the beach towards Von's. When we had trudged through the whiter sand at the top of the beach and were emptying our sneakers on the concrete foreshore, Melanie clutched my arm and said, 'I feel terrible. I just feel terrible.'

I said, 'That's quite a sun.'

We sat on the kerb and she leaned and put her head under my shoulder, in a gesture of helpless resignation. 'You know what I feel terrible *about*, don't you?'

'Don't worry about it,' I said.

She shook her head and leaned back and took a look at me. Was she checking what effect she was having on me? Her breasts were a soft promise against my chest. 'I could *not* think of your name.'

'Listen,' I said, 'a lot of people have the same problem. Unfortunately, there's no easy cure. Only who is Tom Stone? Just in case I ever have to be him again.'

'You won't tell Charlie, will you?'

I said, 'Is this going to be our secret?'

'Can it be. *Please?*'

'Pending something a little darker, of course it can.'

She looked up at me, for a beat or two, and then her lips touched mine. 'Thank you.' Another flattering beat and then she sprang up, as if she didn't really want to. 'He's somebody I used to know.'

'Spencer is, or Tom Stone?'

'Both, as a matter of fact. Mainly Tom. Funny thing is, you're not in the least like him.'

I said, 'That sounds like my misfortune.'

If Melanie's mistake allowed me to be bolder with her, it made her more nervous with me. Her periwinkle eyes carried a hint of accusation; I had made her do something foolish. 'I didn't really know him all *that* well,' she said. 'We skied together a while, when I was into skiing. He was an incredible athlete, and still is, I guess.'

'That clinches it: I'm not Tom Stone.'

'Why did I *do* that? I just can't imagine why I did that.'

'As a matter of interest, did – did Spencer know Tom Stone?'

'Sure,' she said.

On our way back to Charlie's place, Melanie said, 'Can I ask you something? Because what was she like? Mireille. The last Mrs Lehmann.'

'Oh. I thought she was beautiful. But . . .'

'Everyone says she was beautiful. So tell me about the but part.'

I explained that I met Charlie and his then wife, Mireille, in the mid-Sixties. Like so many Hollywood people, they were living in London. I recalled how, when Mireille arrived late and – since Charlie was on location – alone at a loud party we gave in Holland Park, she had only to show herself in the doorway for silence to fall on the room; her appearance was unassuming, but she might as well have been preceded by a fanfare of trumpets. Those violet eyes and the russet hair and the impression of haughty availability excited desire in men, envy in women, admiration in everyone.

The 'but part' was that Mireille dreaded the loss of her beauty so much that she never truly enjoyed her life or allowed anyone else to. When, not long before they broke up, Charlie asked her what she wanted for her birthday, she said, 'Can I have anything I want?'

Charlie said, 'Yes, darling, of course.'

'Then give me yesterday,' she said. 'Give me last week. Give me last year. Give me that, will you, please?'

When the Sixties ended, well into the Seventies, all the Americans who never wanted to live anywhere else left London and went back to L.A.. Charlie sold the house in Chester Square, at a very good price, and went with them, alone. He left Mireille to be taken care of at a highly recommended place in the country. When there is nothing to be done for somebody, it costs a lot of money to do it.

Charlie arrived in California just as the oil crisis was hitting the real estate market. To avoid taxes, Merce Sugarwater told him he had to spend his Chester Square profits on a new dwelling place, and soon. Mrs Magic, the realtor, was so pleased to have any kind of buyer come to her that she kept telling Charlie how lucky he was: real estate was at rock bottom. The whole of Bel Air and most of the Hollywood Hills were going for pennies. He turned down bargain after bargain. Finally, he said, 'Mrs Magic, these bargains are all very nice, but don't you have anything that's overpriced?'

That was when she took him to 1544 and a half, Benedict Canyon. It had six acres of landscaped Hawaiian-style gardens, a guest house for four, ten bedrooms, staff quarters, a tennis court and an indoor-slash-outdoor pool. Charlie looked at the double living room and the fifty-seater cathedral-ceilinged projection room and he said, 'Think there's enough room here for one person?'

Mrs Magic said, 'I don't think a man like you is liable to be short of company for very long, Mr Lehmann, are you?'

Nor was he; but after Mireille died, Charlie did not mean to get married again. Few unmarried producers in green light situations have to suffer from loneliness. On previous trips to the Coast, Sylvia and I had met, and said how much we liked, Julie and Hannike and Wendy and Marie-Thérèse.

'He's had a lot of woman, hasn't he, Charlie?' Melanie said.

I said, 'He's an attractive man.'

'Do you think I'd be good for him?'

'I think you'd probably be good for most things.'

'Please be serious. He wants to marry me.'

'Do you want to marry him?'

'Yes, I do. I do.'

'Why wait for the jury? That sounds like a quorum to me.'

'I so want it to work. Do you think it can? He's afraid. Not frightened; afraid. He's not used to loving people any more.'

'I thought Charlie was only ever afraid of taxes. Do you love him?'

'Why else would I want to marry him?'

'That's right,' I said.

We took the barbecued chicken out onto the deck where the hot tub was and watched the sail boats parading out towards Catalina Island. Now that I was aware of their hopes, Charlie and Melanie seemed touchingly gentle with each other; neither was quite sure whose dream was whose. When Sylvia and I made tactful signals that we ought to leave, Charlie – who had brought us out in his new *café-au-lait* Maserati – absolutely would not call us a cab. Melanie said why not let her make supper and then we could all go back to Beverly Hills. Sylvia went to help her.

'Isn't she the sweetest girl imaginable?' Charlie said. 'And she's clever. She paints, she also writes . . .'

'Don't turn me against her now, Charlie.'

'Only one thing is wrong. When she's forty, I'll be seventy. I'll be *seventy*. How can I ask her to make her life with a man that much older than she is?'

'Seize the day,' I said.

'Do you know what she said to me? She said, "One thing I want you to promise me if we get married, never, never put me in one of your movies. Never try to get the director to do you a favour." Is that something?'

'*Guinness Book of Records* time,' I said.

'That's the kind of girl she is. And she says she wants to marry me. She's never wanted to marry anybody before. She wants to marry me. What do you think of that?'

I said, 'Why think?'

The ceremony was fixed to take place in four weeks' time. There was a picture of the lovers on the front of the *L.A. Times*. The caption was TRUE LOVE. My conferences with Charlie were interrupted by calls from people who seemed really pleased. As Victor England said to me, 'When something really nice happens to really nice people you really like, you just have to learn to grit your teeth.'

And then what happened was this: I used to play tennis twice a week with a coach at a court on Mulholland Drive and one Tuesday, when I arrived in our rented Chevvy, I saw that a stranger was waiting for me. Forrest Stuart, my usual humiliator, had injured his shoulder in an over-35s tournament on the weekend and this big blond guy was his stand-in. We had a good game; either he was sly or I was playing better: I took three games in one set and four in the next and then we went for a Coke.

I said, 'It's strange, but I feel like I know you.'

'I don't think so,' he said.

'Me neither, but . . . I enjoyed this anyway. Can we do it again?'

'Why not. My name is Tom Stone, this is the number of my service; this is my home. Now you know it all.'

I said, 'Tom Stone! You know Melanie White, don't you?'

'I know Melanie,' he said. 'You must know Eduardo.'

'Charlie,' I said. 'I know Charlie. Didn't you see in the paper, she's going to marry Charlie Lehmann?'

'I saw.'

I said, 'Which Eduardo?'

He said, 'Do you ask which Nelson Rockefeller? Eduardo. The man she isn't going to marry. Or who isn't going to marry her. Who isn't going to marry her, whatever she does. Mr Always.'

'I don't get it,' I said.

'You don't live here,' Tom Stone said.

'No,' I said, 'I guess I don't at that.'

'She figured it was time to put a squeeze called Charlie on Eduardo. Even a girl like Melanie doesn't get any younger. She can get smarter though.'

'I think she's really in love,' I said.

'Eduardo thinks so too,' Tom said, 'but sometimes you have to think about your future, don't you? Melanie is a girl who can keep a whole lot of balls in the air.'

I said, 'Her thing with Eduardo finished a while ago, though, didn't it?'

'Did it? I hadn't heard that.'

'You're not saying it's still going on?'

'I'm like you,' Tom Stone said, 'I'm not saying anything. But out here business is business; always was, always will

56

be. Forrest said you'd give me twenty-five dollars. Is that
OK?'

'Pleasure,' I said.

Eugene

Though I had, of course, already heard of him, I first met Eugene Brabant when I went to New York in the early autumn of 1963. We were introduced, young novelist to ranking master, at a private view of work by Arnie Coleman, whom Sylvia and I had met while he and Margie were on a sabbatical in Spain. The paintings, few of which displayed the happy endorsement of a red star, were in the style of Mondrian, whose hard-edged influence, once paramount, was already waning. Arnie's show doubled as a memorial service for the Fifties.

'It's a pity,' Eugene said, 'that Arnold went to Europe just when he did. He might have changed his style in time to avoid embarrassment.'

'Oh surely an artist paints what he wants to paint,' I said, 'not what fashion requires.'

'I observed that you were quite young,' Eugene said. 'I hadn't realised you were born yesterday.'

Gene can only have been in his late thirties that Sunday noon at the Mary Heilbronn Cooper Gallery, but – despite the handsome, unlined face and the crown of dark, razor-cut hair – he advertised the cynicism of seniority. Although we appear closer in age now than we did then, Gene was, and is, only six or seven years older than I. However, his Huguenot provenance gave him a cosmopolitan patina. He was, in feet and inches, no taller than I, but that, of course, was reckoning without his pedestal.

In addition to his other advantages, Eugene had been in the war, from which he had emerged with his profile unscathed and his chest worthily decorated. When he said, 'I don't claim to have been brave, but I must own to being *lucky,'* the combination of modesty and smugness suggested not only that he had done his duty but that he was also the darling of fortune and that there was nothing anyone could do about it. *N.B.*, his best-selling novel about Napoleon – soon, he tells me, to be a major mini-series – emphasises Bonaparte's stipulation that his Marshals be lucky as well as brave. 'Luck,' the Emperor is made to say, in the tones of his creator (Eugene, I mean), 'is the only form of virtue which does not have to be its own reward. It is the only kind to which I care to lay claim.'

Eugene's first novel, with the author white-uniformed, gilt-capped and *jeune premier* handsome on the back cover, created quite a stir: 'I woke up and found myself infamous,' he said, in palpable allusion to Lord Byron. If the critical success of *Now Hear This* was remarkable, the subtlety of the writing prevented its rivalling *The Naked And The Dead*, as its author put it, in anything but quality.

Now Hear This was the story of a war hero whose bravery, as a junior officer, in the battle of Midway was counterpointed by his civilian timidities when he was safely home in the USA. Ambrose Cody proves to fear his mother more than the Japanese; having endured the heat of the Pacific with exemplary cool, he becomes feverish in the chilly face of New England social pressures. *Now Hear This* was written with a wry elegance snugly in tune with the character of Eugene Brabant's charmingly helpless *alter ego*. After spending forty-eight hours in the sea, supporting a dying comrade who once insulted him in a disgraceful manner, Ambrose returns to a mother who reproaches and coddles him as if he were a delicate child who has unwisely got his feet wet. 'Why,' he wonders, 'did I have to be born with a silver thermometer in my mouth?'

Eugene assured me that a squeamish editor had insisted that the thermometer be of the oral variety. 'Cody's *mouth*, you may be sure, was not the first destination I had in mind for it.' Unable to find any good reason not to marry the hard-as-nails slip of a girl, of impeccable wealth and skin tone, whom his mother has, as he puts it, 'booked for him as if she were as irresistible as an ocean-front suite,' he can think of no way out except to tell his fiancée that he allowed his companion to drown because he needed his lifebelt. The dear girl shrugs her shoulders and says that she would have done the same thing. When he indicates, with the delicacy necessary in a 1949 novel, that his sexual tastes do not incline him towards the marriage bed, she confesses that she is still very fond of one of the girls with whom she went to Barnard. '*Amor Vincit Omnia*,' she says. 'That cruel phrase,' Ambrose Cody remarks, but only to a sailor he has met in a Boston dockland bar, 'should be inscribed over the gates of hell.'

However, when his uncle, who is also the family lawyer and a man of antique Boston stock, proves to have embezzled Ambrose's trust fund, his fiancée runs away with another, still rich, young man. Through the good fortune of having a peculating uncle, Ambrose Cody is preserved from respectability, though not from penury. It was, as its author told me, a very moral cocktail with the merest dash of bitters.

As his critical essays and reviews have long proved, Eugene enjoys shocking people ('What other form of pleasure can also provide one with both a living and a library?'), but he provokes outrage in a patrician vocabulary and – during those indefatigable public appearances of his – in a drawling, Ivy League voice. It amused Eugene that he had, in fact, attended neither Harvard nor Yale. 'The South Pacific,' he told me, '*without* Mr Rogers' musical molasses, was my only university. By the time I returned to – let us agree to call it – civilisation, I was too old, and entirely too well-read to want to attend classes with beardless young persons.'

Eugene's vowel-sounds echoed the anglicised Boston 'a' of the president he always called Jack, with whom he had played touch football, many many times, at Hyannis Port. 'Personally, I still *like* Jack,' he told me that September noon a couple of months before Kennedy went to Dallas; it was as if becoming President were a vulgarity which Eugene could only just find it in his heart to forgive. I was too innocent to guess that the sting lay in what Eugene did not advertise, which was his opinion of *her*.

So grand was his manner, and so manifestly good his tailor, that I assumed that Eugene Brabant, like his fictional hero, had been launched on the sea of life on a flotation cushion of old money. Hence, when he asked me, with caustic courtesy, what sort of writing I did, I was defiantly ashamed to tell him that, in addition to my novels, I was driven to do a certain amount of work for television. 'Unfortunately,' I said, '*I* lack a trust fund with which to feed my wife and children.'

'You imply that I have the former and am deficient in not having the latter.'

'Not at all. But facts are facts.'

'Sometimes they are, sometimes they're not. In this case, they are not: I support myself, and my tailor, entirely from the fruits of my own Olivetti. As for my lack – not want – of children, it proves only that I have no wish to bruise the fruit of my loins on what remains of our ignoble century. What are your plans while you're here?'

'I don't know that I spring to plans,' I said. 'I'm doing whatever the publicist at Viking arranges for me to do. Which doesn't seem to be much.'

'This afternoon, what are you doing this afternoon? I'm promised on a radio show. One of those public service open-ended affairs where you can say anything you like as long you don't expect to be paid for it.'

'Lucky you. Or should I say *important* you?'

'Luck is what the happy few have the wit to arrange for themselves. Why don't you come along?'

'If I sit at your feet much longer,' I said, 'I risk being taken for a shoe salesman.'

'Come and be on it,' he said. 'Make a name for yourself among the blind and the senile, the only constituency still capable of understanding words of more than one syllable.'

When we reached KTZ radio station, Gene appeared to be so influential that I was immediately empanelled. Once we were on the air, however, he did me the honour of showing me not the smallest favour or politeness. We clashed most noisily over the character of Lord Byron; when I declared him to be that rare thing, a genuine impostor, a Lord who pretended to be one, Eugene chose to think that I was really getting at *him*. We milled away, as Byron's boxing instructor used to say, right and left, but finally left the studio rather pleased with ourselves, and each other.

He said, 'If you want to write movies, you'd better come out to L. A. I can introduce you to some people.'

I said, 'I don't really like American films.'

'How about American money?' he said. 'I'm not concerned with your taste; I'm concerned about your wife and children.'

I did not go to Los Angeles on that particular trip. However, I did suffer myself to be drawn into the New Wave of English cinema and, for a season or two, I enjoyed a ripple of success. I began to be solicited by some of the Hollywood people to whom Eugene Brabant could have introduced me three or four years earlier. Hearing that I was on the coast, 'Red' Berkowitz asked me to come over to Burbank and see him. His hair was still the colour of his nickname, although the pale face, with its anxiously bespectacled ruthlessness, already had more lines than Duke Wayne.

'Frederic, I want you to read something for me.' He pitched me a thick script with gold lettering on the front. 'And tell me what you think. And then, if you think there's anything to talk about, why don't we talk about it?'

I took the script to the poolside deck of the Beverly Wilshire Hotel, where the sun was not yet carcinogenic and where it was still smart to be called to the telephone. Only when I opened the fat folder did I see that the first draft of *Helen* had been written by Eugene Brabant. As I read his rather grandiloquent version of the Trojan War, I persuaded myself that his heart had not been in it. The script had its sly moments, but they were too often private jokes intended more for 'Red' Berkowitz to miss than for an audience to laugh at. In short, the thing needed work. Before I agreed to do the re-write, however, honour – or cowardice – impelled me to call Eugene Brabant in Acapulco. 'If you don't want me to do it,' I said, 'I won't do it.'

'My dear Frederico,' he said, 'you have a wife and children. You have moral, or at least marital, reasons for being the serious hack I played purely for fun. Make the blind poet turn in his grave yet again, if you can, and give Helen the balls they want her to have. But first make sure you milk the golden calf for all it's worth.'

I did ten very well-paid weeks' work on *Helen*, especially on the dialogue. Eugene himself has remarked, in more than one of those brilliant *New Yorker* reviews of his, that dialogue 'is a field in which the second-rate are at ease'. The loud implication is that he is more at home on the lapidary uplands of narrative prose. However, there were aspects of his structure and tone which I deliberately preserved; it amused me to think that, as often happens when one screenwriter emends but does not wholly efface another, Eugene and I might each be given a share of the eventual credit.

After I had delivered, 'Red' Berkowitz did not press me for a further polish. He wanted to cast the piece first, he told me. I returned to England. It was six months before my then agent called to say that the picture was going ahead and that Dotty Lampard was going to star. They almost certainly had Larry for Agamemnon, Steve for Achilles and they were talking to Marlon for Hector. Marlon had no problem about being dragged three times around the walls of Troy behind Achilles' chariot, but he did want director approval before he bit the Trojan dust.

Not long afterwards, the entire production was on its

way to England. When I spotted 'Red' Berkowitz at the White Elephant and, after I had waved to him, he went on clutching his companion's upper arm as if he had taken an option on it, I sensed that they must have hired another writer for the final polish. One must not take these things personally, although everyone does, of course.

Self-congratulatory advertisements soon appeared in the trades. *Helen* was commencing principal photography, albeit without Larry, Steve or Marlon, the script was said to be the joint work of Stanley Woolf and 'the Great Greek Poet, Homer'. I could hardly complain that the once blacklisted Stanley had agreed to do to me what I had done to Eugene, but I still wondered how much of my dialogue would be heard to pass Dotty Lampard's lips.

I saw Eugene the following month, in San Sebastian, where he was the president of the Festival and had enrolled me on the jury. We disagreed about the merits of most of the films in competition; he thought they were all witless and I thought only that most of them were. We did agree, however, to resist the removal of our names from the credits of *Helen*. Even if it did promise to be ten times more tedious even than the Czech film to which we had awarded the Golden Shell of San Sebastian, we were determined to mill away right and left.

We did, and lost. The Writers' Guild Credits Committee decided that the elements which were not unique to Stanley Woolf belonged to the underlying material, Homer's *Iliad*. Eugene's and my consequent malicicus expectations, not to say hopes, about the film's reception were fully honoured by the reviews. Bosley Crowther was merciless in New York; in London, even darling Dilys failed to be kind. Eugene called from Mykonos to tell me that, according to his Athenian friends, the Greek press had prescribed hemlock all round.

Our unworthy jubilation was short-lived: within a week, *Helen* had broken all box office records in London, New York and, if it matters, Athens. I happened to be in Los

Angeles soon after Stanley Woolf was nominated for an Oscar, along with 'Red' Berkowitz, Dotty Lampard and 'Vincent Vodka' as Eugene always called the director. Eugene and I watched the awards ceremony together. Even if Stanley Woolf had been our closest friend, we might not have been wholehearted in our pleasure when he won the award for Best Unoriginal Screenplay, as Eugene put it, but when Vincent Vodka was named Best Director and 'Red' Berkowitz stepped up to receive the award for Best Film, even Eugene's cool became a little heated. 'They've given that Commie bastard Stanley Woolf *our* Oscar, Frederico,' he said. 'We wuz robbed, robbed, robbed.'

On the back of *Helen*, Stanley became a ranking producer again. A year or two later, he had the nerve (unless it was the gratitude) to approach, and make a deal for, Eugene Brabant to script a film he no longer had time to write himself.

On the weekend after the deckled pages were finally delivered, Stanley called me at the Beverly Wilshire Hotel, where I happened to be, and asked if Eugene had shown me the script. He had not. 'You're a friend of his, aren't you?' he said. 'Because I have a problem. I hate it. I *hate* it. What am I going to say?'

'Have you ever heard of the truth? Try that.'

'Fred,' Stanley said, 'will you read it?'

'That's the poison cup, Stanley. I'm bad casting for Hamlet's mother. Anyway, I don't want a re-write job.'

'I can't offer it to you. I can't even do it myself. I'm contractually obligated to stick with Brabant or dump the project. Don't hang up. I know when the dialogue will play and when it won't. Gene's won't. How can I . . . how can I persuade him I'm right?'

I said, 'Stanley, don't tell anyone it was my idea, but suppose . . . suppose you get a bunch of actors to come in and read his script, in front of you and Eugene. If he *hears* the way his dialogue plays, or doesn't, maybe he'll . . . see it your way, and maybe even volunteer to fix it himself.'

'Freddie, you're a genius.'

'Rumours,' I said, 'rumours.'

'Tell you what, you're so rarely in town, why don't you come by the house, make a party of it? Incidentally, I have a book I've optioned that could be right up your elegant tree-lined street. Come and pick it up. 4070, Benedict Canyon. Monday at eight. I'll have some *hors d'oeuvres* and stuff brought in.'

I went along. Was I a fool or was I a ghoul? Stanley had hired a nice, slightly nervous bunch of young actors. Eugene gave no sign whatsoever of being on trial; he looked more like the judge. When the reading began, the kids really tried to believe in a text whose wooden jokes and overlong sentences defied performance. By the end, however, they had the exhausted air of paramedics who have tried in vain to breathe life into what is irremediably dead.

As they took their hundred-dollar bills and departed, Stanley begged me not to go with them. Eugene looked up and said, 'Well, that was terrible. That was simply terrible.'

Stanley was such a picture of relief that you could have sent him to the framers. 'Eugene,' he said, 'I'm so grateful to you. I'm so grateful to you. In fact, I'm in total awe of your honesty. It really *didn't* work, did it? This is supposed to be a comedy and they couldn't even make *you* smile.'

'It was, *nemine contradicente*, an evening to forget.'

'You do see my problem, don't you? I can't ask Dotty to play Gloria. Because I know exactly what she'll do. She's already threatening to go to Cambodia and look after orphans for at least a week. She'll go for a whole year. She might never come back.'

'Let her go,' Eugene said. 'Whenever the whore of Babylon reaches a certain age, she always want to join the Red Cross. I'll get Elizabeth for you.'

Stanley fidgeted and fidgeted with the Oscar he kept on the mantelpiece. 'Gene,' he said, 'you heard those actors tonight. You said yourself it was a terrible experience. It didn't work, it didn't work, it didn't work. So, seriously, what do we do now?'

'Isn't it obvious? Frederic knows. *I* know: hire ourselves some better actors and read it again.'

That was the moment that Stanley Woolf dropped the Oscar on his foot and broke his big toe. It was the only laugh of the evening; not that I can claim any credit, of course.

Kill or cure

Boucheporn was often in the Sarlat market on a Saturday morning. He was usually wearing an 'English' sports-jacket, correctly creased flannels, leather shoes (nothing casual about Boucheporn), a crisp shirt (ruled feint) and a purplish silk tie with a metallic lustre to it. For all his slightly dated English stylishness, Boucheporn left no doubt about his provenance: his French was authentic to the point of peremptory. Among the stall-holders, neither *s'il vous plaît* nor *merci* figured in his vocabulary. He did not ask; he ordered. He pointed; he watched for a thumb on the scales; he paid. Disdaining slivers of Cantal or Morbier on the slim tip of the cheese-lady's knife, he showed that he knew exactly what he wanted and what he did not. Boucheporn had been around.

Why did he choose to constitute himself our familiar? We seemed unable to avoid him on a Saturday morning. And why did we – or at least I – endure his familiarity in so docile a fashion? My wife dreaded (and often ducked) his button-holing geniality, but I found no way of evading his invitations to step into the Bar de la Boétie for a glass of Alsace. I told myself that I was learning something about *'la France profonde'* as I listened to him exchange ingratiating incivilities with the local characters. He had a certain enviable, if unsubtle, authority; he neither took 'no' for an answer nor easily said 'yes' himself. When M. Peiro, the best of the builders in the region, tendered for the work of reconstruction at the *château* Clairefontaine (which Boucheporn had acquired, at a suspiciously low price, when its owner was on her death-bed), he spurned the estimate and made loud comments on the quality of the work which Peiro was already doing on the Mairie. 'I'm not a Coco,' he said, 'and I'm spending my money, not other people's.'

He had imported his own Portugese couple to look after himself and Madame Boucheporn. He let it be known, by proclaiming it loudly, that Carlos was an expert *couvreur* who would take care of the roof single-handed; he was also a mechanic, a minder and a *maître-plombier*. When Fressengeas, an artisan whose *devis* Boucheporn had torn up in front of his eyes, made a Saturday morning comment concerning the hygiene (and the intelligence) of the Portuguese, the café was treated to a demolishing tirade on the idleness of French workmen and the degeneration of the French character. 'Because let me tell you something, my friend – the Portuguese are a race that understand loyalty.' Boucheporn glared at me as if I had disagreed with him. 'Carlos would die for me; his wife would do the same for Madame Boucheporn. The Portuguese are a race that know the meaning of loyalty. Do the French?'

'We are loyal when we have something to be loyal to,' Fressengeas said.

'I'll tell you exactly who is to blame,' Boucheporn said. 'De Gaulle. De Gaulle.' He scowled at his audience, which raised no evident objection to his analysis. To agree with him did not suffice to gain his favour. 'Why? Because he was an autocrat, do you suppose? On the contrary: because he was not enough of one! He played the strong man, but how strong was he? Ask our friends who trusted him in Algeria. The man was a weakling. You want proof? What kind of a soldier – what kind of a *man* – allows himself to be dominated by a woman? He wore the *képi*; she wore the trousers. A man is a man or he is nothing.'

In London he would have appeared ridiculous, but here, among the wine-rouged faces along the zinc-topped bar, he belonged more to folklore than to some obsolete bestiary. Boucheporn's ideas were obscene, but they were expressed in a vernacular which flattered by its brazen intelligibility.

In his frank presence, one could imagine oneself a bit of a frog. When he asked me whether I followed his meaning, I was pretty sure that I had. He struck attitudes as the cathedral clock struck the hours, regularly and with unconfusing clarity, and always a little louder than you expected.

Boucheporn's wife never came to the market. He shopped from a list, from which he would sometimes deviate with an expansive gesture. He was a *connoisseur* of *moules* and he was not above aborting a purchase of mine just as the booted fish-woman was looping together the handles of a plastic *poche*. 'Not this week,' he would say, 'look at them! White flesh means they've been grown in a tank. They've never been near the sea. Smell!' He grinned at the fish-woman, quite as if he expected her to appreciate his ruining her sale. 'A crustacean should fill its shell, am I right? Of course I am! You don't want shrivelled edges; you don't want' – he indicated with his thumb – 'parasite crabs.' He probed the soft anatomy of the *moule* he had prised open with the fish-woman's own knife and flicked at a lobe of flesh with a suggestive forefinger. 'Does that remind you of something?'

I looked at my watch. 'I must go,' I said, 'Sylvie . . .'

'You're lucky,' he said. 'Your wife can do things; she can be a real wife to you. Whereas mine . . .' He frowned as though I had deliberately raised the subject which he found painful. 'Health! It's more important than money. It's more important than anything. You don't agree? You will.'

My failure to dispute the point seemed to mark me as a coward. Boucheporn's leathery face dropped into reproachful folds. He adjusted his pork-pie hat and went poutily on his way, as if I had wasted quite enough of his time.

I did not see him for a while. He was a man of intermittent regularities; he would appear for several weeks in a row and then disappear for three months. Occasionally we would catch sight of him on the road, wearing dark glasses and driving a big grey Opel with a rumpled wing. Behind the wheel, he never acknowledged my amiable salutes; he had the air of a man of respect. It was no surprise to hear rumours that he had been in the night-club business in Djibouti. A pensioned Dutchman who practised the cello for five hours a day told us that he had heard from an ex-ambassador to Venezuela that Boucheporn had achieved belated respectability by marrying a rich woman in poor health. Madame's money had secured possession of the *château* Clairfontaine and put the swimming pool under its all-weather plastic hood. The rumpled Opel was Boucheporn's own.

One day we saw it parked outside the Vieille Cure when we went there for lunch. Boucheporn was at a table by the big open fireplace where peasants used to huddle on winter nights. He was with a neat, dark woman in a black leather skirt and a blue silk blouse with small white buttons. The glistening hair was cropped quite short on her neck and was shaped above it in a thick, abundant loaf which suggested businesslike sensuality. She looked to be in excellent health. He watched her eat her *escalope de foie de canard* as one might a pet animal; he was both indulgent and proprietorial.

Boucheporn's attitude towards us that day was neither that of his effusive Saturday self nor that of the implacable driver. Only for a second did he appear to recognise us, with a wary bulge of those shameless eyes and a pout of the leathery lips. It was as if he were reassuring Sylvia and me that our secret was safe with him. He blessed the mundane lunch of a husband and wife with the surreptitious allure of an assignation. It was both vulgar and rather endearing.

After Boucheporn had paid, and departed, Madame Guimberteau, the *patronne* of the Vieille Cure, came and stood over our table. I remarked on the chic and charm of Madame Boucheporn, who was not at all as I had imagined. Madame Guimberteau glanced at my wife with female complicity. Surely Sylvia had already guessed what she now revealed? 'That is not his wife. That is his *petite amie*. She is down from Paris for a few days . . .'

The few days became a few weeks. We saw the *petite amie* (in a smart change of costume) in the car of M. Josse, a local estate agent. Word came back to us from our cellist friend that she was after a small property in the region, but not *too* small.

When I next saw Boucheporn in the market, it was approaching high summer. He came up to me with all his old familiarity. Although we had shopped without his help for several months, he took it that I was in urgent need of advice. Did I like pigeon? Had I ever had it correctly cooked? It should *never* be cooked as long as the English cooked it, but then, if I didn't mind him saying so, nothing should. I said that pigeon was not on my wife's list.

'Surprise her,' Boucheporn said. 'Women like to be surprised. They pretend they don't, but they do. They like to be a little bit afraid; they say they want to be safe, but do they? They swear they don't like certain things, but they long for you to do them, isn't that your experience? It's mine. You remember what Baudelaire said about young girls? They're sluts, all of them, the virgins, the innocent-looking blondes, all of them! Never trust them, above all when they tell you the truth! Why is your wife not with you?'

I explained that our children had come for the holidays. She had enough to do at the house.

'Ah family! I only wish I had a family!' He looked at me balefully, as though I had something to do with his failure to find true happiness. 'Alas . . .' I remained poised between compassion and worldliness. 'You and your wife,' he said suddenly, 'you must come up to the *château*. Bring the children! When are you free?'

The sudden assault of hospitality caught me unawares. I knew that neither Sylvia nor the children would welcome a visit to people whom they did not know and whose conversation might not be easy to follow, but Boucheporn was irresistible. He was even carrying a diary (*'on doit toujours porter son agenda,'* he told me, making a moral delinquency of my failure to be equally equipped). A date was fixed. Despite the reluctance of my family, I felt bound to honour it. How often did one get the chance to observe the French in their own habitat?

Although the little gatehouse looked to be in poor repair, the main building of the *château* Clairefontaine had been reappointed with a rectitude that bordered on pomposity. Boucheporn met us in the *cour d'honneur* and took us on a full tour of the newly blonde stonework. When we reached the pool, he demonstrated the enviable speed with which it could be unhoused from its plastic shell for summer purposes. Carlos, doubling for a gardener, was spraying the *massifs* in which pink roses showed a thousand bright buttons.

When we went inside, we found Madame Boucheporn in the big living room, its shelves comely with matched sets of worthy books. She was small and grey under a silk shawl spread over her knees. Her feet were on an upholstered stool of the same Louis Treize style as the throne on which she sat. She was gracious and brave in her role as a *grande malade*. She watched Boucheporn as he opened the bottle of Dom Ruinart which had been lolling in a silver tub. The wish that she could help was implicit in her helplessness. Boucheporn was as kind as we knew him to be perfidious. He spoke gently to his wife and he adjusted the blinds so that the evening sun should not threaten her. He could almost have been an old aristocrat, for whom courtesy and contempt excited the same attentive formality.

Rosaria, Madame Boucheporn's maid, came in with a plate of *Bourbon* biscuits. She served us all, but her concern was for her mistress. Rosaria was dark-eyed but her hair had russet lights in it. She moved with an efficient rustle of skirt and apron; the sound was both decorous and very slightly suggestive of female qualities which were, for the moment, irrelevant.

Sylvia remarked how lucky the Boucheporns were to have such a couple. I asked whether they had any children.

Boucheporn and his wife exchanged small smiles. 'We have to hope not,' Madame Boucheporn said.

'They are brother and sister,' Boucheporn said.

Now we could all smile.

'Carlos used to work for my husband when he was . . . in business.' The mention of Boucheporn's commercial activities seemed to affect his wife uneasily. Rosaria came promptly with a glass of something which fizzed medicinally. It seemed the right moment to take our leave.

On the way home, Sylvia said how sorry she was for the sick, deceived wife. I reminded her – and informed the children, who probably knew already – that the French took an unsentimental view of marriage. Wouldn't a woman in Madame Boucheporn's state assume that her husband had a mistress? One should not import Anglo-Saxon cant into the Gallic climate. The candour of the French eliminated guilt and made reproach inelegant. I was prepared to bet that Madame B. knew all about the *petite amie* and probably encouraged her husband in his conquest; probably she liked him to regale her with the details. We had all heard of *Les Liaisons Dangereuses*, had we not?

'If it's all as cosy as that,' Sylvia said, 'why are they called "*dangereuses*"?'

There was a derelict cottage a hundred metres beyond our house, over the crest of the hill. One day, when I was busy translating Euripides' *Medea*, I saw Boucheporn's rumpled Opel drive up and park, just within view, outside the cottage. If I did not relish the idea of his *petite amie* as a neighbour (I rarely relish the idea of *anyone* as a neighbour), I shook hands politely when Boucheporn knocked at our door and Christine was introduced. Boucheporn wanted to know if there were any drawbacks to our *coin*: were there any mad dogs, for instance? 'No mad dogs,' I said, 'only Englishmen. Oh, and the water supply can be rather unreliable in the summer. And we've got this pair of peacocks in the valley right below us and they wake us rather early. Also, our neighbours do have this stagnant duck pond, which is rather nearer to the cottage than we are, of course, and the mosquitoes . . . well, you can imagine.' In short, I did for the cottage what Boucheporn had done for the fish-woman's *moules*. When I had finished, Christine said, *'Il faut réfléchir.'* I liked the click of her heels and the bob of her breasts in the little black dress she was wearing, but I could not quite look forward to Boucheporn's Opel coming regularly up the hill at five o'clock and leaving again at seven. I was squeamish enough to be afraid he might wink at me as he passed.

The word was that Madame Boucheporn's health was deteriorating. A specialist flew in by air taxi from Bordeaux. He made solemn recommendations. Boucheporn had to be at hand when his wife needed him, but he was no less eager to have Christine at hand when he needed her. The solution was – as the French like solutions to be – logical: Carlos was commissioned to renovate the old lodge at the entrance to the *château* Clairefontaine. Boucheporn's devotion to his wife was matched only by his desire for his mistress. If he could not be in two places at once, he could only make the two places in which he wanted to be as close together as possible.

Whether or not Madame Boucheporn had known of, or guessed, Christine's existence before, it was now beyond concealment. Boucheporn was as uncompromising as he was assiduous towards his sick wife; the arrangements he had made constituted his final offer. If she had been a robust French wife, loyal to the national myth of resourceful femininity, she would have become Christine's best friend and her husband's tolerant confederate. She would have subverted her rival with a thousand kindnesses and piqued her husband with a hint of other interests, but Madame Boucheporn lacked the energy or the aptitude. She had been poorly and she grew worse. Rosaria was with her night and day. Boucheporn, less omnipresent, did his more or less honourable best, in all departments. By the time Christine was installed in the renovated lodge, it was hard to say which looked the more exhausted, the husband or the wife. Rosaria took care of both of them with unsleeping zeal. When Boucheporn whispered that he was slipping away for an hour or so, it was impossible for him to tell whether sympathy or reproach was keener in those dark eyes.

Madame Boucheporn suffered. She suffered terribly. In her strained delirium she told Rosaria of how much she loved the husband who the world said had married her for her money. Why had she failed to make him happy? She blamed the Sisters in the convent to which she had been sent as a child. She remembered her youth when she loved to dance and to skate (how she loved to skate!) and to play tennis. How pretty she had been and how ugly she had become! Why else had her husband done what he had? What good was money when you were going to die? Rosaria wept as she dried her mistress's tears and she listened in anguish to her sorry words. 'How long can it go on, Rosaria? How long? That woman is killing me. The doctor comes and he examines every part of me but my heart, but where else am I sick but in my heart? Do you know the latest? She's going to be here for Christmas. The last Christmas I shall see on earth.'

The next morning, Boucheporn was surprised to find his wife alone when he came to see her. Where was Rosaria? Without her, Boucheporn's life was impossible. He hurried into the garden, where he found Carlos chopping wood. He stood waiting for a moment's pause, but none came: Carlos chopped and chopped and chopped. Boucheporn lost patience. 'All right, Carlos; very well, something is going on. What? Answer me!'

Before Carlos could speak, there was the sound of a shot. Boucheporn glared at the Portuguese, unconvinced by his show of innocent surprise. The two of them ran towards the gatehouse. Boucheporn did not like to run. There was another shot as they reached the freshly varnished front door. A fleck of *tuile de récuperation* fell at Boucheporn's feet. The shot had gone through the roof.

'My God!' Boucheporn said.

The new front door was flung open. Christine stood there on her Louis Jourdain high heels, in her black leather skirt and her blue blouse with the small white buttons. Her facsimile fur was over her shoulders and she had a Vuitton suitcase in each hand. One of them had been packed so clumsily that only a single lock could be fastened. Christine tottered past Boucheporn as if he were a ghost she had not time to see. She carried the patterned cases to her bright red Peugeot – a premature Christmas present – and threw them inside. She got behind the wheel, removed her bracelets and drove away in the wrong gear.

Rosaria was standing in the door of the gatehouse.

Boucheporn said, 'In the name of God . . . what happened?'

Rosaria said, 'I gave her three to be out.'

'Carlos, is that your gun? Did you give it to her?'

Carlos said, 'Could I refuse?'

Christine was never seen in the region again. Madame Boucheporn felt well enough to get out of bed for Christmas lunch. By New Year's Day, she was ready to go to Gstaad where she even did a little skating. Before Easter she was on the golf course. The doctors were amazed (and slightly mortified); Rosaria was not. Boucheporn accustomed himself to the vigorous and demanding company of his wife. When it came to playing together in the Veterans' Mixed Doubles at the Domme Tournament the following August, Boucheporn almost rebelled, but Rosaria told him that her mistress would be cruelly disappointed if she let her down. He went out and bought a new racket.

In the third round (after one bye and one victory), the Boucheporns were up against the cheese-lady and the son of the *pépiniériste* from Le Bugue. Madame Boucheporn performed heroically at the net, but the heat was harder to take even than the cheese-lady's service. After winning the second set with as good an overhead as a woman of her age could be expected to execute, Madame Boucheporn accepted her husband's congratulations and then slumped to the dry, rust-coloured clay and, with a small sigh that a sentimentalist might read for satisfaction, breathed her last. *Comme ça!*

Boucheporn was devastated and dignified. What he might once secretly have craved now left him destitute. A month or so after the funeral, we had him to dinner. He observed our conjugal felicity with mournful approval. Combining what I hope was tact with curiosity, I asked about his future plans. Had he heard from Christine? She had offered to return, he said, and comfort him, but what comfort could she be? '*C'était une pute.*' He wondered, in a deep black voice, whether we knew anyone who would like to buy the *château* Clairefontaine.

I muttered something about time and effort and the consolation of happy memories. With a sudden change of expression, like a criminal who has decided to come clean, he said, 'Look, the page has to be turned. She wouldn't have wanted anything different. Besides, Rosaria doesn't want to live in France. All right, nor do I! We're going to find a house in the Algarve. We both want our children to be Portuguese.'

'A wonderful race,' I said.

Victor

Every student of Hollywood agrees that Victor England has had a long and famous career as a director. Who will ever forget the duet Dick Powell and Jimmy Cagney performed in *On The Lam*? Can anyone, however carping, deny the zest and explosive energy enshrined in *Just Around The Corner*? Victor belonged to the Golden Age when life could imitate *kitsch*: the American dream was still something you could open your eyes to.

He came from a small town in the Ozarks which had never produced anything but chickens. The real-life equivalents of the dear hearts and gentle people who sang that barn-storming final number in *God Bless America* fuelled Victor with an abiding determination never again to live among them. At sixteen, he bummed a ride to New York, where he fetched and carried for Orson at the height of his Mercury Theatre renown. Then he had the luck to step in and co-direct a song-and-dance show for Jed Harris.

When, by way of unnerving encouragement, Jed whispered to him, 'I usually hate musicals and I usually despise the people who do them,' Victor said, 'And do they usually reciprocate?'

Mr Harris scowled and then he clapped Victor on the shoulder and said, 'You're OK, kid. Go to it.'

Victor did. He had the courage of those who have no choice. He would sooner drown than go back to Fayetteville and he did not intend to drown. I did not meet him until the mid-Sixties, just after he had finished shooting a romantic thriller at Cinecittá. *On The Lam* and *Just Around The Corner* and *God Bless America* were already way, way behind him; he was a legend who was not yet forty.

When *The Ides of June* began, as they used to say, to tear up trees, Benny Bligh, in the *Observer*, punned derisively that he sensed that 'the vibes of jejune' ran through the picture, but his tartness only added to its renown. Victor was on top of the heap.

I had recently written a small English picture, which failed to provoke the kind of queues that formed nightly, and even daily, for *The Ides of June*. On the other hand, we had had very flattering notices even from Benny. As usual, the director was credited with all the ideas which had been present in the script long before he was hired; in the tradition of his calling, Clive had no scruples about appropriating all the available laurels.

On the morning Sylvia told me that Victor England was on the telephone, I was more astonished than excited. Victor stood for the very type of Hollywood product to which the New Wave, whose contributing ripple I now fancied myself to be, was committedly hostile. Was that supposed to debar me from accepting an invitation to lunch in Regent's Park Terrace with a lightweight legend? Victor offered to send the car for me, but I said that I would catch a bus. I was still a Socialist.

Victor's house had a Waygood-Otis lift in it. With an impressed sneer I rode up to the first floor, where silk-swagged neo-Georgian windows framed a view of the park beyond the tubbed tulips on the gleaming terrace where an umbrellaed table was already laid for two. Victor himself was disarmingly unpretentious. When he informed me that everyone had told him that the little English film I had written had been brilliantly directed, but that they were wrong because it was brilliantly *written*, my own disarmament quickly followed. Over smoked salmon and caviare, I discovered that Victor was embarrassed by admiration; he preferred to admire others. After I enthused tactfully about *On The Lam*, his brow rumpled with becoming doubt. 'Have you *seen* it recently?' he said. 'It's really not very good.' If he said anything was good, it was certain to have been directed by Billy or Joe (not Losey, Manckiewicz) or Stanley. His most endearing and reliable quality was his eagerness to give credit, in the case of his own work, to those who had performed or written or photographed or designed it. Unlike any other director I knew, or have known, he valued other people's talent more than his own, and insisted on saying so. At that stage Victor could afford to be self-deprecating: when did the golden touch require Midas to advertise its possession?

During London's brief and swinging renaissance, cinematic talent flowed improbably from West to East. Where other American exiles were canvassing for martyrs' crowns, Victor England swore that he had been too insignificant to be blacklisted. He had paid his proxy dues to Republican Spain and even campaigned for Helen Gehagan Douglas against Dick Nixon, but he just wasn't famous enough to be worth hounding. 'I did all the right things and I never got so much as a *sub poena*!'

When Victor suggested that he find a book to option, so that we could work together, I told him that I didn't want to do adaptations or work with other people. 'Unless it's of one of my own books. And you wouldn't like those.'

'Why wouldn't I?'

'They don't have happy endings,' I said. 'I'm not interested in commercial writing.'

'You don't know me.' His voice seemed as rumpled as his forehead. 'I don't always want things to end happily. Except for me,' he said, 'and you.'

'I'll try and think of an original idea worth doing,' I said.

'That would be so nice.'

I walked home across the park convinced that I had kept a cool head. Refusing to be conscripted by flattery proved that my integrity was not for sale. At the same time, I did wonder what price Victor might care to put on it. The sincerity of his praise, no less than the prospect of my first Hollywood deal, stimulated my imagination. By the time I reached Baker Street, one part of my mind was already disgusted by the commercial qualities of the plot which another part was evolving for Victor's seduction. I advanced it tentatively, but when he said it was great, I saw no reason to challenge his judgement. His next move was to ask me how we were going to proceed.

'*We*'re not,' I said. 'Sylvia and I are going to Rome for a few weeks. If you want, you can give me some money and I'll write the script while I'm there.'

'The last time I did that with a writer,' Victor said, 'I never saw him or the script or the money again.'

'That's the risk you have to take,' I said.

Victor sighed and looked down at his monogrammed house-shoes. 'Who do I talk to? Do I talk to Richard?' I had recently changed agents and was now represented by the most feared negotiator in town. 'Tell him not to be too tough on me, will you do that?'

'Of course I won't,' I said.

After the deal was closed, Sylvia and I and our young children were able to drive to Rome in our first, powder-blue Mercedes. When I had finished the script, I sent it with sudden trepidation to England. As if to prove how marginal was my interest in screen-writing, I settled down to write a novel, but even as my Muse addressed herself to worthy work, I kept an ear cocked for the telephone. Victor England had been honey when he wanted my services, but how sweet would he be now that he had paid for them?

One evening, the telephone rang at eleven o'clock. Was it my mother? Was it Gino Amadei, with problems on another script?

'Freddie?'

A writer always knows, as soon as he picks up the receiver, how well his work has been received. Victor's way of saying 'Freddie?' sounded like good news, and it was: within a year, we were in production. Victor gave a dinner at the Hôtel de Paris in Monte Carlo at which, as the famous roof rolled back to reveal the starry heavens above, he told the assembled company that they were all there because of one person; and then he pointed at me. One doesn't forget a thing like that.

Victor and the others made a lovely film. Some people thought it was too lovely: however artfully mounted, it remained a bourgeois romance at a time when Benny Bligh, our most influential critic, was hot for the proletariat and Chairman Mao. Although Hitch himself called to offer congratulations ('Incredible,' he said, 'not a single process-shot!') and André Sarris judged it England's best picture, what Victor always called 'our film' tore up very few trees.

However, I soon had what I (and he) thought another good idea: it was to make a film which was itself a pastiche of cinema history. A romance that began in the silent era, as a silent film, complete with titles like 'CAME THE DAWN', melded into a Twenties musical, then segued through a Thirties comedy into a Forties melodrama and finally widened into a Fifties-cum-Sixties sci-fi extravaganza, without the characters ever noticing that their story had been spread over five decades with all the changes in décor and mores which had blessed or blighted the twentieth century.

To my dismay, no one bought the idea of *Time and Again*, except Victor. The studios said it was too original; they meant too expensive. As money grew tight in Europe, Hollywood went back to Hollywood and so, in due course, did Victor. On one of my visits to The Coast to work with another director, he told me that he had a project with Barbara and Glenn Polunin, authors of a recent *huge* hit. The Polunins believed in working closely with the director. All craft and no art, they hated being left alone by the director to write the script and they liked to be on the set every day.

'Good for them,' I said.

When, on my next annual trip to L.A., Victor asked me to go over to the valley and see the rough cut of *Hooch*, I steeled myself to be taught a lesson in close collaboration. I was determined to be enthusiastic: even if one's dearest rivals have spawned a masterpiece, there are some bullets one must learn to bite.

After the screening, as I heard myself congratulating Victor and the Polunins on doing 'something truly remarkable', I concluded secretly that I knew nothing about the movies or the public. I was furtively relieved – and horrified – to feel, though I would never, never say so, that *Hooch* was a mess.

I could wish that the public had not turned out to share my unexpressed opinion. When *Hooch* opened and closed (Benny Bligh gave it a one-word review: 'Ouch'), Victor tried to be philosophical, but when he read a post mortem article in the *L.A. Times*, in which Barbara Polunin was quoted as saying that the director had ruined her and Glenn's best script and ignored their repeated advice, he was devastated. Unable to believe that she had been correctly quoted, Victor went and called her.

'Barbara,' he said, 'did you see what the paper says you said about me?'

Barbara said, 'Yes, I did.'

Victor said, 'Barbara, you didn't really say those things, did you?'

Barbara said, 'Yes, Victor, I did.'

Victor said, 'Oh, Barbara.'

After the calamity of *Hooch*, Victor had difficulty in getting even a development deal. Whereas the Polunins' career suffered only a bleep and soon recovered its upward trajectory, Victor was denied the only balm available to 'the creative community': he had no work. In most eyes, his situation was scarcely pathetic; not everyone gets to endure the anguish of unemployment in a Malibu beach-house worth eight million dollars, minimum. All the same, Victor was in pain. He had been young, and successful, for so long that the symptoms of age, and failure, humiliated him. He was brave, but how could be pretend to be happy? When he left messages for new people whose work he admired, they did not return his calls. Old friends who were still important players were too busy to be friendly: they might wave, but they never crossed the room to hug and pat him on the back. Who ever thought Victor would miss those things?

I tried to interest various studios in attaching him to scripts which I had been hired to write, but our friendship was no longer a credit to me. When Sylvia and I dined at *Spago* with the Polunins, they seemed as concerned as we were. Barbara had forgotten her treachery and said that she and Glenn were trying to get Victor a job over at Disney, where they were doing something too terrible even to tell us its title. As we shared our gourmet pizzas, all of us agreed that the rarest of Victor's qualities was that he never claimed credit where credit wasn't due. It sounded ominously like an obituary.

One evening recently, we happened to see *On The Lam* yet again, in a French TV series entitled *Les Plus Grands Films du Siècle*. After Cagney and Powell had done the ultimate soft-shoe shuffle, I went and dialled area code 310.

'Freddie! How great to hear you! What's happening?'

I told him how well *On The Lam* stood up. True to form, he said, 'It was all Dick and Jimmy.'

I said, 'What are you doing?'

'Well, as a matter of fact,' he said, 'I'm doing what you do. I'm writing a script.'

I said, 'Great! What about?'

'It's a little idea I had. A love story. In five parts. The first section is a silent movie and then it turns into a Twenties musical and then it segues into a Thirties comedy and then into a Forties-cum-Fifties melodrama and finally it turns into a Sixties sci-fi kind of thing.'

I sat there for a long minute, and then all I could think to say was, 'Oh Victor!'

Concerto Grossman

I have always envied musicians. What could be more virtuously self-serving than to sing for one's supper? Alas, not even when allotted the triangle in my prep school orchestra was I ever able to strike the right note at the right time; at Charterhouse, I was definitively branded a 'non-singer' by the choirmaster. It is bad enough to hear that all flesh is as grass without being banished forever from the number of those who can be trusted to announce it in tune. To one beyond its magic scope, to be a musician is not only an accomplishment, it is to have the entrée to a hermetic and harmonious community. Who would argue with Peter-Paul Grossman when he said, in a recent interview, that he wished that half the time that he had devoted to the cinema had been dedicated to Wagner or to 'the dance'?

Peter-Paul did not disclose exactly what he should have done with the other half of his misused time; he left it hazily clear that it was something of even greater cultural significance than taking yet another dip with the Rhine Maidens. It is typical of his determination at all times to renew himself that Peter-Paul chose implicitly to discount the merits of his 1963 Freudian version of *Winnie The Pooh*, in which the brilliantly re-thought Eeyore was said to be closely modelled on certain newly discovered material on Karl-Gustav Jung. The fact that the imported actor spoke partly in Schweizer-Deutsch irritated some Milne scholars, but I agree that it created a marvellous perspective through incongruity.

It was that seminal *Vinnie Ze Pooh*, and its explosive critical reception, that convinced Gino Amadei, and Gino who almost convinced me, that we should ask my already famous college friend to direct the script on which I had been working for the last six months. It was based on my own story and, in my pettish way, I was not flattered when Peter-Paul said first that he did not normally do commercial crap. Nor was I wholly placated when, after a persuasive lunch at the Trattoria, he relented, on condition that A PETER-PAUL GROSSMAN FILM appeared above the title. The casting of Rosemary Titchbourne as Lola was another non-negotiable demand. Peter-Paul told us that what he valued about 'Rosie' – as opposed to 'some putative star' – was that she could *sing*. Since the film was not a musical, I did not quite see the point. Grossman explained that he saw Lola Gerassi, my heroine, as a woman whom, like Rosemary, life had *deprived* of a chance to sing.

After the film was finished, Gino Amadei said, 'I'm sorry but I have to tell you one thing: the Rosemary Titchbourne has a voice we never hear and the most audible ankles that I have ever seen.' For one reason or another, *The Love of Lola Gerassi* never received a general distribution. As Grossman said in a recent interview, England is a Philistine country in which tolerance is all too often another name for laziness. Only one rare critic applauded the innovatory cutting technique which he guessed had been inspired by Tristan Tzara. Peter-Paul attributed the failure of the film to 'the basically banal *donnée* and, of course, the Bisto-style music.' He had, he said, wanted to create the sound track himself, but 'the producer's vulgar and venal considerations had, alas, prevailed'. However, as *auteur* he had the grace to allow that the blame had finally to be his. When Peter-Paul says *mea culpa*, it is the cue for everyone else to redden guiltily.

The first time I ever saw him, he was wearing blue jeans, Moroccan slippers and a tented beige duffel coat with its hood half-latched over masses of that often photographed, and caricatured, curly black hair. He was carrying his breakfast tray across the third court of St John's College on a

November morning. His porridge was being kept warm by a lustreless tin lid on top of which a much-flagged quarto volume lay legibly open. As he walked, he was reading with intimidating intensity: his corrugated forehead was lined like a manuscript page, ruled and ready for crotchets. There must have been a morning frost, for as he stepped from the paved to the cobbled part of the way to the Bridge of Sighs, his leading foot, in its pointed white holster, suddenly went shooting away and up into the raw air. He skittered backwards and forwards, at once, with his tray and his book. He might have been giving a pedestrian impersonation of Stephen Leacock's man who leapt on his horse and galloped away in all directions. Happening to be on the way to the buttery for my own breakfast, I watched and listened, with malicious anticipation, for the clattering comedown of a man whose reputation, even at the beginning of his first year, both promised eminence and prompted spite. Instead, with elastic inelegance, Peter-Paul repealed the law of gravity before it could be applied to him. He hopped, tottered, lurched, blundered in a cascade of staggeringly balanced improvisations. Not only did he not fall, not only did he not lose so much as a single lump of his porridge, but he also contrived *both to turn a page of his book and to continue reading*. Was there ever a more manifest annunciation of genius?

As recent studies have shown, my generation at Cambridge was top-heavy with theatrical talent. In the 1950s, the difficulty lay less in finding a prodigy to direct undergraduate productions than in recruiting the troops on whom he might exercise his generalship. Emulous contemporaries who could not hold a candle to Peter-Paul were not always ready to carry a spear for him. My modesty was my salvation; I enrolled to play ignoble Romans and rhubarbing mechanicals in a number of early Grossman successes. In his version of *Macbeth*, I doubled as Malcolm and as a branch manager in Birnam Wood; he schooled me to add a neoteric note (not always spotted by the groundlings) to my interpretation of the part of Cinna the poet; as Osric, I spoke broad Devonshire in sly, if slightly unintelligible, allusion to Sir Walter Ralegh who, Peter-Paul postulated, was almost certainly in Shakespeare's mind as the courtier's macaronic model.

The Cambridge *cursus honorum* seemed to be less a ladder looming above Peter-Paul's head than a red carpet leading strollingly downhill, from where he stood, to the highest places in the intellectual sphere. Had I known of it at the time, I should have said in my 1956 farewell profile of him in *Varsity* that he reminded me of that hillside hotel at Delphi where you get into the lift and press a button in order to go *down* to the top floors.

After being laurelled with a research fellowship to study Comparative Anthropophagy, it argued great courage when Peter-Paul quite suddenly renounced his academic career. Since he had been sponsored by men unaccustomed to having their favours set – let alone chucked – aside, Grossman's decision to go to Paris in order to become a *clown* struck some of his intellectual Godfathers as picayune, not to say blasphemous. He justified himself, at a meeting of the Apostolic circle to which he had been elected at a younger age than anyone since Russell, by declaring that, although his thesis was already all but complete and almost certainly major, he had concluded that the ideas of the Hellenist to whose work he had applied himself for the best part of three years were not worthy even of refutation. It was not some Bohemian caprice which took him to Paris, but an out-of-the-blue opportunity to learn 'the rhetoric of silence' offered him by the great mimetic sage, Touvian, to whom Marcel Marceau himself conceded the last wordless word. By leaping into a world of pure gesture, Peter-Paul hoped to come back through a door 'on the far side of speech' and gain a new insight into 'the pharmacopoeia of mundane signs'. The effect of this declaration was heightened, as perhaps I should have mentioned, by the red nose, white face, bald wig, orange braces and baggy pants in which he delivered it. It is typical of the elasticity of the best Fenland minds that no one at the meeting made any mention of the fact that, contrary to the society's Edwardian rules, Peter-Paul was not wearing what is normally meant by a tie.

Sylvia and I were living in Paris when word came that Grossman was coming to study with the white-faced master of the *Cirque Muet*. We were shivering that winter in a couple of rented rooms in the working-class district of Crimée, while I wrote my first novel, but I heard that a fellow-apostle, with money in furs, had lent Peter-Paul a cosy flat on the Ile de la Cité whence he pedalled to his classes in the *Onzième*. I sent him a card saying that we should be glad to hear from him if he were lonely. He must have been studying silence too diligently to be able to respond.

A mere week or two after his unobtrusive arrival in a city where he had announced he knew no one, I saw a full-page interview with Grossman in *L'Express*. Its subject was '*La Musique Totale et la Chose Sociale*'. One phrase was particularly Delphic: '*Pour moi*,' P.-P. G. was quoted as saying, '*la logique est surtout un cri d'alarme!*' When Sylvia said, 'Logic is above all a cry of alarm? What's that supposed to mean?', I replied that I thought that I could give it a sense, but that we needed Peter-Paul for a definitive exegesis. We did not get him until towards the end of that freezing winter in Crimée, when Sylvia and I received an invitation to a '*soirée unique*', directed by Peter-Paul Grossman, in which a critical history of the world was to be encapsulated, with an interval, in terms of music, mime and movement. If I was touched that Peter-Paul remembered us, I was petty enough to frown when I shook the envelope in vain for the tickets I assumed he had enclosed.

Sylvia and I sat very high up in the Salle André Breton, somewhere in the Marais, and were properly chastened as Peter-Paul's little troupe challenged any number of *idées reçues* with a vocabulary, as it were, consisting only of lengths of coloured rope, three beach balls, two window-cleaner's ladders, a bathbrush, a trampoline and a unicycle. I date the decline of existentialism as a commanding humanism from that shamefully ill-attended evening not a hundred metres from the Hôtel de Ville. Some people were so shaken by the iconoclastic acrobatics that they left early, but we stayed to tell Peter-Paul how amused we had been. All at once, his forehead took on immensely responsible corrugations. He looked like a frightening polyvalent labrador who had been threatened with the Nobel Prize for Frivolity.

I chose to think it a mark of favour, though it may have been mere loyalty, that he agreed to be free to dine with us after the show. It had, of course, taken it out of him. Was Sylvia a little tactless when she raised the question of what he had meant by saying that logic was above all a cry of alarm? He responded by opening his mouth in an inaudible shriek which, nevertheless, turned every head in the not unimpressive restaurant to which he had led us. He had, as it were, piped ultrasonically like a bat and transformed the whole room into his belfry. When Sylvia made a weary face, I had to admit that my friend had somehow succeeded in making me feel that my wife had failed to see the point. My mood was not lightened when Peter-Paul deferred to me, instantly, after I had gestured to the waiter for the bill. At the door, the *patron* thanked him thoroughly for the old francs I could ill afford to spend.

Despite and perhaps on account of our affinities, Peter-Paul and I have never become close friends. Over the years, our paths have crossed, but we were never true *compagnons de route*. It was something of a surprise, therefore, when I was contacted by young Giles Carpenter, the president-elect of the Cambridge Union, and asked whether I was free on a certain date in the autumn. The thing was, Giles explained, they were having a debate about Music. When I muttered sincere excuses on the grounds of incompetence, the conniving young man explained that Peter-Paul wanted the word 'Music' taken in a very wide sense, as

91

signifying the domain of the Muses. I said, 'Peter-Paul? As in Grossman?' 'Of course,' 'Ah,' I said, 'and what is the motion exactly?' My question was, of course, tantamount to an acceptance. 'That Today Memory Has Too Many Children,' Giles said. 'He hopes you'll propose.' The motion was arch, but it was not witless. I said, 'Who else was on Peter-Paul's list of putative proposers?' 'Yours was the only name mentioned,' Giles said.

Despite Sylvia's Cassandran warning, I fell for it. As I started writing my speech, I was surprised at the virulence with which my first draft was laced. Intent only on the composition of amiable barbs, I armed more war-heads than I ever guessed my arsenal contained. My original purpose was never to portray Peter-Paul as a polyvalent and peregrinating popinjay, but alliteration, however pusillanimous, trailed savagery in its train. Only now did I realise how angry I was at his perversion of Lola Gerassi or at his appropriation of its *auteur*ship. I had not even forgotten that he never returned the hospitality we could ill afford at the Brasserie de l'Hôtel de Ville. Had I, in consequence or merely in addition, seriously disliked his setting of *Dido and Aeneas* in a Calcutta knocking shop and of *Ariadne Auf Naxos* in the Betty Ford Institute? My vituperation stopped short of saying that he had claimed poetic licence without being a poet, authorship without ever having written a word, and a place in the pantheon only on the strength of being panned, but you could hear the squeal of its brakes. Conscious of my bare-knuckle approach, I told myself that Peter-Paul would certainly give as good as he took, and that I knew him to be very good at taking.

Before the debate, there was a cheerful dinner, with heaps of mashed potato. Today's young men and women in new formal clothes were curious about the world of their fathers, in which Peter-Paul and I had been young, though – as he pointed out – he was younger than I. When we lined up to go into the chamber, my opponent affected horror at the sheaf of paper which I revealed myself to be carrying. 'You've *prepared*,' he said, quite as if this were a breach of all civilised precedent. 'You bet,' I said.

Called to speak first, I was nervous, but I did not tremble. I got early laughs by pouring feline praise on Peter-Paul who, I said, was the very instance of the only child who made all his siblings redundant. His books, his paintings (his recent first show, of ready-made collages, at Maggie Hamling's, had taken the form of a Retrospective), his operatic productions, his stage happenings proved that the brother of the Muses had so upstaged his sisters that they would be well-advised to marry people who could find them jobs in subsidised theatres. There was a cry of 'ooh' at this below-the-belt reference to Rosie Titchbourne's frequent appearances in Peter-Paul's operatic productions. I sorted my papers quickly and proceeded to what I paraded as a sincere tribute to my opponent, who lay slumped on the bench opposite me in a style possibly owing something to Henry Moore's dying warrior. Willing to wound, but lacking the killer instinct, I ended by saying that I looked forward to hearing how many new art forms the great Grossman had conceived during my defence of obsolete forms and old hats. However, I warned the audience not to be too easily seduced by my opponent as he played all the parts in his own Concerto Grossman. He was, I reminded them, a particular virtuoso on his own trumpet.

I sat down to solid applause. When Peter-Paul rose, it was, it seemed, in articulated instalments. He less walked than ramped, like some doomed but dignified caterpillar, to the despatch box. Once there, he groped in an inside pocket and produced a sheaf of paper. So much, I thought, for the sly fox's lack of preparation! He found a pair of glasses – age blights even a prodigy – and piled his script before him. He peered and saw that the sheets were blank. He sighed and turned them the other way up. To his clownish chagrin, he revealed them to be blank on both sides. My feeling of pity was supplanted by apprehension as the audience's rustle of embarrassment turned into a growl of amused complicity. They, and I, had realised that my paper bullets had not even scratched the man whose fire I was now fated to endure.

How shall I describe the fifteen minutes which followed? It was hardly a speech, since Peter-Paul literally did not say one word. In front of my eyes, and with gesture alone, he composed cadenzas and improvised riffs which denounced me as a commonplace novelist, a trudging *cinéaste*, a commercial traveller, a diurnal and pedestrian reviewer, an uxorious husband and a decidedly overrated tennis player. As for Music, what part had I ever played in its inner counsels? I was, he indicated, after tuning an invisible instrument which still failed to utter a tolerable note, never better than a futile second fiddle. He had, it seemed, observed me for years and seen nothing he did not despise. My speech had suggested that he had usurped a dominant place in the arts without being an artist. I was now proved to be wrong: his art was that of an assassin; the Concerto Grossman, which I had dared him to compose, was his silent and cagey equaliser.

When in Rome

Until I got to know Oliver Cork, I thought that I might become a classical scholar. Why else had I spent the unhappiest days of my young life learning Latin and Greek? When I was eight years old I already knew *amo, amas, amat* and all the other conjugations of the Latin verb to love, although love itself was never on the curriculum of any school I attended. Why did I persist along the *cursus honorum* which was so thick with dust and so musty with grammatical oddities? A classical education, I was always promised, provided the only valid apprenticeship if one wanted to have a proper English style.

I continued to impersonate such antique Romans as Virgil and Cicero for several hours a week, for many years, before I had occasion to visit Rome. Although I often gained good marks for my mimetic efforts, I was also capable of plummeting to a gamma minus, whereas, even in the days when he was my undergraduate rival, Oliver remained buoyantly in the alpha class. He had been through the hard school of the Jesuits, where a solecism was like stepping on God's toe and elicited due chastisement. I toyed with Latin; he was devoted to it. There is a vast difference between being clever enough to be a scholar and being scholarly enough to be one.

By the time I had published a couple of novels and Sylvia and I had our first two children, Oliver was Professor Cork in Bâton Rouge, Louisiana. He abandoned sports jackets and flannels for seersucker suits, his Brummie accent for mid-Atlantic respectability and his first, Midlands-born wife in favour of one of his Dixieland research students, an Ovid buff. In the letter he wrote to me defending the virtues of second thoughts, Oliver referred to his new woman as 'Teddy'. When, eventually, they took me up on my suggestion that they visit us while we were living in Rome during the Sixties, I discovered Teddy's pet-name might be boyish, but that her figure was not. It was no surprise that Latin love poetry was the subject of her doctorate.

Oliver had a bulging briefcase and no shortage of academic calls to make. I rather envied the fatness of his Roman address book. We were in Italy because I was writing a film about Lord Byron for Gino Amadei. Working for Gino, however well paid it might be, did not brace me with the intellectual breezes which seemed to blow through Oliver's life. Although his Catholicism had lapsed beyond repair, my friend was soon on caustically genial terms with Monsignorial as well as with Communist scholars. I went with him to a meeting in a Jesuit residence on the Clivo di Cinna where he read a paper on 'Metaphor as the Legacy of Paganism' which both scandalised and delighted his largely clerical audience. It was said that the Pope himself later requested an off-print; as a bonus, Oliver also enclosed his paper on Monogamy and Monotheism.

During the Professor's monastic absences, Teddy seemed happy to go on solo trips to the rich variety of classical sites of which, until their visit, she had only read. In view of what I remembered of Oliver's uncomely first wife, I was surprised to discover how lively and attractive Teddy was. She had long, freckled legs and eager blue eyes and bouncy fair curls; she might have been a majorette if she had not been more interested in the social and sexual strategies of the late Roman republic and early empire. When she lounged at the breakfast table in her maroon velvet robe and serious spectacles, conning the small print in the *Guide Bleu* for answers to topographical questions that had already defeated me, I glanced at Oliver and wondered what secret powers secured him her allegiance.

Oliver was short and plump and dark. His shoulders were already rounded with scholarly application. He smoked a great deal, drank more and was a stranger to all exercise apart from turning pages. Yet he took Teddy's vivacious devotion for granted, quite as if it were he who was doing the favours. And it did seem that she admired and respected him; it was not altogether in a teasing tone that she sometimes called him 'Professor'.

I cannot remember any long conversation with Teddy in those busy, untroubled days before Rome became prey to the Red Brigades and all their leaden consequences, but I do remember her laugh. It bubbled with apparent warmth but I suspected that it was a way of averting rather than encouraging contact. Teddy was a cat who liked to prowl alone. I was surprised when, one morning at breakfast, she asked whether we would like to come out to Tivoli with her; she intended to go first to Hadrian's villa and then to the adjacent Villa d'Este. How about it? I was busy with revisions to Lord Byron's overlong adventures and had not time. Teddy said that was no problem because she and Sylvia were big girls and they could go on their own, couldn't they? I was left to collect our children from the Montessori school where they were learning *'uno, due, tre . . .'* and the two women took the train to Tivoli.

That night, Sylvia had nothing piquant to report. Apparently, Teddy had been more informative about the past than forthcoming about the present. For some undefinable reason, I suspected that she had said something to make trouble between Sylvia and me, though I could not imagine what it might be. The undignified result was that I began to make a particular effort to amuse Teddy, if never to seduce her. Christmas was coming and when I mentioned that I was going to the Piazza Navona for the toy fair, she wanted to come with me. Did Sylvia mind? On the contrary!

After Teddy and I had strolled round the *piazza* together for a few minutes, she went off to find, as she put it, a few surprises for everybody. I am afraid my heart sank: it seemed to indicate that our guests were going to stay for

Christmas. The *piazza* was crowded and, once Teddy had gone, I failed to find her again. I dived into the crowd repeatedly but, like some incompetent predator, I always emerged without success. Finally, I took my collection of hand-made stocking-fillers and went home alone. To hell with the woman!

She came back an hour later, laughing that laugh of hers. She had looked everywhere for me, she said, and finally decided that I had dumped her. I was forgiven, of course, but her forgiveness seemed to enrol me in a conspiracy whose purpose I did not understand. When, a few days later, she and Oliver told us that they had found a little apartment off the Via Cola di Rienzo, adjacent to their favourite libraries, we made no effort to detain them. Promising that we should come and see them as soon as Christmas was over, we drove them to their new address with urgent reluctance. In the event, quite early in the new year, once Lord Byron had been reduced to a slim hundred and twenty-eight pages, we returned to London without my having had any further contact with our visitors.

Shortly before we left Vigna Clara however, Sylvia ran into Teddy at the hairdresser's to which she had introduced her and where Teddy's golden crown of immutably tight curls excited a sort of shrugging admiration. Only when we were dining at the *Côte d'Or* at Saulieu, on the way home, did Sylvia tell me that Teddy had begged her to have lunch and then disclosed, over some of Alfredo's *fettuccini*, that she thought she was pregnant.

'How much of a disclosure is that?' I said.

'A bit of one. In the sense that she hasn't – or hadn't – told Oliver about it.'

'That sounds a bit coy for someone of Teddy's liberated outlook. I kept half-expecting her to call you "man".'

Sylvia said, 'She's conceivably taken liberation a little further than you think. Note the word "conceivably".'

I said, 'Oliver's not the father, is that it? *Seriously*? Is she *sure* it's not Oliver's?'

'Yes, yes. Yes, because he can't make babies, owing to something that happened in an earlier chapter, and yes because she knows whose it is.'

'She told you all about him when you went to Tivoli with her, did she?'

'She gave me a few indications. Did you know she and Oliver weren't actually married?'

'These days,' I said, 'who is – apart from you and me? What do you think Oliver will do?'

Sylvia said, 'It's not only Oliver. There's also Daddy to be considered. Or not.'

'Do you happen to know who he is?'

'Some Italian she bumped into somewhere.'

'*Dio mio,*' I said, 'it wasn't in the Piazza Navona by any chance, was it? You can get all kinds of Christmas presents there all right!'

'She didn't expect to see him again. You know Italians.'

'Instead of which?'

'Exactly,' Sylvia said. 'He wants her to leave Oliver and . . . go and meet his mother. He says he's "*un uomo sincero*" and he had a right to raise his own child. She was relying on his being a shit, so this sincerity of his has rather let her down. All she wanted was a spoonful of syrup, as you might say.'

'Pity she didn't let me know.'

'She did think of it,' Sylvia said, 'briefly, but I . . .'

'I bet you did,' I said.

As I have indicated, all this took place more than twenty years ago. We can now dissolve, as movie people say, to a few months ago when, by chance, we were again in Rome and when, by coincidence, the Corks were also there. If I tell you that they came to Europe to celebrate their only son's winning the Prix de Rome, for his translations of Martial, you will know that Teddy decided, all those years ago, that she would cleave to her husband, once she had persuaded him to marry her, and that she did indeed fly back to the US, and academic life, with Oliver.

We have seen them, and the brilliant Julius, only infrequently during the intervening years. Teddy is still a good-looking woman, although the curls are now sprigged with silver and the figure is generous to the point of expansive. Oliver has renounced alcohol but his undiminished flow of erudite publications prove that he achieves almost equal mileage on *acqua minerale*.

When the four of us lunched at *Giovanni* behind the Via Veneto, we grew nostalgic about a time when we were in reality much less at ease with each other than we chose to remember. Teddy still enjoyed the wine which Oliver denied himself and, since she now has a lectureship herself, in Classical Women in Translation, she was less inclined to defer to her husband. Over the sliced peaches (hers with acquavit, his without), she said that she seriously wanted to know what we thought about something: should she inform Julius' father of his son's success? 'I guess I owe him that much, don't I?'

Oliver ate his *penne alla matriciana* as if the rest of us were discussing an abstract problem in physics to which he could not be expected to make any contribution. There was something about my old friend which unnerved me by its coldness. Quite suddenly, I could understand why Teddy had turned to some Italian stud for a little heat in her life.

Being with Sylvia gave her courage, she said, so could she come back and call Virgilio, Julius' father, from our hotel? Relieved to hear the emotion in his voice and the gratitude on his lips, she arranged to meet him the next day on the first landing of the Spanish Steps. Oliver and Julius would be attending a conference on Love Poetry in the Late Empire, which was not her period.

Of course I cannot be sure exactly what happened, since all I have to go on is hearsay, or rather *her* say, but it seems that the meeting began sentimentally. Virgilio was more handsome, in a silver-winged kind of a way, than she remembered; he said that she was more beautiful than ever, at which she said she laughed (I could imagine that

100

part all right) and murmured, '*Eheu fugaces* . . .', although Horace's lament for the fleeting years rang no consonant bell in her lover.

As they ambled up the steps to *Trinitá dei Monti* and then past the Hassler, where Gino Amadei was staying, and along the Via Due Macelli, Virgilio's mood changed. He was not content to muse on the passing years or to find consolation in what might have been. He might be fifty years old, but he had not yet lost his capacity for passion. Teddy's usual deprecating laughter did not appease his urgency. She should leave this dry professor of hers, Virgilio said, while there was still time, and come and live with the true father of her child.

Teddy was touched, but her companion's fire did not quite set her alight. If she had taken his arm, it was out of kindness, not desire. His puzzlement gave way to indignation. When he began to weep, Teddy was indulgent; when he started to shout, she became alarmed. When he chose to appeal to passers-by, she detached her arm from his and walked away. He caught her by the sleeve and promised, huskily, that he would control himself, provided she did not leave him. She said okay then, but behave. As they walked together towards the Trevi Fountain, she could positively *hear* Virgilio's reproachful silence.

The Trevi Fountain, where Marcello Mastroianni and Anita Ekberg walked on the water in *La Dolce Vita*, is no longer the reserve of wishful lovers or loitering sightseers. There were many tourists, but there were also many hustlers. If it had always been a place where street photographers did not have film in their cameras when they took your money and promised prompt delivery of the prints, it was now flagrantly thieves' row. The few policemen did nothing to allay Teddy's anxiety. She was glad of Virgilio's arm. He led her to the centre of the crowd, murmuring to her in an Italian she did not entirely understand, although she heard and understood '*ti amava, ti amo, ti amaré*' clearly enough. She sighed and said that she sure wished some things were different. Virgilio took a five-hundred-lire coin from his pocket and held it up to her. 'Wish, and throw it in the fountain. Do it, Teodora!'

Teddy said, 'I'm truly sorry, but it's too late, Virgilio.'

He looked at her with his unchanged brown eyes and they brimmed with appropriate tears. She gave him her best smile, as one might give one's last piece of small change to a beggar. He said, 'Come and live with me here, in Rome.'

'Virgilio,' she said, 'you don't understand. I can't. Not now. It's too late.'

'It's never too late, if you love someone.'

'Virgilio, I have *tenure*.'

He slapped her stingingly across her freckled cheek. 'You don't want me, then why call me, uh? To prove that you didn't, uh? *La prova dell' indifferenza*! All right. All right. I have a son, he doesn't even speak Italian. Thank you. *Disgraziata*! Thank you and good bye. *Addio*.'

She said, 'Virgilio, don't leave me, not here!' but he had turned away and he did not turn back. She felt the surge of the crowd like a rip tide in which she had forgotten how to swim. She was conscious of eyes on her and on her handbag. Several young girls, whom she had seen in a group before, converged like virgin sharks. Somehow she knew that they were after her. She thrust the shoals of Japanese cameras aside and scampered to a small hotel and asked, breathlessly, to use the telephone.

When it rang our hotel room, I was alone, having just come back from a meeting with Gino Amadei, who still almost had all the money needed to make that film about Byron I had written (and rewritten) a quarter of a century earlier. Teddy begged me to come and get her from the hotel lobby she was afraid to leave. I grabbed my coat, checked that I had my money and my passport and ran, like a grudging Galahad, to find a taxi.

There was something both flattering and presumptuous in the way Teddy had summoned me rather than her husband or her son, whose scholarly activities rendered them immune to interruption. I saw the sign of the hotel she had named and veered towards it. As I neared the door, I was surrounded by several girls who spoke to me in an insolent *patois* I failed to understand. I stopped and bent down to hear more clearly and that was my mistake. As soon as I was stationary, I was sunk. I felt many hands all over me and, being an unworldly writer, not a man of prompt action, I thought of the scene in Lawrence Durrell's *Justine* where the hero goes to a child brothel and becomes the target of a similar soft assault. I had, of course, already been robbed by the time I feared I might be. For a moment the girls were all over me and then they were dispersing in all directions and I was aware of my empty pockets and started yelling 'Stop thief!'

Teddy had come out of the hotel in time to see me pursuing the girls, whose bare brown legs were so much more agile than mine. As it happened, I did manage to corner one girl against an ice cream cart and held onto her fiercely, though without much idea of what to do next. She knew exactly what to do: quite calmly, she torn open her dress so that one pale breast popped out like a sudden puppet. She then began to scream. In rage and astonishment, I let go and looked for a policeman. The girl's screams earned much quicker attention than my calls for help. She stood there with her breast on show and began to cry and point at me, opening her dress all the way down in order to demonstrate the falseness of my charges and the brutality of my assault. I looked round and saw Teddy. She was laughing. She was laughing her damned laugh.

'I've lost two hundred thousand lire. *And* my passport.'

Teddy pointed to the ground. There was my passport. Somehow its having been thrown down increased my humiliation. 'Damn it to hell, Teddy, why couldn't you call Oliver if you wanted someone to come and pick up your goddam pieces?'

'Oh come on,' she said, 'you know Oliver when he's in a seminar. The great untouchable.'

The girl had put herself together and slipped away. I did not even try to catch her again. My money was doubtless already tucked away under some respectable matronly skirt, where it would stay until the distribution of the girls' daily dividends. Still grinning, Teddy put her arms around my neck and kissed my sweaty, unsmiling face. 'I'll never forget this,' she whispered.

When, over the usual *cappuccini* she told me what happened with Virgilio, I said, 'It's all a long time ago and maybe it's all for the best, but tell me the truth: what the hell made you choose some Italian off the street to be the father of your child?'

'Some Italian?' Teddy said. 'I'd have you know that Virgilio once won the Vatican Prize for Latin Verse. Do you think Julius would ever have won the Prix de Rome if you'd been the father?'

Merce

When I told Victor England that I needed a Hollywood lawyer, he said that I couldn't do better than Merce Sugarwater. Victor arranged for the three of us to lunch at the old Brown Derby on Wilshire Boulevard. After we had been introduced, Merce said, 'I'm an old, old admirer of yours.'

Victor England said, 'Is that right, Mercer? I only knew about the "old, old" part.'

In fact, at that time Merce was not yet fifty, but he had been moving in the best Hollywood society ever since Darryl first hired and promoted him as a young counsel. Merce Sugarwater rarely lost a case, partly because his cases rarely came to court. 'I don't like lotteries,' he used to say. He was an apostle of compromise who could be trusted even by his own clients. Men liked to see things his way; women liked to see him. However, when one glamorous female client sought to prove her gratitude in a way the Internal Revenue Service would have no way of taxing, Merce told her that he was sorry to disappoint a client, but he was a very married man who practised law exclusively for the money.

Lucienne Lafayette Sugarwater was no mere wife; she knew enough about modern art to teach (and sell) Billy Wilder a thing or two. The Lafayette Gallery started out on Robertson, but it soon moved to Rodeo Drive. How did Lucienne ever find time to raise Murray and Paula *and* run the business? In addition, she was a renowned hostess at 2070, Bel Air Drive. The Sugarwaters' secret was that each had expertise the other never presumed to share.

If Merce loved his wife, he doted on his children. Pictures

of Murray and Paula were silver-framed in his office. Whenever he looked up, he could see why he continued to work so hard. Paula had her mother's tastes and she was prettier than her pictures; Murray was smart and very athletic: he was in the Beverly Hills High School tennis six when he was fifteen.

Merce told Victor and me about the first time he recruited the kid to make a four with 'Red' Berkowitz and Carter Crosby (in the days before he was famous as TV's Mitch Beazley). After Carter had been aced a couple of times, and they were changing ends, the actor patted Murray on the head and said, 'Hey muscles, since when do you get to make a monkey out of your dad's top clients?'

Murray said, 'Watch the foot-faults, sheriff, OK?'

When he and his father pulled a little too far ahead, Merce spooned a few easy overheads to their opponents.

'Come on, dad,' Murray said. 'Concentration.'

'Are we playing for money here?' Merce said. 'I didn't realise it was that heavy.'

'I wish,' Murray said.

After the boy got his place at Yale, Merce bought him a classic green Mercedes 280 SL, which had been used in a movie 'Red' Berkowitz produced over at Universal. It was waiting in the car-port – next to Merce's Silver Shadow and Lucienne's Alfa Romeo 2800 Spider – when Murray came back to the Coast for his parents' twentieth wedding anniversary.

'Hey, dad, you didn't have to do this, you know.'

'Why else would I?' Merce said.

'Right! Pity the green's not metallic.'

Once the kids were in college (Paula majoring in Fine Art Appreciation), Lucienne was busier and busier (and richer and richer) with the Gallery. Merce became suddenly and vocally aware of mortality. Victor England patted his friend's incipient paunch and sent over an exercise machine. He threw in a book of Dr Pritikin's punitive recipes for longevity. 'Forget dairy,' he said, 'and remember: I'm going to need a good lawyer for a long time yet.'

One day, after a brutal murder right in back of them, on Stone Canyon, Merce bought a gun. New locks were fitted on all the doors and he discouraged Lucienne from keeping valuable paintings up at the house. The Balthus nymphet, for obvious instance, had to be removed from the bedroom to the Gallery. Lucienne hung a 'not for sale' notice on it. That soon brought the right offer.

Once Conchita had gone home and the Mexican gardeners had turned off the sprinklers, 2070 could be quite a lonely place. Merce kept his gun behind a false brick near his bedside console. When an unarmed-combat coach advertised executive self-defence courses in the *Hollywood Reporter*, Merce had his assistant call the number. He could not say who the enemy was, but he meant to be ready for him.

Not long before Merce was due to turn fifty, Lucienne had to go on a buying trip to Europe. A week later, she called from Schipol Airport, Amsterdam to say, number one, he should stop by the printers and check the proof for the Silver Wedding Party invitations and, number two (wouldn't this just have to happen?), she wasn't going to be back in time for his birthday.

'I'll just have to celebrate on my own,' he said. 'Unless I can get hold of this blonde number who "Red" says is so great for his insomnia. What's her name? Harriet Hellcat? How about you? Is Helmut Steinglitz still wanting to make sure your bedside light works OK?'

'Helmut is still being the soul of tactful courtesy, but then I'm used to disappointment, big guy, aren't I? I miss you, Mercer.'

'And I miss you,' Merce said. 'You're still as great-looking as the day I met you. I just wish it was going to be you and me on the hearthrug with that bottle of Krug, same as always, but . . .'

'Keep it cold for when I get back. The bottle. Have you heard from the kids?'

'They're fine,' Merce said.

'Meaning you haven't. You will, though.'

'Meaning you've already bought them what they're going to give me?'

'Would I do a thing like that?'

'Maybe I should give them a call.'

'Tell Harriet to be out of there before I get back. And straighten the bed, you bastard, or else.'

'I love you, lady. Always have, always will.'

'Me too,' she said. '*Hasta pronto*.'

The night he hit the half-century mark, Merce took a birthday tongue sandwich from Factor's (triple, on rye, hold the mustard) and a stack of contracts into his den and prepared to bludgeon himself into tiredness. Around eleven o'clock, he heard the clink of something against glass. There was a lot of it in 2070, Bel Air Drive. He had once said to Murray, after one of the kid's less controlled parties, 'People who live in glass houses don't get stoned.' The sound could have been a branch from the patio's tree being blown against the French doors. They had mentioned the Santa Anas starting up again, but supposedly not for a couple of days. Was that a glass door sliding in its oiled groove? Not even the Santa Anas slid doors open.

Merce padded, in his socks, to his *en suite* bathroom, without turning on any new light. In the mirror behind the throne, he glimpsed the glint of movement in the living room behind him. Jesus, what was that? The clumsy bastard must have walked into one of the Balinese umbrellas. Before he could have time to recover his poise, Merce launched himself across the floor with a tutored yell of martial venom and bracketed the intruder's head to him with a forearm locked under the chin.

'Holy Christ!' the man said.

'No,' Merce said, 'I'm just the man who lives here. And you're the man who doesn't. You to play. Make it good.'

'You are some mover, mister. I didn't know there was anybody at home. They said . . .'

'Did they? Who did? Who told you to come up here?'

The man said, 'I was looking for some people is all.'

Nylon parka, oily jeans, jogging shoes, blue work-shirt: as his eyes became accustomed to the smear of light from the poolside lights, Merce checked off the wardrobe of the no-hoper. 'You're a cheap two-bit thief, am I right?'

'No, sir, you're not. I didn't come here to steal nothin'.'

'What were you doing, looking for a party?'

'I'll tell you something: you're in pretty good shape for a man your age. You're in *damn* good shape. Really.'

'Someone tell you different? I want you with your hands on the mantelpiece. And now spread your legs.'

'You don't have to do this,' the man said, 'unless you want to. It's under my arm.'

'What is?'

'My piece. What did you think? My *dick*? Listen, give me twenty bucks, mister, what do you say, and I'm out of here?'

'Why do you have this with you?'

'OK, so I'm a thief. What do you expect me to carry? A clarinet?'

'So what did you come for? The pictures? They don't happen to be here any more. What?'

'What does it matter? Gimme ten. Gimme ten and I'm out of here, OK?'

'No,' Merce said. 'No. No it's not OK. Fuck you.'

'Don't get excited.'

'Don't tell me what to get. Just . . .'

'It gets some people in the pants, having someone in their power. I know this from experience. I know you're a lawyer . . .'

'How do you know that? How do you know that?'

'How do I know that? Maybe they told me; they told me. You're famous. Didn't you know? It make you horny, doesn't it? Power. So don't be surprised is all I'm saying. Ten bucks and I'm history. Car fare.'

'How did you get here?'

'I took a bus and I walked.'

'What kind of a burglar doesn't have transport? How were you going to take anything?'

'I was told there was cash.'

'No, you weren't, because there never is. The bus driver carries more cash than I keep in this house.'

'Whatever.'

'Are you listening to me?'

'I listen good with a gun in my nose. What?'

'I'm going to turn you loose.'

'I appreciate that. How about the ten?'

'And then I'm going to call the patrol. I'll give you a coupla seconds and then I'm going to call the Bel Air patrol and if they catch you, well, then they catch you.'

'Two-way bet. That figures. Let's do it.'

Merce marched the intruder to the door. Once he was out under the flame trees, Merce stepped back inside, snapped the locks, and called the Bel Air Patrol. Then he threw the man's cheap gun on the bed and rummaged behind the greased brick for his own. He went back and picked up the Balinese umbrella and then, with the Smith and Wesson in his hand, he opened the front door. He figured he would get into Lucienne's Alfa, back up and around and shine the headlights down the drive. That way, if he was still around, the intruder would be flushed into the path of the incoming patrolmen.

As Merce approached the 2800, he saw the man in the driver's seat, trying to wire the car. Merce nudged the gun right against his temple. 'Now you listen to me,' he said, 'I'm very, very nervous. I'm so nervous I'm liable to kill you if you do anything at all. Even like breathe maybe. So now get out. We're going to play statues till the patrol get here.'

'These damned imports. They have the craziest ignition systems, don't they?'

'Get out when I tell you, you fuckin' freak.'

'Easy, Mercer . . . you don't have to talk that way. I understand your feelings.'

110

'I want you in there. I want you in there and lying down on the floor. In the hall. Be careful of those.'

'What are they exactly?'

'They're antique boxes from Nepal. You make one move and I'll kill you.'

'Relax, fellah; I'm still the same guy. Did I make any moves before?'

'How dare you try stealing my wife's car?'

'How did I know it was hers? Did you seriously call the patrol?'

'Damned right.'

'That's a nice automobile, but it's a crazy ignition system they have on those things. Excuse me, but is this a service you actually *pay* for?'

'They'll be here,' Merce said. 'You called me something back there. What did you call me?'

'Call you?'

'You called me by name. Who told you my name?'

'How would I know your name?'

'Is my question.'

'Unless they told me. What did I say it was? And was it?'

'You're a devilish little lying bastard.'

'That's summarising. It's not all I am. By any means.'

'Don't try charm. Not on me. Not now.'

'OK, so we won't get married after all.'

'You called me Mercer.'

'I think they're ripping you off. The patrol. They're ripping you off. You don't seem to be on their A list. It was me, I'd make a stink.'

'Keep your face down on the floor. Eat that rug.'

'I can't afford to eat rugs this good.'

'When I tell you to.'

'Sir, can I ask you one more thing? Right up your alley. Which is, can you recommend a good lawyer? Mercer is your name?'

'You know damn well it is. But how?'

111

'I think we have company,' the man said. 'We have company.'

The patrol car's headlights were swaying over Lucienne's rare tropical shrubs. The man rolled his eyes for permission and then he was on his feet and offering his wrists to the patrolman. He and Merce almost smiled together and then Merce was alone again. He turned on the TV and watched a tennis tournament, live, in some city where it was still light. At three in the morning, he had wound down enough to tell himself to go to bed. He lay there, counting his heartbeats. How many more would there be?

The telephone woke him. 'Dad?'

'Murr! What's wrong, son?'

'I'm at LAX. I'll be right over. Talk to nobody till I get there.'

'Who am I going to talk to, six in the morning and your mother's not here?'

When Murray arrived, in fawn slacks, cashmere sweater, hair wetly combed back, no shirt under the Giorgio Armani bad boy jacket, he said, 'What's going on suddenly? How come you're all by yourself?'

'Mummy's still in Europe.'

'On your birthday? That's unconscionable.'

'This has been some night,' Merce said. 'I had a break-in here. I had a punk break in and I nailed him, Murr. I nailed him right there where you're standing.'

'Is she going to be back for the anniversary?'

'Sure.'

'Sure she is. The invitations are out, right? She wouldn't miss a thing like that.'

'I have to go collect them. What are you doing here, Murray? What brings you to L.A. all of a sudden? You don't have to tell me her name if you don't want to. Hey, you didn't lose your job, did you?'

'It lost me,' Murray said. 'I don't want to be a lousy photographer.'

'There aren't any, are there?' Merce said. 'They're all highly talented.'

'This character broke in here . . .'

'I handled him. I was shaking, but I handled him. You'da killed him.'

'We don't have too much time. Dad, he's why I'm here. This is something else you're going to have to handle. Alan is why I'm here.'

'*Alan*? Do I know an Alan?'

'I thought he maybe told you his name. You had your gun up his nose as I understand it . . .'

'His gun. I had his . . . He's someone you *know*?'

'You're going to have to stay cool, dad. Because . . . Dad, how much do you know about me?'

'Well, I know you recently combed your hair, so there has to be something you want. Presumably something that folds and fits neatly in the back pocket. Are you doing drugs again? What's going on around here?'

'Alan could make one phone call, OK? He called me. Now come to your reasonable conclusion about what's going on.'

'I conclude he had his damn nerve. He took advantage of you, Murr. I never presumed to choose your friends, but this character is a low-life. He's a menace to society. I can see why you liked him, but . . .'

'Alan never had an even break in his whole life.'

'Well, don't look at me to give him one now. If by an even break you mean dropping the charges. He came in here with a gun.'

'And you've still got a hard-on, haven't you, just thinking what a fucking giant-killer you were?'

'Is that how you talk to your father?'

'Dad, I'm sorry, but it was always going to come out. I thought you'd both be here, you and mother. That's why he came here. The way you always are. Alone. With the Krug and the hearthrug. Of *course* I knew.'

'What was he going to take? We don't keep any pictures

113

up here any more. Your mother's jewellery? She keeps nearly all of it in the vault.'

'Dad, make an effort. Try having your worst suspicions.'

Merce said, 'You sent him up here to kill your mother and father? Are you smiling? Is that a smile I can see on your face? I want you out of this house, right now; and forever. I want you out of my sight. You don't exist.'

'You want to get some breakfast? Let's get some breakfast. We have a negotiation in train here.'

'I'm still trying to believe that this is some kind of a joke.'

'Why not? Why not call the patrol and tell them exactly that? Better still go down there. Sincerity is always better in person. The whole thing was a practical joke, officer. You cracked the case, dad. Damage-limitation always was your preferred field. I'm going to get some juice at least. Want some?'

'You send a man up here with a gun . . .'

'You still have it?'

'Damn right.'

'Thank God. We can deep-six it right away. There goes their case. We have every chance of getting Alan out of there before he has an asthma attack. He has asthma attacks in stress situations.'

'Imagine your mother when she – '

'No, *you* imagine. Imagine the happiest couple in the whole world, deeply respected and admired, with a Silver Wedding coming up in just over two weeks. Everybody's due to be there. I can't wait; Paula neither.'

'I can't think how she's going to take this.'

'Oh heck, spoilt little bitches just have to learn how to handle disappointment sooner or later. Part of the higher educational process.'

'Murray, you're an evil little bastard. Don't you dare bring your sister into this.'

'She's in it. How about ART EXPERT DAUGHTER CO-DEFENDANT IN MURDER PLOT? Quite a party topic, right?'

'Who are you? I don't know you. Who are you?'

'Hold up, Dad. Paula's a big girl today. Shall I tell you what she likes to do? Shall I tell you what *I* like to do? With Alan? Alan is not just some punk; he's some punk I happen to love.'

'Love! You talk to me about love?'

'You know who started me on the slippery road to butt-fucking? Your old buddy Carter Crosby. Come to think of it, you negotiated his deal, didn't you? You set it up. And then shut your eyes. Tight.'

'I WANT YOU OUT OF THIS HOUSE. Do you hear me?'

'Nope. Nothing coming through, I'm afraid.' Murray drank juice from a high glass and rolled his eyes towards his father. 'OK, suppose I was exaggerating. Suppose Paula didn't know how far this was going to go. Suppose she just thought we should shake you down for a few grand. Does that help you feel any better? Or think any clearer? Because what I need you to come up with is a good reason why we really and truly need to spring Alan and have you and mother get the place straightened out in time for the party. Here's a clue: think Paula.'

'You *touch* her, either of you.'

'You're not grooving, you're not grooving. OK, try it round another way. Why did you have mother take the Degas and the Dufys and the Balthus out of the house and down to the Gallery?'

Merce said, 'Because I didn't want valuable things hanging around the house. Now get out of my life.'

Murray was being steady-handed with a fresh slug of juice. 'They have women's jails in this country too, you know.' He looked at his father and then sipped his V8. 'How come you're so sure those paintings were valuable? Genius may be immortal, but not even Claude Monet went on painting pictures forty, fifty, as much as sixty years after his death. And it is naughty, not to say indictable, to sign his name to water-lilies he never

115

floated.' Murray looked at his slim watch. 'Nine a.m.! Opening time at the Precinct House! Put on a nice smile and let's got to it, shall we?'

Merce was steadying himself; he had both hands on the Cuisinart.

'You should never have encouraged Paula to study *genuine* moderns, should you, Dad? If she'd stuck to Renaissance, she'd maybe never have realised her mother was rich and famous out of peddling fakes. Paula's lover is Jamaican, are you aware? Are you in favour? Walford. What's the latest liberal position on that?'

'Her life is her own.' Merce's voice was very white.

'Alan gets sprung, no one ever ever knows. Except it might be a good plan to close the gallery, while mom's still ahead. She should maybe spend more time taking care of fatso. You're looking older, Merce. She can warm your slippers. Something different for her to do on the hearth-rug, come next anniversary!'

Merce said, 'I'll go get the car.'

'I think you'll like Alan,' Murray said, 'when I bring him to the party. Tell you what, I'll even take the pictures. I'll shoot the party for you. Is that a deal?'

It was almost a year later when the community read in the papers how Mercer Sugarwater had surprised a burglar jiggling the combination on Lucienne's new jewellery safe. As Victor England tells it, but strictly not for publication, the man did not argue with the Smith and Wesson, but he warned Merce, as the lawyer reached with his free hand to call the patrol, that he would serve only maybe a year in jail at the outside. 'And then, soon as I'm out, I'm going to come looking for the guy who turned me in. Think about that, mister.'

Merce thought about it and then he shot three, four, five bullets into the man's chest and head. The coroner was satisfied that a respectable lawyer would only do that sort of thing in self-defence, but 'Red' Berkowitz, with whom I happened to be eating sushi a few days later, asked me why

116

I thought Merce had fired that many times, and in his own house.

'I can't imagine,' I said.

Costa Christmas

Our friends the Foulders have lived just outside Torreroja for almost thirty years now. We were young and poor and artistic together on the Costa del Sol when Torreroja was an ill-favoured fishing village on the road between Malaga and Gibraltar. The Guardia Civil patrolled in surly pairs, wearing portable-typewriter hats and the most common form of transport was a donkey.

Every Christmas we would escape from the cold and wet of London and rent a tiny house with a flowering patio and a view of the sea. The Foulders were our neighbours and would come over to share Christmas lunch in the sun on our patio. Gerry was a bow-legged painter, always in a jeans outfit. He was already creased by middle age, although he was not yet thirty. He had worked in advertising in New York City; Margie had been art editor of a glossy magazine. They had made a little money and they were determined to devote themselves to Art. He was an abstract expressionist; Margie worked in clay. They were looking for somewhere to buy and settle permanently. Why didn't we come in with them?

'I'm afraid the simple life is still beyond my means,' I said.

'There's this great property in the hills. Pennies! At least come and see it. Olive trees; figs; a great view.'

'I'll gladly come and see it,' I said, 'But that won't put cash in my account, will it?'

My failure to grab half of the hill which the locals call La Chica, when it was just five pesetas a square metre, is one of the great dropped catches in the history of real estate. Gerry and Margie did their sums several times, but even at that price they could afford only half of 'The Pretty One'. Ramon Delgado sold it to them and used the money to buy a dump truck. The Foulders built themselves a studio on their half of the hill. La Chica was so called for obvious anatomical reasons: it was twin-peaked and resembled the splendidly rounded breasts of Juanita the gypsy girl, whose yellow-sweatered charms gave her father's flamenco evenings an appreciative following.

In due course, we left Spain, with a promise to come back and see the Foulders next Christmas. Gerry painted; Margie sculpted; I wrote some movies and made enough to think of buying that winter hideaway on the costa. By the mid-Sixties the prices were rising; I missed yet another bus. While I dithered, someone else moved in. Ramon Delgado's sons, now in the construction business, arrived to build the newcomers' house. It was a small fortress, with barred windows and a studded door. There were heavy gates and a barbed wall. The Pinzls were rumoured to have come from Brazil.

The Foulders watched as the Costa del Sol exploded into garish prosperity. Towers of Babel rose in tiers where gypsies once strutted. Dry old Andalusia yielded to watered golf courses and supermarkets bigger than the Ritz, and ritzier. You rarely saw a donkey.

One sunny day, the Foulders heard the whoop of sirens approaching La Chica. The Guardia Civil had long since abandoned their cloaks and the Lee Enfields; they now came in cars as creamy and colourful as ice-cream sundaes. However, their birds had already flown. The Pinzls, it was rumoured, had been crated in boxes and exported to Israel to answer charges about their earlier life.

Gerry and Margie were properly shocked when they learned of their late neighbours' iniquities, but they were also understandably anxious about what would happen to El Marqués, the Pinzls' bunker. There was talk of a high-rise hotel, then of a disco-development. The Foulders had survived, financially, but they lacked the resources to protect their privacy by buying the other breast of La Chica. The asking price was half a million pounds.

The Foulders waited, but not for long. A maroon Rolls came, its occupants saw, and were evidently conquered. The car went away and the Delgado brothers and their bulldozers arrived. The Pinzls' little redoubt was swept aside like a shanty. A mansion was soon being put together. New and wider gates were put up, with electronic security. The lane had to be widened. How else could you get a pantechnicon, with a full-sized snooker table in it, up to the new house?

On yet another sunny day, Gerry was working in his studio when the antique bell jangled. Two men had come to see him. One was very large; the other was Charlie Bruin. He was smoking a Havana, wasn't he? And he did the talking. To come to the point, how much did Gerry want for his half of La Chica? Gerry laughed. The two men did not. Margie came in and wanted to know what was happening.

Gerry said, 'Nothing.'

'Look, don't get me wrong,' Bruin said, 'I want to be a good neighbour, all right? I'm a naturally friendly person, aren't I, Tich?'

'Nearly always,' Tich said.

'Only I thought maybe I could do you a good turn. Because this house – forgive me for saying so – but it's a bit archaic, you might say, isn't it? I take it off your hands, at a figure to be agreed mutually, and everybody's happy. You got in early, they tell me. Clever.'

Gerry said, 'And we're staying late. We don't want to sell.'

'Absolutely the right tactics,' Charlie Bruin said. 'Exactly what I'd say. No sale: up goes the price. OK. Two hundred thou, in any currency you say. Fair?'

'It's very nice of you . . .'

'No, no. No, no, no. Nice don't come into it.' Charlie looked through the big windows on the low-walled terrace. 'Not got much security here.'

'We don't have anything anyone would want,' Margie said.

'Them gypsies is scallywags,' Charlie Bruin said, 'from what we hear. All right, two fifty. You just made fifty grand in a couple of minutes.'

'We're not selling, thanks.'

'Must be very fragile,' Charlie Bruin said, admiring one of Margie's terracotta goats.

Gerry Foulder's father had been a cop. He had once eaten Lucky Luciano's spaghetti – and lived. Gerry could recognise a crook and his ways without breaking sweat, but he was still alarmed by Bruin's intentions. The Spanish authorities might not welcome Charlie and his fugitive kind, but his money gave him leverage, not to say immunity.

For the moment, Charlie Bruin persisted with amiability. He joined El Esmeralda Golf and Leisure club complex and invited Gerry to swing a club. He asked the Foulders to little parties for three hundred at El Rey (the house was now a palace next door). Charlie asked Margie to design him a birdbath, 'big enough to take Jumbos, darling'. The Foulders were polite but they were not seduced. When they refused three hundred grand for their half of La Chica, hints were dropped of less diplomatic methods. Their VW became rather mysteriously prone to punctures. A studio window was shattered by a stone.

But Charlie never turned nasty personally. He would slow down in the Roller – or the Range Rover – and offer lifts. He suggested that the Foulders try the new diving board at El Rey. One way or another, he wanted that other hill. Meanwhile, he set about making himself popular on the coast. He played golf with celebrities. He invested. He hobnobbed with the classier crooks. He talked to the yacht poeple at Puerto Banus and set about buying a forehand from Lew Hoad. Okay, so he had had a bit of a rough past, but now Charlie wanted to live nice.

This new appetite for decorum did not mean that Charlie

lessened the pressure on Gerry and Margie. Their dog grew sick. They suspected poison. They were brave, but they were anxious. How long could they resist the pressure of a man without scruples and with no shortage of the ready? They were out-gunned and they knew it. They began to think in terms of settling for a fortune, despite their long affection for La Chica. They asked us to come down to the Costa del Sol for one last Christmas. How much longer could they resist Charlie Bruin's unsubtle pressure?

Charlie was going up in the world. The Sheik asked him to his pre-Christmas shindig. The Sheik's place made El Rey look like a shanty. In his own country, of course, the Sheik would never have offered Dom Ruinart; up near Estepona, the champagne flowed like the oil which made the Sheik rich. By the time Charlie and Tich came rolling home in the Corniche, they too were well oiled. If they now fancied themselves as gentlemen of leisure, they had not lost their jungle instincts. They both spotted the open windows and the flare of surreptitious light. 'Bloody nerve,' Charlie said, 'someone's doing his Christmas shopping.'

The gypsy was quick, but Tich was quicker. They cornered him in the laundry room. He had a pocketful of cigarettes and an agate lighter worth a few quid. 'Stocking fillers, is it?' Charlie said.

In a different mood, he might have told Tich to bung the poor little sod a few pesetas, but when he tried to do a runner and made the mistake of kicking a bit, they decided to teach him a good lesson. They gave little Paco a right spanking. Then they threw him out into the lane.

Gerry found him in the morning, half-dead. He put him in the VW and got him to Malaga hospital, just in time. Charlie and Tich were well pleased with themselves. They promised Gerry that no one would be messing about with his car again in the future, or breaking his windows, because it was obvious who'd done all that business now, wasn't it? Oh and by the way, there was going to be a big New Year's Eve do at El Rey. The Sheik was coming. Gerry and Margie had to come, and bring their friends. And another thing, they hadn't forgotten about his final offer, had they? There was such a thing as the top of the market, wasn't there? Never a good idea to miss it. See you.

Paco was in hospital for a week. Soon after he came out, Gerry saw Charlie and Tich in the Roller with a couple of blondes of distinction, waiting at the closed gates of El Rey. They couldn't get the automatic gates to open. 'Bloody Spanish rubbish,' Charlie said.

A day or two later, Tich came round to the studio, while Margie was throwing some clay. He wanted to know if the Foulders were having any trouble with their water supply. They weren't. Charlie was. There wasn't a drop at El Rey and Rita had the runs from eating some fancy muck at Puerto Banus.

The next thing they heard, the swimming pool had turned 'bright brown'. The filter was bust and it couldn't be repaired before New Year. Sounds of frustration and displeasure were audible over the wall. The phone was no longer working. Charlie couldn't call the plumber or his stockbroker. It was unbelievable. By the time we arrived to stay with Gerry and Margie, the electrics had packed up at El Rey. The Rolls had three flat tyres on Christmas Eve. The Range Rover wouldn't start. Charlie hurt his hand punching the wall on the patio, he was so angry. He came round to see Gerry, because Gerry spoke the damned language, didn't he, and maybe he could do something?

Gerry said, 'No one in Spain ever teaches a gypsy a lesson.'

'He was thieving,' Charlie Bruin said, 'he was a scallywag. He was out of order.'

'They have long memories,' said Gerry, 'and a great many cousins and they can walk through walls.'

'All right,' Charlie Bruin said, 'all right. Ask the little sod how much he wants. He wants a Christmas present, he can have one. He wants a grand, I'll put a bloody bow on it for him. But I want the place straight for Christmas.'

'What he wants,' Gerry said, 'is to stick a piece of holly up your ass.'

'Well he can't,' Bruin said.

Gerry did his best, but Paco was not to be bought. He wanted to see Charlie Bruin on his knees. No other Christmas present had any appeal for him whatsoever. Charlie thought of strong-arming the little crumb, but no local muscle was eager to deal with Paco or the consequences. On Christmas Day, Charlie and Tich and Yolande and Rita moved into a five-star hotel which had two golf courses. We and the Foulders had a marvellous feast on the terrace in the sunshine.

The best was yet to be. Before we returned to foggy London, a pantechnicon came for the snooker table. As the tail-gate was being closed, Paco rode past the gates of El Rey on his pretty donkey, Platerito, who dropped an appropriate memento in front of the abandoned house. Then he rode on up to Gerry and Margie's with a fat basket of dried figs. He denied that the disappearance of Charlie and his friends had anything to do with him

The Foulders' sick dog recovered all his snap. Their windows were never again shattered. They did not, however, have an altogether happy New Year. They have just heard that Charlie sold his place to Iranians, who are putting up a sixty-room hotel and health farm. 'You can't win 'em all, *amigo*,' Paco said.

In the other room

Bridge, they say, is a funny game, but you would not always guess it from the manners and ruthlessness of those who play it. When my old friend and ex-bridge-partner, Jack Fryer, invited me to join a team he was taking to a European Bridge Congress, I responded with eager reluctance: flattered to be asked, I thought I was probably too rusty for top company. 'No one's talking about top company, old boy,' Jack said, 'or I shouldn't have called you, should I? This is a friendly little celebration of European Unity. A better man than you has let me down; please be the first to take his place! It's all happening in a little ski-resort called Kotzbue, do you know it?'

'Any relation of Kitzbuhl?'

'None whatsoever. I had to look it up myself, but Kotzbue is a custom-built ski resort about fifty kilometres from Ravensburg, nothing but charming concrete blocks and *pistes* as wide as an *autobahn* . . .'

'In Switzerland?'

'Germany,' Jack said. 'Why the silence? We leave on Thursday, we're back on Tuesday. We can ski in the mornings and play bridge the rest of the day. I think we've got a decent chance in the Flitch. Véro is playing with Georges Ratier, for old times' sake. What do you say?'

'What's a Flitch?' I said.

'You remember, surely – a team-of-four event and there has to be a female in your quartet. Véro's our ace in the hole.'

Jack has to be in his mid-seventies, but his zest for life is quite unwrinkled. He belongs to that generation of refugees whose chances of election to nice golf clubs used to be impaired by the space on the entry form which demanded 'Name of Father, If Changed'. However, Jack proved to be the kind of ex-Finkelstein who, in due course, was welcomed by every club he wanted to join. When he was interned, during the early part of the war, he soon became the preferred bridge partner of the commandant of his camp on the Isle of Man. Once released, his precociousness as an engineer secured him privileged recruitment into the British army. Faced with the problem of a brand of water-lorry which constantly broke its back, in desert conditions, he was alone in diagnosing that it had been designed and tested when empty. His reinforcement of the main-frame reduced the number of thirsty soldiers and earned him a commission. After being demobilised, Jack did not go out of his way to make money, but it seemed to grow on the trees overhanging his path. As an uncomplaining but also unforgetting survivor of the old Europe, living well is his best and, so far as I know, his only revenge.

After his first wife was killed in a road accident, his second, Beryl, reacted to bridge widowhood by running away with her husband's accountant. Jack was greatly distressed (Harry Carson was a very good accountant indeed) and decided to renounce conjugal life, if not female company. However, his *coup de foudre* for Véronique changed all that and he now had a wife who was half his age and who, it seemed, shared all his appetites.

My wife shares most of mine, I hope, but she likes neither playing cards nor sliding down mountains. I therefore travelled to Kotzbue alone with Véro and Jack, who had made smooth arrangements for our journey. 'I never fly to Munich,' he observed as we sipped our first-class drinks, 'without thinking of poor Neville Chamberlain. He lost his virginity flying to see Hitler, you know.'

'Darling,' Véro said, 'he was already an old man!'

'And he'd never flown before. He was frightened and he was sick and then, instead of a nice game of bridge, there was Hitler to meet. And all we're faced with is Georges Ratier!'

'*Plus ça change!*' Vero said, but only to amuse her husband. I had been discreetly surprised when I heard that Georges Ratier was going to be in our team. He had been Véro's partner before her marriage and was, it was said, only somewhat married himself, to a rich and jealous German international, the Baroness von Munster.

Georges has the reputation of being a character, which he fosters by the raciness of his remarks, the garishness of his waistcoats and the eccentricity of his bidding. At the table, he confines his outrageousness to making 'psychic' bids, which are the bridge-player's equivalent to a bluff in poker. A 'psych', as the cognoscenti call it, is meant to put off the opponents, by making them believe that the bidder has more high cards or greater length in a given suit than he has, in fact, been dealt. If the bluff works, the pair with the better cards may be inveigled into missing a game or even a slam which would have been available to them with a less mischievous opponent. However, psychic bids are a dangerous weapon, which can explode in their exponent's face. Since it would be cheating if the bidder's partner were given any undisclosed indication that he was using this particular form of bluff, the psychic bidder, like the traditional spy, is on his own: he has to hope that his two opponents will, as it were, be more deceived than the player sitting opposite him.

When we drove up to Kotzbue, the snow was still thick, despite the spring sunshine; the functional greyness of the concrete was rendered *gemütlich* by its creamy camouflage. Our limousine rolled past the usual parades of shops where skis could be hired and T-shirts individualised and where the sale prices were higher than the full prices anyone dared to ask a thousand metres lower down. We slithered through the vertiginous bends on the way up to the Hotel Mozart 2000 where the congress was being held. The flags of all the community nations were grouped over the front door. Neville Chamberlain would have appreciated their peaceful pageant.

Before the opening session of the Congress, the terrace was a salutary Babel which, for optimistic ears, established the reality of the great European concord of which visionaries dreamed for so long. Having been absent from the bridge world for a couple of decades, I recognised only the elderly and the famous, but all the gestures were familiar. Instances of appalling luck or implausible good fortune seemed to be dubbed into a bridge player's *esperanto* which allowed everyone to understand everyone else's stories. Life-Masters such as Lennie Turman (who looked rather icily in our direction, I thought, as if he suspected Georges of some imminent frivolity) or Giovanni Stresa were the Lord Justices of Appeal who adjudicated on this bid or that, one line of play or another.

The Flitch was not due to be played until Saturday. On that first evening, Jack and Véro played together in the Pairs, while I was partnered by Georges Ratier. It was a hair-raising privilege. At one moment he would be hunched over the table, frowning at the cards as if they were in some code he should be able to decipher, and at the next he would fling himself backwards, his chair tilted on its hind legs, staring at the ceiling for heavenly inspiration. When opponents made a disconcerting bid, he would glare closely at them, as if inviting them to think better of their folly. When he considered that they had gone too far, he announced that he was doubling their contract by drawing a large cross on the green baize in front of him with his forefinger.

Georges and I ended the evening with the third prize of a magnum of Bollinger and two large Bavarian salamis for which Georges was able to suggest a loud and improper use as soon as he and the Baroness were upstairs. I noticed that his wife was not as delighted by his ribaldry as Georges was.

Jack had said that the Congress was to be a light-hearted occasion, but the Flitch was over sixty boards and the first prize was a new Peugeot 305 or its cash equivalent for those teams who did not wish to share wheels. Light-heartedness might not be easy to sustain in such circumstances. Jack invited me to ski with him in the morning; Véro and Georges proposed to perfect their bidding tactics in preparation for the main event. On the *piste*, Jack had the enviable effortlessness of someone who had skied all his life. I arrived back at the Hotel Mozart 2000 ten minutes after him, with my vanity bruised but with unbroken limbs, in time for the big match.

As we took our places, the atmosphere grew less festive. I knew enough about the undercurrents of the bridge world to have heard that Lennie Turman and Georges Ratier had, to say the least, had their differences. If Georges had been tactful, he would not have provoked Lennie, but tact was not Georges' strong suit and provocation was his pleasure. He was a smiler who also had a knife and he particularly liked sticking it into Lennie. Hence his first 'psych' of the evening had to be at Turman's expense and was – as we discovered at half-time – devastatingly profitable. Georges and Véro made a small plus score while, in our room, Jack and I bid and made a vulnerable game on the cards which Lennie and Heinz Nordheim had held.

On the following hand, Georges twisted the knife in Lennie's wound; this time he really had the aces and kings which he had only pretended to have on the first occasion. Lennie Turman's partner was lured into an indiscretion, upon which – so we were told at half-time – Georges drew one of his famous crosses on the green baize. Technically, this was an impropriety, since all bids are supposed to be made verbally and in a monotone. Injury was added to insult when Georges and Véro punished their illustrious opponents by getting them four down vulnerable.

When scores were compared during the interval, our team was lying third, two points behind the Milanese and only nine behind the Greek leaders. In the course of the ten-minute break, when we all had coffee and ill-advised cakes, I noticed Lennie Turman in earnest conversation with Giovanni Stresa and then with the Tournament Director, Manfred Mauser, whose office it was both to see fair play and to control the elaborate movements which would ensure that, by the end of the evening, every team would have played six boards against every other one.

We finished our refreshments and the teams split up, one pair from each returning to the 'closed room' in which they would play the remainder of the hands. In her usual ebullient way, Véro put her arm round Georges as they left us and with her other hand waved to her husband. When the Baroness Von Munster observed Véro whispering in Georges' ear and giggling, her glance at Jack invited him to be as displeased as she was.

'The Baroness is afraid that Georges is going to use that Peugeot as a getaway car!' Jack said. 'Perhaps we should let him. But first we have to win the damned thing.'

The extraordinary thing is that we did. At the end of the last session, which took until half past one in the morning, we had scored eight International Match Points more than our nearest rivals, Giovanni Stresa's Milanese. Georges Ratier and Véronique had achieved two more stunning coups; in one they made a small slam although they were missing two aces and in the other Georges managed another of his 'psychs', at just the right moment, and bluffed the Milanese out of a cold seven no trumps. The result was greeted with generous applause by most people, but Lennie Turman's hands were quicker to grab Manfred Mauser's sleeve than to honour our victory. After a few minutes, it was announced that there had been an objection on which a decision could not be made before the next morning.

The allegation was that Georges and Véro had an illicit understanding. Jack and I were exempt from direct accusation, but we were as indignant on our team-mates' behalf as we should have been on our own. Georges might be a rogue, but he was not a cheat. If the charges were upheld, his and Véro's reputations – and international prospects – would be ruined.

It was obvious at the breakfast buffet that the harmony of Europe was shattered. Some players came out of their way to express their solidarity with us; others were frigid. Conversations were muttered, but not entirely muted; one could guess at their content. The main charge was that Georges' rather abrupt lurches and movements of his chair were not capricious but had been calculated to indicate to his partner when his bids were genuine and when they were 'psychic'. Lennie Turman claimed that, after half-time, he had asked Manfred Mauser and Giovanni Stresa to keep note of Georges' more extravagant gestures and correlate them to the results of the hands, with damning consequences.

How can one be absolutely certain that one's friends, or even one's wife, has not cheated? I had no doubt that the charges were false and I also guessed what I did not care to mention to Jack, that the Baroness von Munster was somehow involved; it would suit her very well if the partnership between her husband and Véro were declared illicit. As for Jack, he was certain that our victory had been fairly won, but he declared himself unwilling to spend the whole day in recrimination when we could all be out on the slopes.

Véro said, 'You can't just let them take it away from us.'

'I've lost more than a motor car in my time, my darling,' Jack said. 'Why don't I just buy us each a Peugeot *and* a Bavarian sausage and let Lennie Turman take the hind-most?'

Véro did not smile, as I hoped. 'You're afraid of them,' she said.

Georges said, 'Véro, *allons, allons!*'

'He doesn't want the Germans to think badly of him. He wants them to think he's a British gentleman. He wants them not to know what he really is. He's still afraid of Adolf Hitler.'

Jack said nothing. He sat there looking at Véro with an expression I should have preferred not to see.

When Giovanni Stresa came in late for his coffee and *croissant*, he walked straight across and shook hands ostentatiously with all of us. 'Listen,' he said, 'Lennie can't believe anyone can ever beat him without cheating. So, whatever Manfred decides, we're not going to take the prize, all right?'

Georges stood up and put his arms round Stresa. '*Razza disgraziata d'Italiani*,' he said and then kissed him on both cheeks.

Jack was still looking at Véro with that expression which I wished I was not there to see. The sun bounced from the snowdrifts and through the big windows. The *télé-ski* moved with inviting smoothness up the mountain, but the joy had gone out of the occasion.

At half past ten, all the interested parties assembled in the lounge for Manfred Mauser's judgment. 'Ladies and gentlemen,' he said, 'I have considered this matter with all the gravity it deserves and you would expect of me and I have concluded that the victory of Mr Fryer's team should stand.' If Manfred had had the sense to deliver this verdict and then say no more, all might have been well. 'However,' he continued, 'I have to say that I do not think that any malice was involved in the objections raised and that, in some respects, there were irregularities of conduct on the part of some of the winning team which should not be repeated on another occasion without due sanction. As far as I am concerned, however, the matter is now closed. Thank you. I suggest that we all now go out and enjoy the excellent snow.'

Giovanni Stresa was the first to stand up and applaud, with his hands held high, in our direction. Jack, however, got up and walked out of the room, knocking an ashtray off a table as he went. There was a general movement towards the slopes. I put on my ski clothes without enthusiasm. Véro was in the locker-room. I proposed that we go out together, although I was still shocked by what she had said to Jack. We buckled our boots and pretended that nothing was wrong.

Towards lunch-time, most of the bridge-players went right up to the top of the big mountain overlooking the resort, whence a long gently twisting *piste* took you down at speed, but without conspicuous danger, all the way to the hotel. I saw Manfred Mauser and glared at him when he waved to us. The striped and luminous Baroness von Munster was with him. Véro glanced at Georges where he stood penitentially behind his wife and said, 'Do you think Jack is jealous, is that why he isn't here? Does he think something went on between me and Georges?'

'You must ask Jack. But I doubt it.' In my own mind, I was thinking that you can never be absolutely certain what is going on in the other room.

We delayed for a moment or two, hoping that Jack might appear from the *télé-ski*, but eventually we moved off, a little behind the rest of the group. There was a steep part of the mountain to our left, where *hors-piste* experts had cut what seemed an almost vertical path. As I did my rather laborious turns, I saw a solitary figure, wearing a blue *salopette* and a T-shirt, push off from the top of the path. By the time he joined the main stream, he was no more than a hunched projectile. He went past everyone on the *piste* with the pace and disdain of the born skier.

I could see that there was writing on the back of his T-shirt, but his speed, and distance, prevented me from reading it. After a series of turns which sent arcs of snow over Manfred Mauser and the Baroness and Lennie Turman and anyone else within range, the solitary exhibitionist made a wide turn to reach the entrance to the Hotel Mozart 2000 where I arrived just in time to see him come to rest and lean down to release his bindings. I realised then what I might have guessed earlier: it was Jack Fryer. His back was still to me and I was able to read what he had had printed on his individualised T-shirt: YOU HAVE JUST BEEN OVERTAKEN BY A 76-YEAR OLD JEW.

The rest of the bridge-players laughed and applauded as Véro kissed her husband and then, as they went in together, put a mitten full of snow down his neck. Georges Ratier looked as though he wished he could do as much to the Baroness. Neither Manfred Mauser nor Lennie Turman seemed at all amused. As I mentioned before, bridge is a funny game.

We are members of
the Guardia Civil

'Quiet tonight.'

'Quiet enough.'

'What's that bus? I don't recognise that bus. There isn't usually a bus at this hour. Ten to ten. Where does it come from?'

'Algeciras. It's a special. Plane was delayed. Manolo told me at the Post Office.'

'Delayed?'

'There was a telegram for some *estranjero*. Engine trouble. I don't know. Something. Who knows?'

'It will be cold before the night's over.' Ramon drew his cloak around him and let it swing free again. Salvador could see his colleague across the lit street. The lights were sconced in the sides of the flat, white houses. They marched away down the long, silent street. The two Guardias went after them. They advanced on the darkness at the end of the village. It grew darker for them as they went forward. Salvador swung his cloak too.

'I suppose you are right.'

'You will see. How is your cough? Is it better?'

'Cough?'

'You had a cough. Is it better?'

'It was nothing. It's better.'

'You have to be tough for this life.'

'This is the life we have,' Salvador said. 'It's better, the cough: in a week, two weeks, it will be gone. It doesn't disturb me. Things of that kind don't mean anything to me.'

They walked. They stopped for a moment by the common fountain and turned to face each other, Ramon and Salvador, as if a third person had ordered them. They leaned on their rifles and then they turned again and continued to walk. Ramon ruffled his moustache with a mittened hand and blew out his cheeks.

'My father at one time had to patrol alone,' he said.

'Alone? Truly?'

'Truly. In his day it sometimes happened, a Guardia had to patrol on his own.'

'Things are not like that now,' Salvador said.

They walked.

'You suffer from the cold, do you?'

Ramon said, 'I? No.'

'You said it would be cold tonight.'

'It will be cold, but I do not suffer from it.'

'I thought perhaps you suffered from it.'

'I? No. Never.'

A light from an approaching lorry swung full in their eyes as it came round a corner. Salvador fumbled for his torch. The lorry charged between them, leaving a tail of diesel fumes. It rattled away behind them towards the village they had now left.

'They always accelerate on that corner,' Ramon said.

They walked.

'You were asking me something.'

'About your father.'

'My father! What a man! He once took on three anarchists single-handed. Strong as a bull. He was a bull, my father. Enormous! His moustache – you should have seen it. It was like a bull's horns. That was the style with the Guardia in those days. Like a bull's horns! What did your father do? What kind of a man was he?'

'He was a shoemaker.'

They walked.

'The sea is calm tonight,' Salvador said.

'It must have been engine trouble. Sometimes it is the wind that is wrong, but this time I think it must have been engine trouble.'

'It's calm tonight. No wind at all.'

'But cold,' Ramon said. 'It will be. The stars are like nails.'

'In Tarragona.'

'What?'

'My father. We lived in Tarragona.'

'Ah, Tarragona! From up there us.' Ramon waved in the darkness, towards Cordoba or Jerez de la Frontera or Estremadura even. 'Is he alive today?'

'No. He is dead. Is yours?'

'No.'

'Dead,' Salvador said.

'Dead.'

They walked.

'You should have seen his moustache. It was exceptional even for those days. Did your father have a moustache?'

'My father was clean-shaven. Always.'

'Did he die recently, your father?'

'No. Did yours?'

'He died many years ago, many.'

'And mine.'

'My father was killed in uniform,' Ramon said.

'Mine was not,' Salvador said.

They walked. The road went inland, leaving the long silver beach glistening under the eaves of the sky.

'My father was killed,' Ramon said, 'in 1934. Over there. Anarchists. Twenty-five years ago.'

'Mine in 1936. Almost the same.'

'In Tarragona?'

'That's the truth.'

'It was Red, wasn't it, Tarragona?'

'For a long time,' Salvador said.

'He once took on three of them at one time. But when they finally shot him, he had no chance. It was an ambush.'

'Was he alone?'

'No. He was with others. They were far from help. There was nothing to be done. They killed many of their attackers, but it was an ambush. There was nothing they could do.'

137

They walked.

'Your father, what happened to him?'

'He too was shot. They shot him.'

'The Reds,' Ramon said, 'they would kill us today.'

'The sixteenth of July, 1936,' Salvador said. 'There is a light showing in the house of José Menendez.'

'His aunt and her children.'

They walked.

'Your father was killed by his workers?'

'He had no workers. He was a poor man.'

'What had he done?'

'Nothing. Nothing.'

'He was killed for nothing? My father too was killed for nothing.'

'Your father was a Guardia,' Salvador said.

'They were mad; they were bedevilled,' Ramon said. 'If he was a shoemaker, why was he killed? What kind of person was he?'

'A good person. Quiet. He made no trouble.'

'In Tarragona he was killed.'

'Yes. At the beginning. He was taken away. They came for him. He was taken away.'

'In the early days,' Ramon said. 'I understand. He was a worker.'

'Yes.'

'An anarchist?'

'He was nothing. But they shot him. A mistake perhaps.'

'Perhaps. In war . . .'

'He looked like someone maybe.'

'He should have had a moustache.'

They walked.

'Then he would not have looked like whoever he looked like.'

They walked. The road sloped down towards a bridge. There were eucalyptus trees in the river bed. The moon was coming over the brim of the hill.

'Let's smoke,' Ramon said. 'It's an hour now. Let's have a smoke.'

Salvador crossed the road to his colleague. A car passed, salting the landscape with unmasked light. *'Estranjero,'* Salvador said.

The match flared. The men saw each other yellow in its light. Ramon had a big moustache. 'He was shot by us, your father.'

Salvador said, 'Yes.'

'Life is hard for men,' Ramon said. He took bread from his pack and broke it and held some out to Salvador. They held the bread while they finished their cigarettes. 'They suffer from mistakes. And when there is war . . . there are many mistakes, many.'

'Many, many.'

'It will not happen again, Spaniards killing Spaniards for the sake of *estranjeros*. We will not allow it to happen again.'

'Never.'

'Who suffers? Spain suffers.'

'And no one else.'

'The poor suffer. We too were poor. Sometimes there were delays with pay. It was hard for a Guardia to find credit. You live among savages.'

'I know.'

'Did you weep when your father was killed?'

'I wept.'

'Did you?' Ramon said. 'I did not.'

'I am surprised that you did not.'

'And I am surprised that you did.'

'We must go on,' Salvador said.

They walked.'

'What do you think of the new chief?'

'He is a chief,' Ramon said.

'He is a chief, it's true.'

'Strict.'

'Strict. A chief has to be strict.'

'He has no choice.'

'None.'

'It must never happen again, what happened before. Not again.'

'Who wants more blood?'

'Our sons must not fight. They must love each other. Your son, my son.'

'They will.'

'They do not want to fight.'

'They want good things. They want American music, American clothes.'

They walked.

'We are all sick of fighting, sick of death,' Ramon said. 'Because who profits? Not Spain. Not the people. Not the poor. Above all, not the poor. When did they profit from blood? Never!'

'Why did you not weep when your father was killed?'

'I do not know,' Ramon said. 'I was at home with my mother and they came with his hat. I comforted her and I did not weep. I did not think to weep, not then, not later. Then because I did not think, later because . . . I did.'

Ramon stopped. Salvador stopped. Ramon warbled softly. Salvador crossed to him.

'There is someone under the bridge. I saw a match.'

'Smugglers?'

'Who knows? Perhaps.'

The sea was a silver wing on the shoulder of the hill that sloped down to it from the bank of the river. There was no wind. They eased themselves from the road and lurched into the vineyard below the shadows. They slithered on their heels to a bamboo grove that whispered on a level with the dry river. Ramon touched Salvador's arm, a finger to his lips. They could see the pull and wane of the cigarette under the hood of the bridge.

'There's only one,' Ramon said. He was unslinging his rifle.

Ramon led the way through vines. The cigarette was put out. The moon caught the spokes of a bicycle. Out at sea, fishermen were shouting at a catch. Ramon was a few yards ahead of Salvador and Salvador took quick steps to be with him. The effort made him cough. Salvador had coughed and the man was alerted. He was thrusting his bicycle at the steep bank to get to the road, but the side of the bank was crumbling on him. Ramon was quickly up the shoulder of the road and running along it in his loud boots. What could the man do? He could not run because he needed his bicycle. He needed it to carry the stuff and he needed it for his future. He had to get his bicycle up to the road so that he could pedal towards Los Boliches. But Salvador was racing out of cover now. The man was between two fires. They could see him now, both of them. In the moonlight he had a silver face, like a baby moon himself. His bicycle was an awkward loaf under his arm. He began to run with it, along the *rio*, hoping to outflank Ramon. Salvador coughed as he ran, and ran as he coughed. Ramon was outflanked and Salvador had to catch the man on his own. The man looked back and saw Salvador and he pushed at the earth and tried to climb the tilting world that seemed to push him down when he wanted to go up.

'Stop!' Salvador said. 'Stop!' He clawed for the man. He was close enough to touch him. 'Stop now!'

The man's face was eclipsed in the shadow of a tree as he swung himself up with one hand on a branch. He was up on the road. Ramon fired as he turned to mount the bicycle. The shot whined in the silver light. Salvador could believe he saw it. The man was not hit. He was straddling his bicyle. Salvador used the tree too and he could see him as he stood into the pedals of the bicycle. Ramon saw him too. Ramon would not miss again.

'Stop,' Salvador said, 'stop or we fire!'

The man leaned all his weight on the pedals and bent his back with effort. Salvador was running. He was saying 'Don't shoot!' at the same moment as Ramon fired. This time the bullet came close and stopped. The bicycle fell sideways. The man was sitting on the road. He was holding his thigh. Salvador was standing over him. He said, 'I am shot.' He mumbled to himself.

Salvador said, 'Be polite.' He could hear Ramon breathing beside him. Was that why he drove his foot into the man's rump?

'Don't – '

Salvador did it again. 'I told you . . .'

The man was silent. He kept his curses in his mouth. He pouted with them.

Ramon said, 'We could kill you. You ran.'

The man shrugged.

'My father would have killed you.'

Salvador shone his torch in the man's face. It was the face of a boy. There was blood on it and there were tears. The boy had wiped blood from thigh to face. Ramon was kneeling to look at the wound.

'It's nothing.'

'What was I doing? Why did you shoot?'

'I told you to stop. Why did you not?'

'I was frightened.' The boy was white from a fresh shave as well as from fear and pain. His beard scarcely showed.

'Where have you come from?'

'I was seeing my *novia*.'

Ramon said, 'You lie.' He kicked the boy. It was a duty. 'Don't lie to me.'

'I do not lie.'

Ramon kicked him again, with the other foot. 'That is a lie too. That's two lies too many.'

'I have been seeing my *novia*, I swear it.'

'Her name? Her name!'

'What will you do to her?'

'Nothing you have not.'

'What's this stuff?' Salvador said. 'In here. Did your *novia* give you these?' He showed Ramon the cigarettes in the saddlebag, American and English.

'Did you hear what he asked you?'

'I found them. They're not mine.'

142

'You found them? You went fishing, I suppose, and up they came!'

'Cigarettes, tobacco . . .'

'I found them. There is the bag.'

'You kept the bag just to show us! And where did you find them?'

'Under there. Under the arch. I stopped for a smoke and there they were. They must have left them there.'

'Your friends?'

'I don't know.'

'You stole from your friends?'

'I thought it was . . .'

'Contraband. And so it is. And where were you taking it?'

'I don't know. I don't know. Please, I – '

Ramon smiled. Salvador saw his teeth like the bones of a filleted fish. 'Where were you taking it?'

The boy said, 'To the Guardia post. I was taking it there. To the Guardia post.'

'He was taking it to the Guardia post. And who did you think we were? If you were taking it to the Guardia post, why did you run away from us?'

'I thought perhaps you were *contrabandistas*.' Hope anaesthetised his pain. He almost stood up. 'I was afraid that you were . . . anarchists. I was afraid you would kill me.'

'You thought we were anarchists! Do anarchists wear uniforms and carry guns? You were ordered to stop and you ran. Do anarchists have rifles today? Is there no such thing as the Guardia Civil?'

'I was frightened. I did not think.'

'Think now.'

'I thought the smugglers were coming back. I've done nothing. I am a poor man . . .'

'You are a poor boy,' Ramon said. 'You are not a man at all. You weep. Men do not weep.'

'My father is dead, my mother relies on me. She has no

one else. I am the oldest. If you take me away, who will she have? She'll starve. You can take the stuff. Take the stuff. I don't want it. I only want my bicycle.'

'He wants his bicycle.'

'You can take it if you want it.'

'We can take everything,' Ramon said.

'I know. I know.'

'You're wounded,' Salvador said. 'How will you get home?'

'I'll crawl,' the boy said. 'I'll get there. My mother will look after me. She knows what to do.'

'She's done it before.'

'She knows about such things. Take everything.'

'And let you go, is that it?'

'I'm in your power,' the boy said. 'Do what you want. You can do what you want.'

'Who told you that?' Ramon said.

'Everyone knows. You do what you want to do.'

'That is not so,' Salvador said.

'It is by no means so,' Ramon said.

The boy said, 'You are not rich . . .'

'That is so,' Ramon said.

'That we are not,' Salvador said.

'Then why – ?'

'Why?'

' – do you not take the stuff and – make what you can. I'm not going to say anything to anyone.'

'That's a good idea. Starting now.'

'I swear. You are not rich. Why do you take me and give me to the rich, to the powerful? What will you get? You will get nothing. I am a poor man – '

'You are a poor *boy*.'

'I am poor. My mother has no one else. You have mothers.'

'We have mothers,' Salvador said.

'Then you understand. I have done *you* no harm, have I?'

'Come on,' Ramon said. 'We've done enough talking.

144

We're off in an hour. The chief wants to talk to you. He'll make us stay while he does it. There's a lot you have to tell him.'

'I know nothing. I found the stuff.'

'You'll think of something when we help you, and we will. Come on, on your feet.'

'I can't. I'm hurt.'

'On your feet.'

'I know nothing. What will he do to me? I'm eighteen years old.'

'We'll think of something. He'll get it out of you one way or another.'

'You have mothers,' the boy said. 'Why are you doing this to me? What did I do to you? We're all poor people. Why do you do this?'

Salvador said: 'We are members of the Guardia Civil.'

They started to drag the boy back along the road.

Stolen property

No one has to believe this story. I am not sure that I entirely believe it myself. It all began with my writing a film about a real-life Don Juan. I happened to read about a young Spanish aristocrat who, in the seventeenth century, consciously decided to model himself on the mythical amorist. He dedicated himself to more and more unscrupulous and outrageous seductions and provocations until one day, in old Sevilla, Something Happened; whereupon his whole life changed direction and he became a model of penitential sanctity.

Having written the screenplay, I offered it to my old producer friend Gino Amadei. I often threatened to take my uncommissioned work elsewhere, but who else was likely to believe in it with quite the same quibbling enthusiasm as Gino? A month later, he called to say that he had shown the script to Hansi Pollock and that he wanted to do it. Hansi is recognised by every film journal as a serious *auteur*, which means in practice that he is intolerant of any talent but his own and cannot see a joke even with his glasses on. I never much liked Hansi, or his films, but who could deny that his wife, Poppy Langton, would be perfect as Elvira? If Poppy were American, she would be a great star, but in London she was regarded only as Hansi's beautiful but over-rated wife (the English always call people over-rated when they under-rate them).

Having acquired a director, our next problem was casting. When Gino told me that Hansi wanted us all to go up to the Royal Exchange Theatre, Manchester and see Bill Napier in *The Bacchae*, I said that I was sure we were wasting our time. How could an uneducated rock star, who had never been nearer to Thebes than the Cypriot restaurant opposite his agent's office, became a Greek god as sly and ambiguous as Dionyos? 'Nevertheless,' Gino said.

In her businesslike spectacles, Poppy studied the cocky little performer as though he were a difficult text. Was she impressed? Was she dismayed? How little one ever knows about women, especially when they are being actresses! As for Bill's performance, it was, quite simply, a revelation. When we went round to congratulate him, he watched Poppy's entrance in the mirror and, on noticing the cheerful coarseness of his grin and the gleaming chill of the look she returned, I suddenly wondered whether they had a history together. They certainly had a future.

Naturally enough, the budget did not allow me to travel to Spain with the team whose employment had depended on the stack of pages which Hansi had now appropriated, rewritten and for which he would, in due course, claim all the credit. However, I heard word, through Maggie in Gino's London office, of the usual dramas: after they had been told that it never rained in Sevilla, it poured for five solid days; two sets of rushes had gone missing and had been traced to Grenoble where the French customs would not release them; Gino's wife dropped in unexpectedly to find him in intimate conference with an undressed dress-designer. And Bill? Judging from the rushes I saw, he had transported his innocent effrontery from provincial England to Andalusia while at the same time blending it with the Latin coldness which I had imagined in Juan. As for Poppy Langton, if she was acting the part of a woman attracted despite her better judgement, she was doing it superbly; on the other hand, if she was genuinely excited – and alarmed – by Bill Napier, her feelings were being turned to good cinematic effect by her unfathomable and unsmiling husband.

When Gino telephoned me, a few days before they were due to finish shooting, he said, 'Hull-er?' in a questioning manner, as if he had better things to do than take the call which he had instigated.

I said, 'How's it going?'

Gino said, 'Look, why don't you come down here for once? To be honest, I think the writer should be on the set.'

'And I think he should be better paid and more respected; do you think there's any connection?'

Gino fell silent and then he said, 'Wha-at?'

I said, 'What's gone wrong?'

'Look, to tell you the truth, it's Bill Napper, whatever his name is.'

'Is he having it off with Poppy?'

Gino said, 'Is he? Yes, probably. The *real* thing is, I don't know why, we have a problem wiz him.'

'Because of the script? Because of Hansi? Why?'

'Why-ee? That's the question and I want you to ask him. After all it is your film, and we've been shooting around him for three days, we're running out of places to waste our time and money. The girl will give you the tickets.' As he hung up, Gino said, 'By the way, how are you?'

Terry, the unit driver, met me at the airport and took me to the Alfonso XIII, where the stars were staying. Gino had left word for me to come to his suite. He said, 'I'm glad you're here. I would have come to the airport.'

'Except that you didn't.'

'Because, look, I want you to find Bill as soon as you can.'

'He's *missing* now?'

'Look, please . . . I've brought you here . . . find him and get him back off the set, I'll do anything you want. Within reason.'

'That's a pretty tight budget, isn't it?'

Gino said, 'Wha-at?'

Eventually I found Bill Napier in the Barrio de Santa Cruz. I walked into the old Jewish quarter, with its narrow white streets and the deep shadows that fell into them from the tall houses with their tiled balconies and their air of neat secrecy, and I seemed to be drawn to a shady square where orange trees hung their heavy fruits over the cobbles. Bill was sitting on a tiled bench beside the fountain in the centre. I sat down beside him and said, 'People are worried about you.'

He said, 'I thought you'd understand what's happened.'

'Well,' I said, 'quite frankly I don't. Because no one's told me what has.'

'I've fallen in love,' he said. 'How many women have you had in your life?'

'Never mind that,' I said.

'I can't count,' he said. 'I could once, and I did, often, but I can't any more. A lot more than a thousand and three and now, for the first time in my life . . . You'll have to tell Hansi. He'll take it from you.'

'If you want Poppy,' I said, 'you'll have to tell him yourself.'

'Poppy? Poppy's nothing. That's over, that is.' Quite as if Hansi had directed the scene, an orange fell from a tree into the basin of the fountain with an alarming splash; I smiled, Bill did not. 'All right,' he said, 'I met this woman. She was an extra. They went out and found these women, tourists, people from all over, because Hansi had this idea of a crowd of all sorts of faces, only Juan didn't want any of it because they were too easy. It was a sort of crumpet buffet, if you know what I mean.'

'I think I do,' I said. 'Probably because it was in my original script.'

'Anyway. Do you think I'm a nice person?'

'Why not?'

'Because I'm not. But I can pretend to be. That's why I was nice to the extras, all right? Went and took my lunch with them.'

'That *is* nice.'

'Only because I wanted madam to think I was going off her. Poppy. I wanted her to suffer a little.'

'That isn't.'

'So I go over and all the girls start creaming themselves as usual, all except this dark girl sitting all by herself reading a book. No interest in me whatsoever. Know what a book was in our house when I was a kid? A book was a magazine. We didn't have book books. I had to go up to her. Guess what she was reading, this black-eyed bird. She was reading a book *backwards*. I watched her. She turned the pages from the back towards the front. I thought she was winding me up.'

'Hebrew.'

'How did you know that? Do you read like that?'

'To the Jews, the whole of world history is a flashback. When the Messiah comes, he will admit us to the Garden of Eden once again and we shall never need another book because we shall finally be back to page one.'

'Is that what you believe?'

'Not a word of it,' I said. 'What was the book?'

'She wouldn't say. They were calling for us to go to make-up and stuff, lunch-time was over, I had to go, so I said, "Will you be here later?" and she shrugged. As if it mattered! It mattered to me. That afternoon we did the scene where my character provokes this duel with the brother of a woman he's been with, knowing that the man will get killed, just for the fun of it: another kind of shafting, all right? Then we had a break and then there was going to be a night shoot, the scene where I meet this funeral and realise that it's my own, all right? So I say to laughing boy, Hansi P., will he call this girl for the night shoot, because I think it might be an idea to have her around. He says to me, "Think she'd take her clothes off? Because I've had this idea of this naked girl walking behind the coffin. Think she would?" I said, "Ask her." I see Hansi go up to her during the afternoon and ask her and she looked at him – well, the way she looked at him – he should've turned into a frog, but your film directors never do, do they? I found my way over to her and I said, "It wasn't my idea. I swear to you. Only please come tonight. They pay double at night." She said, "Do you know what's wrong with you?" She had this voice! "What's wrong with you is, you don't even know anything *is* wrong." I hadn't noticed until then that she had this gold chain round her neck, the kind some girls have crosses on sometimes, only it went down under her dress – she wore a dress, not jeans or anything like that – and I couldn't see what was on the end of it. "Well what is then," I said, "wrong?" She said, "This film of yours, it's a fake. It doesn't tell the right story and you don't even know it, do you? Because Don Juan was, him and all the others, he was a *thief*! A thief and a murderer." Just the job before I had to go and do this scene with the brother of the girl.'

'I saw the rushes,' I said. 'They were very good.'

'They burnt people at the stake in this bloody city,' Bill Napier said, 'in this bloody square. Right where we're sitting. They enjoyed it, you know why? She told me. Because it meant they could keep what they'd stolen.'

'She came that night then, did she?'

'She stripped off right there in the open and the way she did it, it was a way of refusing to do it, that's how it struck me – contempt, not . . . surrender.' Bill Napier might have been scanning some private monitor for a second view of what had happened. 'I was supposed to come out of my house, having got back from Corsica, after doing the business with my sister, and I hear this music and along comes the funeral and I have to ask whose it is and Hansi has the idea I should ask *her*. They told her to say "Don't you know? Don Juan is dead!" I said she should have a wad of extra dosh if she had a line and Hansi agreed. He lets the girl know it was my idea and she gives him one of her looks. So we're doing the shot and the funeral goes by and there she is, this naked girl, and I ask her the question and what does she do? She doesn't say anything. She just gives me this look and, bang, I start shaking. I start shaking, and I can't bloody stop. Hansi finally says to cut, Ernie's got the bloody camera half way up me hooter and they're all saying what a great performance, in spite of the girl forgetting the line and I still can't stop shaking, all right? They check the gate, everyone's happy and they want to do one more, so they look around for the girl and she's gone. Vanished. Puff of smoke time. And I say, "Well, that's it for me, I'm off." And I was. I walked the bloody streets like a maniac, all night, looking and not finding. Finally, I go back to the hotel. I got to the desk and I ask the snotty bugger in the monkey suit for my key and what does he give me? This gold chain with this key on it. That's right: it's not a room key, it's an old key, with all these elaborate lumps and notches on it and you know and I know where it comes from. There's a piece of paper in my cubby hole and it's got this address on it: "My house", that's it: message ends! Never mind, it's not the first come-up-and-see-me-sometime key I've had in my life, is it? I ask where the Plaza Doña Elvira is – it's just about dawn at this point, clammy and cold, good old sunny Spain, and I'm running across the road and into these narrow streets where the Jews used to be about five hundred years ago, and I'm like a kid and the first girl in his whole life has said tonight's the night. I'm flying. I can imagine her sitting there, with those hot and cold black eyes on her and this great crest of black hair and the red lips and I don't know what I want to do to her, I want to do everything, I even want to kill her, just a little bit. I'm in a panic, as if the whole place is going to vanish before I get to her: knees like water! I run up to where this number ought to be and, bloody hell, there it is – one of those tall, narrow houses with this bloody great solid door with a little barred hole in it you can see through into this patio. I get my key and I'm trembling so much I can't hardly get it in. What's funny?'

'Nothing,' I said.

'I give it a twist, thinking I bet it won't work, and it turns and the thing's open and I'm in! I'm in her bloody house. There's lots of pot plants in the patio and up the steps to the sort of landing with lots of doors off it and I'm wondering which one is hers. I try one and it's open and I'm in this room with all these paintings and the silver mirrors, all the usual fancy junk, smells of polish and clean dust and I realise I don't even know her name. Much it matters, only where the hell is she? I go out onto the landing again and what do I do? I make a sort of noise. I can't describe it; it was a sort of howl, a cry of triumph and anguish, as you might say. Longing and . . . hope, at that point.' Bill Napier looked at me with huge, wet eyes.

'And no one came?'

'They came! Doors are flying open and about eight men come out, various ages, various expressions, from murderous on up, because after all, it's seven o'clock in the morning and . . . they're jumping all over me, like they all want tear off a piece of me for a souvenir. They say I'm a thief and they're going to call the police, all the usual forms of welcome. And I'm saying the same thing over and over again, "Where is she?" Finally, one of these crazy *señors*, he recognises who I am. He doesn't know anything about the film, but he's been to one of my concerts in London. Bit of luck. So then I'm the honoured guest and everyone's calling for the *muchacha* to get up and make some coffee and I'm thinking maybe, maybe *she's* the *muchacha* – but not a bit of it; she's some Fraulein learning the language. I describe my . . . my . . . I describe the woman I'm looking for and they've never heard of her. No one remotely like her ever lived there. I must have the wrong house. Then I show them the key. "Now tell me it's not her house." Do we get another mood change! They look at each other and I'm thinking, "Whoops!" because now I know: I know she's landed me in it *and* she's landed them in it, all in one diabolical go. She's used me to give them the message that they're living in her house and that whatever they do, it'll always be hers and they'll always be a bunch of thieves and murderers.'

I said, 'I don't think you can blame people today for what their ancestors did to your ancestors five hundred years ago, do you?'

'What do you mean her ancestors?'

I smiled, and then I stopped smiling. Bill Napier looked as if he was never going to smile again. 'Bill come on – '

'You know your trouble? You don't believe in things. You write things and you don't believe in them. That was her house and she'd lived in it. The wandering Jewess. And now, as you're here, you can go and tell them what I've decided to do, can't you?'

After he told me and I had, at his request, repeated it so that there should be no mistake, I went back to the Alfonso XIII and found Hansi Pollock and Poppy and Gino in the enormous breakfast room. Their pallid faces turned towards me for the good news I could not give them. I said, 'Are you ready for this? He's going to give away all his money and all his possessions and become a barefoot friar.'

Gino said, 'A barefoot *what*?'

'Monk. He's renouncing the world, the flesh and the devil. All three of you.'

Hansi Pollock said, 'Where the hell did he get an idea like that?'

'Well,' I said, 'I expect he stole it from the script, don't you?'

An old, old story

We were living in a rented cottage in East Bergholt when Major Wakefield disappeared. Kennedy was President-elect of the United States and I was writing plays for television to supplement my publisher's meagre advances. The Old Mill had an asparagus bed and fruitful raspberry canes and a lawn where our small son's pram could go, but it compared poorly with Stour End, which was a smartly converted Suffolk barn at the top of our high-hedged lane.

The Wakefields had spent money on a patterned thatch roof and keen paintwork. A man in a green baize apron worked regularly at the roses (Dorothy Perkins grew in a pink arch over the gate) and, in due season, did knowledgeable things to the apple trees. The back lawn was kept perfect for the merciless courtesies of croquet. We would hear the calculated clunk of the balls as we wheeled the pram, with its new and demanding freight, past that unchipped gate. A three-litre Bristol and a sharp red Mini-Cooper announced our neighbours' lack of false modesty.

One Sunday morning, several months after our nodding acquaintance began, Bill was doing something competent to the Bristol's carburettor – or was it carburettors? – when we walked past. 'Morning! I say, why don't you pop in and have a drink with us? Molly's just opening a bottle.'

It was an excellent Sancerre, beaded with evidence of cool premeditation: the Wakefields knew how to live. It must have been a May morning, because blossom was pinking the espaliers around the croquet lawn. With her deliciously undulating walk, Molly brought the bottle and glasses to where white furniture was waiting for us under a medlar tree.

Our seduction was charmingly accomplished. The Wakefields even confessed to having seen something of mine on the television a week or so before, though they said they had no idea that they were living adjacent to a famous writer. I did not regard my contribution to a series entitled *Probation Officer* as a certificate of fame, but it was nice to be recognised.

When my wife remarked on the beauty of the garden, Bill offered her the short tour ('You'll be away inside a couple of hours!') and he soon had her laughing as they inspected Brocket's neat, 'maidenly' achievements. Meanwhile, Molly took me into the house. There were nice antiques (Mrs Jenkins, the gamekeeper's wife from the big house, polished twice a week) and there were some unexpectedly agreeable pictures, including a Whistler etching and a small Stubbs which Molly had picked up, for Bill's forty-fifth birthday, at a country house sale near Coggeshall. On the baby grand, I saw a black and white photograph of Molly when slightly younger and more conventional; her hair was done in officer's wife fashion: neat, not showy. Bill was silver-framed, next to her, in his regimental polo team. His unassuming manner suggested that he was its star.

'Was your husband a regular soldier?'

'Regular?' Molly said. 'As regular as he had to be.'

'Does he miss it?'

'Yes and no,' she said. 'But not always in that order.'

She appeared to be amused by my diffident curiosity. People who have been at the centre of a scandal, however parochial, tend to suppose that everyone knows all about it. In fact, I had no idea of what we were later to discover: Bill's reputation, when he was a Lancer, was notorious. Women and ninepins were interchangeable as far as he was concerned. Yet men neither feared nor even resented him; if he sometimes cuckolded a brother-officer, he could be relied on not to humiliate him. Wakers had no use for marriage, but he respected marriages; he might be a bit of a poacher, but he was no home-breaker. The light touch enabled him to cut an appealing figure, even on the thinnest ice. He was brave and he was loyal and he was, to a degree, discreet; quick to kiss, he was slow to tell.

Bill and his colonel, Piers Chadwick, had been at Sandhurst together. They waded out, side by side, to one of the last ships to leave Dunkirk in 1940 and they were companions in arms across the desert, up Italy and into Germany. Piers was capable and responsible, born to command. Bill was his ideal adjutant; he imposed discipline with a smile, whenever possible, and with a chillingly straight face when smiles would not serve.

During the fighting, of course, there had been no problem with regimental wives. The army travelled light and Bill was able to love and leave with patriotic punctuality. In Germany, on garrison duty, things were rather different. Piers had long worshipped the lovely girl whose photograph he had carried throughout his campaigns – she had been a convent schoolgirl of sixteen when he met her at a point-to-point in the summer of 1939 – and he now proposed to go home and marry her. Bill, of course, was his best man.

Piers was a fine soldier, with the DSO and the MC to prove it. At the age of twenty-nine, he knew more about killing than loving. He was not used to female company. Although he very much wanted his wife to be happy, he feared that she was not. The newlyweds had started married life under comfortable auspices, but the colonel knew that things were not working out, though he did not know what to do about it.

One evening, over a bottle of liberated Schnapps, he asked whether Bill had any suggestions. He could speak frankly. Bill did; he gave his friend a crash course in basic bedroom tactics. Piers listened dolefully. He admitted that one or two of the recommended wrinkles were unknown to him (and not particularly palatable) but he still felt that the trouble was due to something more . . . emotional. The old girl was moody and listless. Would Bill have a word with her? Piers was a planner; he needed someone else to mount a recce and then he could decide how to proceed. Would Bill *please* be a pal?

Bill was so reluctant to have the promised *tête-à-tête* with Molly that he went out and had several pink gins, and an amenable Fraulein, before sitting down to their frank, and fatal, conversation. The trouble with their marriage, Molly was not slow to reveal, was that she had fallen in love with her husband's best friend. Such a thing had, no doubt, happened to millions of people before, but it had never happened to her. In that low, delightful voice, she said she was more sorry for Piers than for herself. Bill said that the whole thing was impossible: Piers had saved his life more than once. 'And you his,' Molly said, as her eyelids slowly lowered and slowly opened again. Her bosom heaved. It was a facer all right.

They swore that the thing would go no further. Molly devoted herself to her husband; Bill put in for a transfer. Meanwhile, he applied himself, with dismaying joylessness, to the pursuit of other women. Previously, he had never dreamed of Molly as a possible prize – how else could he have been so attentively charming to her? – but her confession now licensed his imagination. He had never thought of her 'like that' before; now he could not think of anything else.

Bill Wakefield fell as passionately in love with Molly as she had with him. A man who had always maintained that females were objects of pleasure, but never of enduring affection, was suddenly obsessed by the one woman whom he was determined to deny himself. Molly tried as hard as he did to do the right thing, but denial fed desire; opportunity made it irresistible. While Piers was in London doing some red-tab business at the War House, Bill and Molly found themselves snowed up together after some God-awful New Year's shindig at an American base near Wiesbaden. Someone who should have known better told someone who did not and, by the time Piers was back in Germany, rumour was ready to do its poisonous stuff.

Bill went to see Piers. He was honest enough to confess what he would have preferred to deny. He was as straightforward as he was ashamed. He was sure that Piers would recognise that it was the last thing in the world anyone wanted to happen. Bill said that he and Molly were immensely fond of Piers and they would do anthing he said, but facts were facts: there were bound to be casualties.

Piers was both noble and deeply wounded. His restraint was worse than a shout; his generosity cut more keenly than sarcasm. He would not stand in the way of his wife's happiness, but he warned her, when all three of them were locked together in his quarters, that Bill would love her and leave her, just as he had all the others. He would not prevent her, but she was making a terrible mistake which would result in her finding herself bruised and alone. He was prepared to bet.

'I've changed, old man,' Bill said. 'This is love. The genuine article. Everything I always said couldn't happen to me.'

'You'll never change,' Piers said. 'And I don't want to see Molly hurt. I don't matter; she does.'

'I promise you, Piers – give her a divorce and you'll not live to see the day when I'm not with her or not faithful to her. My oath as a Sicilian!'

Piers had to smile, just. They had had a guide through the sewers of Enna, during the Italian campaign, who promised them – with justice – that he would lead a platoon safely to the crest of the craggy town and he had been as good as his Sicilian word. The two men shook hands and Bill and Molly left the colonel's office together.

The story is short; the agony was not. Piers stiffened his upper lip and granted Molly the divorce which mortified him. Bill resigned from the army and made the best of the last thing he wanted to do. The Wakefields bought Stour End and settled down to gorge themselves on their mutual passion. Molly was a delicious wife; Bill was a stylish husband. They were happy.

In their happiness, they found time to spare a thought for Piers. They wrote him; they sent him Christmas cards; they hoped like hell to hear that he had met someone else. If only he could be happy too, the tiny flaw in their blissful existence would be repaired. He neither answered their letters nor found consolation.

We never became intimate friends with Bill and Molly. We kept the cottage at Bergholt but we went abroad for a long spell so that I could write a novel without being distracted by *Probation Officer*. When we returned to the Old Mill House, they had gone away for a while. By the time they got back, our brief routine of mutual visits was broken and was not repaired. The glimpses we had of them were of a Bill apparently as attentive as ever and of a Molly unaged by satisfaction. For some reason, however, they did not choose to ask us in. They waved, but they did not beckon.

One morning, there was a jangling ring on the ship's bell that hung by our front door. It was Molly, in a housecoat, without make-up and with those blue eyes boozy with tears. Had we seen Bill at all? She had come down to breakfast, a little late, and the house was empty. I said that he had probably buzzed off for a quick eighteen holes: it was just the day for it. Her anguish was excessive and immune to appeasement. 'Would he take all his photographs with him if he was only going to the golf club?'

I went back with her to Stour End. It was soon obvious that he had taken not only his photographs but also his clothes, regimental mementos and sporting gear. I was stupefied; in my innocence, I could not begin to guess why a man so manifestly infatuated with his wife, who had – against all the known form – honoured his word all those years, could suddenly elect to vanish.

The Wakefields' breakfast table was uncleared. *The Times* lolled against the toast-rack. Molly sat on a tall stool staring without interest at the rosy garden. My eye was drawn to the folded newspaper. The Deaths columns was uppermost and in it I saw a paragraph headed *CHADWICK*,

PIERS. Brigadier Piers Fisher Chadwick, DSO, MC, late of the 12/14th Lancers, had been drowned in a boating accident. It was asked that neither flowers nor letters be sent. I looked at the item again and imagined what was not said, that Piers Chadwick had contrived an 'accident' to cover a suicide which it would be tactless to commit more obviously. Neither self-pity nor accusation was worthy of an officer and a gentleman, but once his life had no further regimental responsibilities, he owed it to no one to go on living.

I did not like to look at Molly. I realised now that Bill Wakefield had kept his promise to the letter: Piers had indeed not lived to see the day when Bill was not with Molly or not faithful to her, but his death released his old friend from his honourable bond. Rover boy, I suspected, would never come home again.

The Latin Lover

Ten days before the end of Cricket Term, Gilbert Master-man was fifty years old. The senior Classics master carried his voice low on his chest, like an Order. In school, he sported corduroy trousers, with thonged sandals – Iphicratic, he called them, when in amiably didactic mood – over clocked socks. Iphicrates, he informed the Sixth, was the Athenian who hastened the decline of Sparta by redesigning military footgear. He exacted the annual tribute of a collective groan when he declared that the Attic general defeated the hoplites by hopping lighter than they. However, on the night of the square cake with its candles in an L ('Roman fifty for you, Gilbert!'), he paraded a greening dinner jacket, burgundy-cummerbunded evening trousers and silver-buckled shoes.

The celebrations in Tennant's Hall had been arranged by Dickie Dicks, the modern Languages man ('*Merci* to him,' as Mort was sure to say). The beaks' common room, whose panelled hall bridged the Gothic archway to the school grounds, was named after H. S. de M. Tennant, Second Master (O.C. 1824–1913). The beard of his bronze bust, at the top of the stairs, once inflicted a trivial, mortal nick on a haemophiliac junior master whom it shaved too closely after a bibulous evening. His uncommemorated name was Porter, or was it Potter? In every school one can find an archivist who knows that kind of thing.

Gilbert's party too was bibulous, but not at all fatal; there was nothing more lethal than chaff and 'champagne'. 'Actually,' Dickie Dicks said, 'it's *Méthode Champénoise*, but you can't tell the difference can you, Gilbert?'

'Not I,' Gilbert said, with his *flûte* to his lips.

Long-skirted, nag-shouldered beaks' ladies – their *cache-tout* evening dresses had the lineaments, and charm, of overalls – asked each other, again, why Gilbert never married; surely he couldn't be happy, living alone in Gamekeeper's Cottage, could he? Receding tides of boyish glances had washed over the older masters' wives. Looking back on the untelevised years when not even the sixth form included a female pupil, they were now free to smile, if bleakly, at desires which they had been forbidden, in those days of monastic curiosity, ever to entertain: legend still recalled what happened to Nurse Bartlett. One version spoke of *both* the Bailey boys.

The younger wives, and staff, were not obliged to the tradition of draped drabness. Mrs MacGlashan (Penny) reminded Gilbert, openly, of deep-bosomed Aphrodite, and secretly of other things. Pat Marsh, the freckled Manchester engineer, a titan for outdoor work apparently, arrived alone but did not stay so: Hesketh and Chard, the Eton man, were keen to join her class. She had practical experience in the East and a cracking backhand too.

There were toasts and jests for Gilbert's half-century. 'Good old Gilbert,' some said, and others (Darwin, of course Darwin) rallied with 'Less of the old!' Even Alex MacGlashan was seen to wince a smile, methodic bubbles up his nose. Alex was sombre with good luck; his Glasgow graduate wife was a prize, but where did Penny go on the mountain bike on Thursday afternoons when Alex had the Under Sixth for double Plantagenets and Harry Houjego (Hockey Blue, buffoon) was free. Harry was not talking to Penny just yet; but then would he be when MacGlashan could see him? The unseen, as Gilbert knew, in Latin and in Greek, was what one feared the most.

Chris Mortimer clinked coat-of-arms-lengthened spoon on glass and gave the old friendly speech. 'Tonight we can let our hair down, while we still have some, some of us,' etc. Chris's hair was visible, H.C.I. whispered to Percy Porritt, the chaplain, mainly because his hat was in the ring for Master. Mort went on (but not on *and* on) to treat Gilbert to well-prepared spontaneity. Pinching a rag of tongue between his teeth as if the administering of jokes were a form of punishment, he gave Gilbert six of his best, including a new antique about Tommo Thomas, who once called the school wicket-keeper 'The Ancient Mariner'. Why so? 'Because he stoppeth one in three.' Penny MacGlashan didn't get it: why should she? Hesketh explained; Bill Riley, the Bilge man was jealous, he found, on Houjego's behalf (strange organ, boys, *and* girls, I see, the human heart!). Christopher lifted his glass and gave them – and not a moment before time! – Gilbert Masterman. Everyone's chair scraped as the company did the right thing. '*Vivat*,' they all said, some before others, and then, 'Speech!' They had come for that.

Gilbert held up the glass which modesty had forbidden him to sip and told them how much he preferred what it contained to milk and honey. Sometimes, he reminded them, there are more amusing places to be than the promised land. Such company as tonight's was, he said, his consolation, as he entered what might well be the second half of his life. '*Il faut être réaliste, mon gros*,' he said, and clapped little Dickie Dicks on the *épaule*. 'I have to say, and I might say it even if I did not, that the Second Master struck just the right note this evening, and – I am relieved to say – not too often. He made the jokes and Janny, I am told, made the *vol-aux-vents* which (with the very greatest respect, Christopher!) seemed to me slightly the fresher and crisper!' Christopher winced sporting amusement; Janny smiled wider, whiter pleasure. It was a smile she had been taught in second-year drama school; in the third she met Christopher and never learned to frown.

The Mortimers had four children, three already at the school; as a toddler, the five-year-old fourth ('Caresse! Imagine,' Ivy Porritt said, 'calling her that, even today!') would always run onto the football pitch whenever the school scored ('In other words, rarely,' Gilbert was telling them). Blonde curls bouncing, Janny turned up to teach drama, and English, on Tuesdays and Fridays; darling Gilbert, Gilbert darling, had been her Falstaff in the Christmas play. The Sixth Form master came down a peg, three times a week, to teach Latin to James, her oldest, in Remove.

Gilbert's gracious teasing and fluent modesty ('If I cannot manage wit, I can – at a pinch – be relied on for brevity') were received with appreciative thumps on the table and only a single glance at a watch (trust H.C.I. for that). When he sat down, it seemed to announce the end of a term to which exams – already in progress – had, alas, yet to supply their final demands.

'Where are you going this summer, Gilberto?' Janny said.

'Italy, I think; Italy, definitely. You?'

'You know Chris and the mountains.'

'They won't come to him; he must go to them.'

'Oh Gilbert,' Janny said (he was never darling off the War Memorial stage), 'I wish you'd join us.'

'You have a Volvo; what need have you of a donkey?'

'He should, shouldn't he, Chris, come with us?'

'Indeed,' said Mortimer, 'why not?'

'I'm not a mountain man,' Gilbert said. 'Thanks all the same.'

'*Flammantia moenia mundi*? I should have thought they were very much you. Aug Four, we leave.'

'Unfortunately for me, and luckily for you, I've already booked my ferry.'

'Your coin in Charon's palm? Let him keep it: you're a long time dead.'

'Often before you know it,' said H.C.I.. The white-haired Germanist slipped his *mots* into alien conversations *en passant*, like one of those car-park drifters who leave flyers under windscreen-wipers in a second and are gone.

'You *always* go to Italy, doesn't he?' Janny said.

'Always. *Ergo*, I'm going again.'

'Too much *ergo* can seriously limit your horizons, Gilbert. Ought you not to try a little *propter* for a change?'

'You know something, Morty?' MacGlashan, glass in hand, was threatening to be bolder than usual. 'You know something?'

'Not I; but I await instruction. What?'

'You're always so considerate: you have tags for the Latinists – hullo there, Gilbert! – vulgar fractions for the mathematics people . . .'

'And what have I got for you, Alex? Dates?'

MacGlashan backed off, tilted his chair one-legged to give him better eyes. Was that Pen, behind the silverware, and was that *him*? 'No offence, Mort. No offence. It's nice of you.'

'Your wife's looking very pretty tonight,' Mortimer said.

'Where?' MacGlashan lifted his chin and his glasses went moony with candles. 'Where?'

Gilbert passed the nuts, assorted, in a silver dish, *ex dono* some pre-1914 Latinised O.C., who had done well in the Argentine after passing out none too high from the Army Class, only just above the gallant Cannon, F., and decorated Fodder, C. Their names, on the left as you go into Big School bogs, now needed regilding in Memorial Cloister.

'You should come and see us, Mr G.,' Janny said, 'for a couple of days. Do you know the Val d'Aran?'

'Sound like an ice-skater,' Gilbert said. 'I don't.'

'Tell me, G.M.,' Mortimer said, 'how's Jimmy faring this term?'

'Still the occasional spondee in the fifth foot,' Gilbert said. 'It's probably all that Lucretius he gets at home.'

As an undergraduate and Mowbrayed dandy, with a waist, he favoured green corduroy trousers (buttons, not zips), and a green velvet jacket, canary waistcoat, bone buttons. Before the day that porter came out to hang his framed disappointment on the Senate House railings, young Masterman frequently carried a cane. He was to be spotted in double-ended bow-ties and sometimes a ruffled shirt (they were just coming in on austerity's tail). He was as clean-shaven as a sixth-century *kouros*; if his tongue was abrasive, stubble was never his style. Having few enemies, Gilbert did his best to humour them; he treasured his butts. What had Donald Bunker done to deserve such allusive lampoonery? And why was Davy Upfill-Jones, Mr Eliot's unsmiling clone, so good for laughs? Gilbert's labels stuck: victims walked round with them like paddock badges. Remember 'double-decker Buss', the Downing heavyweight, and Danziger, Stoyan, counterfeit count, whose mother Gilbert alleged – after Stoyan denied borrowing a Huxley first edition – was descended directly from Dracula? Gilbert met him in tears in Piccadilly one November day in 1956; he went to jail in 1974.

Who would have guessed, in those Arcadian times (before all this and only just after all that), that Gilbert Masterman would ever be a schoolmaster? Actor, producer, wit (as the Master of the College helped himself to baked hake, Gilbert observed, 'The Master is eating his own kind!') and *arbiter elegantiae*, he might have become a quoted critic, say, and no one doubted him a don-to-be. In the formal Fifties, he was already older than men of his own age. Capable of folly, but rarely of foolishness, he danced publicly but once, alone, all night, by the light of a candle, in the rooms of a Latinist called Harry Hotchkiss (ex-Major, the Greenjackets), who had received a Fellowship before he took Part II, one of a kind. *Hinc illae lacrimae* (Terence, not Virgil, Mortimer).

Yes, he had danced and danced (Gilbert, Gilbert) while others drank and drank to the end of the year. His year was ended, and his donnish dream (it wasn't the end of the *world*, though, was it?). He would never be a young Fellow, as he had never been a Major: first flat feet, then flat hopes. He mimed Marlene (on a 78), Falling In Love Again (who never had), while others reprised Footlights songs and imitated Goons, my capitan, till dawn. Gilbert looked undamaged; a dandy always could, and always must: he seemed sleeved in his loneliness as if cut out for it. On

Gilbert's silver knobbed cane, the motto was: SIC FUIT, SIC SEMPER ERO. He did not recognise the regiment, but he knew he belonged to it.

When, as he switched out the lamps, Hotchkiss remarked that his machine was overheating and this tango must accordingly cease, Gilbert said, 'I should never have been Gilbert, you know, Bangers, I should have been Horace. Not that I should have wanted to be.' Was that wetness weeping? Hotchkiss mentioned the church as a genuine alternative to academe; Gilbert had already thought of it, though not as genuine. He decided, but never aloud, to go back to his old school: after all, he had never been happy there.

As a beak, Gilbert became notorious among his colleagues for mocking the school's antique affectations. It was said to be one of the five best in England, which implied the fifth position, though no one could say on what calculus it was merited. The place had been founded by Jacob Legge, a reformed pirate, pious with West Indian dividends and in a hurry, Gilbert presumed, to secure uncommon entrance to St Peter's celestial college. Suffering from the stone, he heaped a hill of treasure in the Home Counties, where a heavenly examiner could not miscount his ostentatious deposit. Unfortunately, *avec l'usure des années* (Dickie Dick supplied the phrase), it had recently been necessary to launch a Tricentennial Appeal. The brochure was complete with talented photographs by an O.C., who had also done the Queen. There were colour views of Quaritch Quad, Challenger's Green and the Bernstein benefaction; the text did not recall how young Bernstein had been blackballed when undergoing Christian treatment at Mr Lock's house. His recent lordship now figured in the marginal committee of honour which called for convenanters' cash to pay for a new roof for Headlam Hall and, more important, the Arts and Sciences extension (in the building-permitted, arrowed space between Green and Little Lea). It was strange, Gilbert was bound to say, how few great men so great a school had spawned. How lucky that, with the new mixed Sixth, they could now look forward to great women!

Before Italy, Gilbert provisioned himself, at Shop (the school omitted definite articles as a descriptive rule), with spiral notebooks – 'Better have another one of those, Mr Fish, for second thoughts!' – and a pot of washable blue. Ideally, he would have persisted with a dip pen, but the nibs had a tendency to snag. Some of the younger chaps – for instance Hesketh, who by the end of term had lost Pat Marsh to Chard (Robin's family money apparently compensated for his family looks) – hesitated between scorn and envy when they witnessed Gilbert's egregious self-sufficiency. Hesketh first called him *porcus* when seeking to amuse an unamused H.C.I.; the Germanist never appreciated the malice of others.

Gilbert had said goodbye to his waist when he said goodbye to *her*. Already at thirty-five, he was 'Fats' to the Remove, despite a certain agility: his feet still seemed to dance, at times, but too often towards the cake tin. Nowadays, he ducked and turned his bulk and was into his Renault 5 ('*décapotable*,' Dicks ironised, '*tiens!*') before anyone could quite see how he had done it, again. On his way to the continent, while jiggling from second into third, he passed MacGlashan, who had taken up jogging ('Not that he'll ever catch her,' H.C.I. muttered, knee to chin as he put on his bicycle clips, the verticle ones, never the hoops).

Gilbert had spent uncertain time in front of his shelves, choosing holiday books; he did not like to take anything he had not read, or at least begun, before. He had his essential provisions (the plaided drum of shortbreads, the tommy-gun magazine of mints), but he needed a ration of dust to supplement the English papers he feared he would buy more often than he did at home (time future, Upfill would say, was already, in some sense, time passed). He selected some Tacitus and Clough's *Amours de Voyage*, yes, and Quintus Horatius the flak, and, oh, that ex-pupil's thing he had, with prompt politeness, congratulated him on, before reaching the indexed end: *Roman Holidays* by Brian Yardley. Look, he had stuck a flag in page 69, to mark where he had flagged indeed. '*Ricominciamo*,' Gilbert muttered; time to apply emery paper to rusting Italian!

He closed and locked the door of Gamekeeper's Cottage. After all these years, he still had no right to call it his: the lease was inalienably the school's. M.C.C. 'Tommo' Thomas had been living there when Gilbert left Mr Lock's house to go up to Cambridge; he was still there, eighty-seven not out, when Gilbert returned to teach the Fifth and wait for the Sixth. M.C.C's innings closed at ninety-two; pink and tender-fleshed, he taught physics and coached the XI in catches on the boundary (their hands were red when he had finished with his steep circuits) and took those with unbuttered fingers back to Gamekeeper's cottage for tea and, before it was bad for them, the occasional Craven 'A'. The lichened fountain in the dense, but narrow, garden supported a tip-toed nymph with mossy bumps. Tommo left his body to science, if it wanted it, and instructions not to prune the roses; they were not that sort.

From the start, Gilbert relished the polemics of scholarship more than its drudgery. *Odium academicum* supplied an elixir of eternal middle age and stored its victims in immortal pickle: what formaldehyde could ever match Housman's prefaces when it came to keeping enemies pellucidly suspended in a solution of ridicule? As an undergraduate, Gilbert preferred notes and introductions to the texts they bracketed; he was more eager to read reviews than the books they barely recommended.

In the blue leather chairs of the U.L., he found that love of learning was not enough to make a scholar: it proved hard to study in one's sleep, though not to dream. He had told Mortimer, J., as much, when the boy dozed, and twitched like a puppy, in double Virgil: 'Beware lest – *cave ne*! – Circe turns you into a dormouse (*dormiglione*)'. Oh how one wished that one had learnt the very things one taught! Somnolent or not, Gilbert enjoyed the security of libraries; he played the detective in intricate catalogues and relished the lonely thrill of tracking a numbered spine to where it leaned in its place like that Impossible She who turned out, against all expectation, to be there, at home, when called upon. In Gilbert's single case, her name was Frances, which rhymed with dances, glances, trances, but not quite with fancies.

He had always been at ease with books. His father bound (and rebound) them in a Fenland city hardly bigger than a village. Calfskin and gum and harmless vices were the tools of his trade. The father died; the mother dried, a Quaker lady by the cathedral close. At school (state-aided Exhibitioner), Gilbert was not athletic, yet comely and lightly feared (the father's death aged his tongue and tone). In his last term, he composed a particularly good paper on *Julius Caesar* for the Shakespeare Soc.; everyone who understood it enjoyed the remark about the redemption of Cinna the poet. Subbing for a gravely ill Head Man, M.C.C.T. initialled 'We all wish him well at Cambridge' on his last report. Gilbert still had it somewhere, though the fold in it was now a gangrenous caesura.

After Barnaby's death, the mother's age was added to the boy's; Gilbert thought of her too much and could do too little. In the vacations, he could be seen in his ruffled shirt going there and back to the shops. He invited Upfill to come and look at the reliefs in the cathedral; they rubbed some brasses. On a walk before tea, Gilbert showed him where the bindery had been (they found it stacked with tiles). In the evenings they played draughts. Then Upfill went to New Zealand.

Gilbert never tired of the machinery of scholarship, though it made him drowsy. He smiled at footnotes with their daggered and starry references; he was glad to observe the wheeling in of foreign artillery of various bores; German, Spanish, French, Hungarian. He had no originality (that stomach announced small appetite for research),

171

but he did crave modest publication; in 1971, with Donald Bunker, he co-authored a little textbook (since reprinted three times), *Latin Now*. It did well in Ghana and Nigeria, until something political changed out there; it remained standard in New South Wales, for the few quid that was worth. The royalties had paid, in their day, for Pompeii, Venice and Ravenna; *forse* they might still stretch to Brindisi if some Maecenas cared to share expenses.

Gilbert was content to explore beaten paths. He came to like what he liked already. He deplored the term 'serendipity' as keenly as he practised that careless habit; he valued everything he dug up, polished and displayed. If parody was his style, he often repaid more than he had borrowed. In the same spirit, when he wrote skits for end of term shows, his waspishness had no sting. He mocked himself more cruelly than he derided others, and with more accuracy. As he had annual occasion to remind his pupils, scholarship and mimicry were cousins; the straight face was their common feature. To mitigate the indigestible gammas in their exam results, he had told the Remove, in the final lesson of the year, that the miracle of the Classics was that they offered a mine from which every generation took something new and yet which, on reflection, grew deeper and richer with every excavation. Even false readings had their canonic place, as Winckelmann's aesthetics – and possibly his ethics – proved. Gilbert watched for signs of puzzlement; the cleverest were those who frowned.

'Was there really someone called Winckelmann, sir?' young Mortimer had asked, as the clock did its hum and click and the minute hand jumped a space nearer the vertical that would release them all into classless summer.

'I used to eat winkles,' Gilbert said, 'raw. On wartime beaches. I winkled them out with the head of a pin. They tasted like wet India rubbers. Yes, there was: a great scholar, though possessed by, alas, dubious theories.'

'Why alas, sir?'

'Because, Transom, his ideas were more beautiful than

the truth. Much. You have played for a draw, young Mortimer, and you have succeeded. To your shame, I trust. Be gone. Be gone.'

Young Mortimer went clattering home; all-alphaed Transom loitered, clapped his specs in their case and seemed to want no holidays. 'What were his ideas, sir?' The boy's cheeks bulged so ingratiatingly that an old-fashioned usher might have suspected bull's-eyes in each cheek. Transom was a pupil pregnant with the half-holiday (and accompanying brief popularity) which, a few years from now, his Oxbridge award would eventually procure him. 'And about what exactly, sir? He doesn't sound like a real person, sir, does he?'

'Do I? Do you? Is there really someone called Transom, Transom? Winckelmann was, you might say, if only you remembered what I told you, the inventor of modern Hellenism, assuming that by "modern" one means the Hellenism that is now out of date. Do you know the story of the man who failed his exams at Oxford because he began his essay with the words "Democracy is a word that comes from the Latin"?'

'No, sir.'

'Yes, you do, Transom; yes, you do. Reflect. Don't you? Winckelmann saw Greek art as men had never seen it before, including, of course, the Greeks. Greece itself he never saw, except reflected in its marbles, which had once been gaudy with colour and not at all the refined things which our friend took them to be. Imagine if he had seen how they treat their donkeys, Transom.'

'Is he still alive, sir?'

'Is he still alive?'

'Winckelmann, sir.'

'He was born in 1717. He is not. Tell me something, Transom.'

'I will if I can, sir.'

'These texts I set you, what do you really make of them? The mother and the jointed child, for instance. What would

173

you say if no prizes depended on it, no alpha wriggled on my book?'

'Isn't it a fertility myth, sir? How long did he live, sir?'

'Winckelmann? Until he died. Until he was murdered. He was murdered, Transom. As Euripides reminds us, life is basically bloody. Admire too much perfectly proportioned marble and you lose your proper suspicions of the body's uses and its frailty. Admire too unguardedly and you too may find your own slabby place *à la poisonnerie*. Am I right?'

'Presumably you are, sir. Who murdered him exactly, and why?'

'And where?'

'If you like, sir.'

'A cook, in Trieste. Why? Because he was there – on a stopover between Vienna and another look at the wretched Apollo Belvedere, I shouldn't wonder. And the cook? He was there, I suppose, because . . . he had some cooking to do, and did it. He cooked Winckelmann's goose. A dishonest answer, and a true one. Frequent, puzzling conjunction; watch out for it, it's sure to recur. No one quite knows the motive; probably robbery. Let us hope so.'

'Why, sir?'

'Why are you who you are, Transom?'

'I don't know, sir.'

'Life is chockablock with imponderables; it has no easy algebra. It is unfathomable; we fish for the truth, but we never, never trawl the bottom. Because it is no great scandal to be robbed, although it is always a little foolish.'

Gilbert was walking Transom, or Transom Gilbert, through Cloister towards Challenger's Green. (Cyril Barker Challenger made a double century in a single day, in June 1904, and then took six for twenty-eight; after that, he went into a bank, where he made little and took nothing.) Transom cantered with Gilbert down Pinkus Steps and slowed along Founder's Walk. Was it the romance of scholarship which made him more loyal than Mortimer? Or was it – it was, Gilbert feared – that Hawke, B.D.J., was waiting for Transom, by Lib.? The master's pedantries were less dreadful to Transom than Hawke's clarity, and for that reason perhaps less attractive.

'If it wasn't robbery, sir, the motive, what do you think it was?'

'Could it have been money? The Attic tetradrach in the scholar's lumpy purse? Do you solicit honesty from me, Transom? Would your mother like it? Are *you* being honest with *me*? The knowledge is all there, as Socrates proved geometrically in the *Meno*, which will soon not be beyond you; it is all there in your head. You know it all, did you but know it. Between the scholar and the cook, what motive for murder existed, do you conjecture? Perhaps the great Johann tried to teach Giancarlo Spaghetti the Golden Rule. Perhaps he sought to pass on the elements of Greek verse composition. What better warrant for a blade in the bladder? After all, you could kill me sometimes, couldn't you, Transom?'

'You, sir? No, sir.'

'Who then?'

'I couldn't kill anyone, sir. Was his name seriously Spaghetti?'

'Clearly, you have yet to finish your education, Transom. Come back next term. Happy holidays to you.'

Hawke, B.D.J., was rich; Transom, R., was poor. When he felt like it, Hawke hawked on the floor of the Charles Wadsworth Greene Annexe and there was ten quid for the scholar who bent to sup the splat. Transom craved what he dreaded, Hawke's coercive smile; there were books in it. Schoolboy stories do not always end in winning runs, though there is often a hush in the Close. Did Gilbert not guess why Transom looked across – checking that he had his specs – towards what the Classics master's blah had helped him postpone? Should Transom be asked to tea? No doubt he preferred to taste cold stone and Hawke's unseasonable oyster. Yet the child wondered, like an innocent, what motive there could be for violence! He meant apart from the pleasure, presumably. Had Transom not yet even dreamed of Hawke astonished by agony, metal in his ribs and a spewing wallet in his hands? Hawke and Transom would be ministers in the same government; Hawke with family trusts behind him, Transom melodious with sincerity, taking stick, but proud to be where he was. Forbid bullying and how are our future leaders to be found and formed? Deny a boy his tormentor and he may never have a lasting relationship in his whole life.

Gilbert ached for Transom, but not with desire; he could not scrounge an emotion to go with whatever he felt; he simply felt it. Oh yes, on the other hand, he could imagine another inviting the boy to a bath and things; absence of desire was what licensed its growth. Alone in the July glare, watching young James on his last visit to Tucker ('Double scoop and a bun, no the Chelsea one, please, fat Fred!'), he thought with envious pity of what the Transom child would agree to endure. Like any clever, servile Greek, he would still call a master 'Sir', no doubt, after nothing was said and everything was done; outrage would come later, if it came at all, and might well require a prompter. Transom would survive whatever he suffered as if it were a favour; he had intelligence. The boy was pure temptation; he excited ideas he could never embody. G.M.W.M. had already given him an excellent report, with a sincerely flattering caveat: *nec nimis negotii.*

Gilbert could imagine with what reproach Transom *père* might ask his son to translate and speculated whether, in punitive honour of the boy's merely indoor achievements, he would sentence him to golf lessons, or to formative gardening, in the long holidays. The flavour of misgivings still soured Gilbert's mouth as he reached Portsmouth and had to wait for France. Frances had been his college-garden Beatrice. She had dark hair and a ready mouth for tart phrases. Gilbert reminded her, and the others, that Shakespeare's girls were boys; all his sweet talk was hermaphroditic.

Frances wore plum-coloured boots at damp rehearsals and a tartan blanket-coat. ('What plaid is that?' he asked. 'Oh, Jaeger, isn't it?' she said). She was the first to drop the book (as Janny Mortimer would say, to remind him that she had her Equity card). She was Gilbert's early ally, Frances, girl playing boy playing girl: taking his point all right, she wore her voice high in her nose, straightly comic. He was the slim one then, in summer's livery: fawn linen suit, the bow-tie with the white spots, the cane, the boss.

By careful chance, they left rehearsals together – languid, fair producer, squarish dark girl – and agreed on Dutch coffee at the Dorothy. She wondered how he could both produce and play the Duke, but then again, if he didn't mind her saying so (he didn't), how could he bear not to be Benedick when he was so much more Benedictine than, well, some people? She had dropped her clever voice after rehearsal and came down a register. It was a grant of nakedness which never undid a button: sensible female, Frances.

The outdoor production was a wet triumph on the first night ('Rain did *not* stop play,' said the *Cambridge Daily News*). The company was praised by G.R. in a London daily; if the caustic, clumsy Benedick was unaccountably admired, Beatrice was 'very right,' while the duke (the gracious Gilbert himself, of course) was 'a droll delight'. Frances had no greater ambition (she acted only for the exercise) but she had the wit to ask if Gilbert had thought of the theatre as a profession. What else did he want to do? 'The Classics,' he said, 'if all goes well.'

'Oh it will, it's bound to. Why ever shouldn't it?'

He blamed the printer at first, when he looked at the framed lists on the Senate House railings. How could it be that Bunker, D. St.G, was in the First Class and Masterman, G.M.W., was not? He was surprised that he could walk back towards the College. He resigned his youth in Trinity Street and put on middle age without anyone noticing. When he met Frances in the Taj Mahal, she took him for a grown man and said, 'Put it out of your mind. What's wrong with a Second? Tell you what: I'm going down to the country, my parents' place, come and stay. You did very well really, Gilbert.'

He assumed that her parents would be at the cottage too; perhaps with their only-wanting-to-play dogs, how-do-you-doing relatives for lunch and a cautious cat ('What's your name then?') who really liked people only when they were leaving. It was an old Suffolk barn near Diss; he and Frances had it to themselves.

'They *always* go away, Gilbert,' she said, 'always. What do you mean, *"arranged"*?'

It rained; they sat indoors and her hopes were his fears.

She said, 'I'm not bored. Are you?'

'Not a bit.'

'Were you all right in that bed? Did you sleep? It sags.'

'It's fine; it sags where I do,' Gilbert said.

'There's always mine,' she said.

'Frances, I'm sorry . . .'

'Gilbert, there's nothing to be sorry *for*. I understand.'

Poor Frances! He recognised small calculation, still less cunning, in her. He had to stoop to put them there. Yet so it ended, pain without pleasure; divorce without marriage; flop, then flight. It might not have called for much to make them happy, but – like Clough, A.H., his *compagnon de route* – Gilbert lacked the vocation. After he had redeemed his solitude, his body turned against him, or he against it; his flesh became a double scoop.

Frances wrote him a letter (one hesitates, but one always opens them, doesn't one?); she did not blame him one bit as she hoped he did not blame her. They both wanted only to make sure they were both absolutely all right and each promised the other that that was so. Once that was settled, she went mad; hair unwashed, hat always on. Thenceforth, she capped everything: cosies for unlit candles, *capotes* for chairbacks, whatever came to a point or a boss had to be dressed in a bonnet. Gilbert went off to Pompeii (for the first time, in a bus).

There must always have been something wrong with her. She chose the wrong men because men were wrong for her. He scented madness like catnip and was well out of it. How right she had been for Beatrice, and how wrong for him! That had been a quarter of a century ago, and more, as boring buffers always said. No woman had left her upstairs life ajar for him since then or said, 'Oh come on in,' through a muffler of silk and buttons.

Now he was fifty. Men he had known in the Union were in the cabinet. One boy he had taught was dead, Baxter, E.G. He had initialled a tribute to him for the mag, before going to check his oil, and slipped it into Percy Porritt's pigeonhole. G.M.W.M. writes: 'I shall always remember the generosity he showed to less gifted boys and how little trouble it was for him to take trouble over unrewarding tasks.' G.M.W.M. did *not* write: 'Eddie Baxter ran like a young God, skied the javelin – for an unbroken school record – as if before the Skian gate, god-guided bronze it might have been whirring death to some great-hearted hero, unless he had a deflecting god footsying at his side. Why should love not be aesthetic? Oh that planted foot, braced flank, bracketed shoulder, flung arm! And then the human totter on the whitewashed line, the body falling back and forwards all in one, the hair dashed from the brow, the downward ambling look as measurers trotted to confirm the mark.' Why should one not be Pindar any more? How did Eddie die? In some bloody silly desert ditch at the wheel of a charitable lorry full of tinned promises.

'Hullo, hullo! Off then, are you, Gilbert?' the padre said, reaching for what had been left for him almost before Gilbert took his fingers from it. Oh goodbyes! Why did some people always make them an excuse for hullo, hullo?

'Yes, Percy, just off.'

Luggage strapped, on the way down Goodge Hill, free at last, Gilbert was thumbed by a Blood sporting a first XI square and had to do the right thing: leaned horizontal to open the far door.

'Thank you very much, sir, not going to the station, are you?'

'Not until you asked me, Hawke. Good term?'

'I can't complain, sir. You?'

'Oh I can complain,' Gilbert said. It earned him the complicity he craved, the craven. Young Hawke was as slim as Gilbert's obsolete shadow. There was a soft frost of moustache on his smile as he watched the master play the chauffeur. What wet wicket widow would help him break his duck when the weather turned foul on his father's cricket tour of Devon and Cornwall? Gilbert said goodbye to him with relieved regret. 'God, that's my train!' the young god said. 'Thanks, Gilbert! Cheers!' The centaur smiled and waved.

Was there a hearse on the ferry? Did Gilbert see a black cat at the customs? What did he do when the ship creaked and insulated cups tilted – 'Sorry,' said the German salesman, 'my friend' – and puddled the cuffed table? Gilbert withdrew his new notebook too late to escape a brown Australia-shaped stain, but no large damage was done; it was quite all right. Later, did he dream, and of what, in the engineered pullman seat? Oh how much better are the highlights than the whole match *in extenso*! Having left his Tacitus in the locked Renault, he had to read the passengers instead. What would he have said, or not said, what footnote would he have supplied, had he seen Penny MacG hand in hand with Houjego, swinging a litre of the old Duty Free? Whose business was it what they did, and then again – more problematic – whose pleasure? There is really not enough of life to go round, Gilbert thought: once miss your turn, you wait and wait. In truth (that flat old thing), the passengers were a text he had not seen before and did not closely con.

After the usual show of early morning patience, he drove off the ferry, past stalled lorries, clank, clank, clank, and there he was in France. Ah the sha-sha-sha of Napoleon's poplars before prosperity put its saw to them! *Ecce guber-nator*, the prompt sheet said, as the rough wind congratu-lated what remained of his hair and he slid south on the green slope of summer. He was not even sorry when it rained, a little, on his open lid. At Albi (where once, surely, there had been an imperial *mansio* or staging post), the storm broke and basted the blush-pink city until it resembled a summer pudding, bricked with raspberries. Gilbert hoisted canvas on the Renault and wondered what, in all honesty, there ever was to admire in the hulking *Bavarois* of the cathedral. Great Giles Gilbert Scott! What was Upfill up to these days? And why in Auckland? Gilbert admired the provincial parquet in the Lautrec museum.

The heat of Provence soon rouged him into a Falstaff who needed no slap. ('False Taafe' Byron had called his Pisan friend, but why? And why did the false always ring so true?) Having to wait behind lorries at Ventimiglia, he strolled back and forth and talked English with other GB's, as if nothing pleased him more than the company of those he had driven so far to escape. He stood and smoked a cigarette (better to seize the day than stretch the years), one Iphicratic sandal on the parapet, while he watched the waver of ghostly cutlery spooning the wind-scuffed surface of the sea. The joy of the holiday with which he had threatened himself was that it had no firm dates or destinations: he might get as far as Trieste and he might not. Perhaps he would be there in a few days; perhaps he would travel hopelessly and never arrive. He would drive until he was tired and stopped; and when he was tired of stopping, he would drive.

He took the turning to Lucca. On the subject of triumvirs, did Lepidus ever write his memoirs? How many happy, third-rate things were lost, and might yet be found! The disabused perspective on Octavian and Antony's Third Man might be delicious; history was often tastier for a loser's salt. Housman had spent the best of his qualities on the unworthy Marcus Manilius, on whom Scaliger and

Bentley had already bent their minds. How nice to be Lepidus' editor (if the manuscript was not *too* corrupt), with notes! One could always recruit Bunker – or unretiring Hotchkiss – if one was in a hole. How enduring enmity was and how eager to be of service!

Under the tree-topped, circumambient walls of the triumvirs' *rendonsnous*, Gilbert stopped to fill the Renault's tank. The *ragazzo* piping the *benzina* masked the now prudently panamaed Gilbert from the figures on the clunking pump. When he snapped off the juice – that kerjoink was an antique sound it was poignant to hear once more – and made his claim, it was Gilbert's first sublime moment of the journey: deceit had such a piquant taste when one had a thirst for it. The dark youth had called the cheating price a little too casually; he wanted only a touch of tactful direction to have done it perfectly. Gilbert's heart went out to him, like a jack-in-the-box: here, catch!

'*Ricominciamo*,' Gilbert said. '*Quanto è? Posso guardare?*'

The velvet eyes (see under *Lovers, Latin*) were worn like wounds and lidded with reproach: how could Gilbert doubt the justice of the price, when it had been cooked especially for him? The figures skittered away (*ceu fumus in auras*, Virgil had Eurydice vanish) and the pump wore as unmarked a face now as its attendant, who repeated his price. When Gilbert shook his head, the lad (ah, A.E.H., what would you have said or done, or, better, composed?) called to two boys, one pillioned behind the other, as they snarled past on a Vespa. 'Sandro, Peppino, *aspettate . . .*' His frown incriminated Gilbert, but his friends went, *ceu fumus in auras* (cow fumes in our arse), astride their blue wake, towards the city gate, one with a hand upraised, as if to leave the room.

Daring agreement, Gilbert repeated the price of what he had not had, and heard it asked again. But now it seemed to be for some different service and, with those unsoft eyes still on him, he was almost pleased to count brown notes into a gold-ringed hand. The necessary jeans (palm oil-stains on each sirloin), the FORZA LUCCA vest (gold-chained cross teed on a rough of black hair), the wetted lips (artful, dodgy!), the lacquered curls (no trace of Transom's sorry summer snow), and the crowded crotch made threats and promises all one. The ruffian's insolence spilled over the recent quinquegenarian like some stinging cornucopia. While the *pompista* rang up the sale, he shook his tar-dark head, the victor victimised. Desire was no part of Gilbert's enjoyment of the scene: desire can be satisfied, where satisfaction never can. God the Father saluted his creation, man, with just such a languid hand as Gilbert turned over now for his puny change.

'*Senta, prego, c'è un pensione, non troppo caro qui vicino?*'

'*Un pensione? Un pensione?*'

Gilbert, corrected, said, '*Scusi: una pensione.*'

'*Meglio così. Forse.* How long you want to stay?'

'*Non so. Una notte? Forse due, tre . . .*'

His name was Mario; his uncle's *Pensione Tiberio* was not far from the *Piazza del Duomo*. He wrote the exact address on a Shell card; Gilbert looked at those fingernails. 'I see you there later.' Did he catch a scent of Gilbert's doubtful hope? 'I do some cooking there at night.'

The *Pensione Tiberio* was a steep, lichened house with a walled garden (and indicated *Trattoria*) at the back. A mattress lolled from an upstairs window. Inside, the hall was cool and chequered. A wall-eyed girl's slow rag encircled a shining puddle of her own creation. After climbing two flights, *con la signora*, Gilbert agreed to an unluxurious room. The counterpane on the brass bed was zebraed with sunlight from crutched shutters. There was a shower and a basin with a spider in it. From the front window he could see the dumpy *duomo*; at the side he looked down at the narrow path to the restaurant and its advertised shade. '*Comoedi scenam, comedones quaerite cenam,*' Gilbert remembered, teacher and pupil in one.

He refused to be lonely, by being his own companion. He proposed a walk and was its seconder. He would first see the cathedral (ecclesiastical outsides were always sweeter than interiors, yet one always had to go in) and then do postcards. There was a pivoting rack of them outside the *tabaccheria* in the cobbled *piazza*; an Englishwoman – who else would wear that off-white panama, so like Gilbert's own, or carry a plaid-lined mackintosh in the blazing blue of the morning? – was making a pursed selection.

'Hullo, Gilbert, all alone?' Had she spoken or was it the ventriloquial voice of the past that made her so familiar? 'You don't recognise me, I suppose. You've aged. I haven't.'

'Are there any other cards, I wonder?'

'I undid one button and you ran. Are you going to run again?'

'I think I shall look elsewhere.'

'Refusal complicates everything. "Yes" never takes long; "no" lasts forever. You refused to be young; I refuse to be anything else. You left me in the garden among the roses and they never fell.'

'You must excuse me.'

'But can you excuse yourself? *Quis custodiet*, isn't that the question?'

'Then again, if they must, there are those who ask for whom the bells tolls.'

'Do you find you get out of breath when you run?'

'Should I run to find out? The best dogs are those that sleep.'

'In order to sleep, do they have to lie?'

Gilbert took Horace into the *patio* and waited for his *rigatoni*. Was there ever a poet who used less mortar in his masonry? The words fitted as snugly against each other as the great stones the Incas laid; yet, in Horace's case, the courses could be alchemized into fluency and the syllables run like sand in an hour-glass, each grain clean and distinct from its neighbour in unjostling felicity. The failed candidate never ceased to take once again the papers he had taken but once.

Out of courtesy, Gilbert winced, here and there, at the Loeb's choice of English, but he would not gratefully have dispensed with the *en regard* opportunity. The beauty of the verse, which made no effort to be beautiful, primed Gilbert's impatient hunger with an ancient grace: how appetising to admire the poetry of a poet who was not himself admirable! Horace too had thrown away his shield, nor did he, like Archilochos, prate of acquiring a new one; yet he had made cowardice as respectable as he made respectability louche. Horace was a fellow-traveller with whom anyone might choose to travel; entertaining no great hopes of the voyage and *arriviste* as he might be, he attached small importance to arriving. By making light of everything, he turned the burden of life into hand-baggage. His euphonious sighs and smiles did not lead him to enlarge the commonplace with a solemn lens or engorge it with penny-a-lining prolixity. *Basta!* That was quite enough food for thought: it was a relief for Gilbert when the *rigatoni*, with a wasp-waisted *mezzo litro rosso*, was brought to him (a little disappointingly) by the wall-eyed girl. At the same time, a bustle of other *pensionnaires*, who had timed a mini-bussed morning with precision, dispersed to their several metal seats.

'Are you English by any chance?'

'Whether by chance or by design,' Gilbert said, 'I am.'

'I have a conundrum for you.'

'Thank you,' Gilbert said.

'Because take a perfect cone. Slice it in a perfect section, straight across. Are you with me?'

'Let us allow that I am not against you,' Gilbert said.

'Schoolmaster? Now, having made your section, answer me this: is the circle at the top of the lower portion greater than that at the base of the upper? Hotchkiss.'

'No, I'm afraid not. Masterman.'

'Is my name. Basil.'

'Oh I see. I use to know a Hotchkiss.'

'My brother probably. I've got several. Younger, older. People often find they know one of us. Is it or isn't it?'

'Is that the conundrum?'

'That's the conundrum. Because consider: in an ideal section how could it be that the bottom of one half should not fit exactly on top of the other? This has been bothering me all morning at the Devil's Bridge, *Ponte di Diavolo*, have you seen it?'

'Nor yet know of its existence,' Gilbert said. How comfortable it proved to resume his gown! 'Why should it bother you?'

'Because, look you, if the circumference of every section, wherever cut, is identical in its dimensions with what lay below it, the cone cannot in logic taper to a point or fatten to a base. All cones become cylinders. You should go.'

'Zeno's spear whirrs and whirrs but never comes to its mark.'

'Indeed. Meaning?'

'We are all immortal, but only for a time.'

'I'm afraid I've annoyed you,' Hotchkiss said.

'I'm afraid you have.'

'May I ask why?'

'I have come a long way to get away from myself and find that, despite all my devious detours, you remind me that I am the same man I came away with. How should the messenger not be as vile as his message? Compare the dancer and his dance.'

'A classicist!'

'Indeed.'

'Harry.'

'Gilbert.'

'Is the brother you used to know probably. Much older than I.'

'Your conundrum is hardly Zenonian,' Gilbert said. 'A section has no depth, hence of course the circumferences are identical.'

'I really only wanted a chat. Forgive me.'

There followed a pork chop with wet *spinaci*, a whiff of Gorgonzola and a pear in red wine with a husky flavour of cinammon. Offered the coffee he would have liked by his leaning-over-backwards neighbour, Gilbert chose to hurry to his car. He drove to Viareggio, quoting an air from Turandot as he passed Puccini's house (Gilbert's god was an unsleeping examiner for whom one never stopped writing). He trudged down the beach, infected with gloom by youthful noises from the sea. Since hedonism had an alibi, on what calculus, he asked himself, did he appropriate a dry, untidy dune and oblige himself to endure the happiness of others? To his right, a fisherman was burying the corked hafts of two rods, having buttressed them against a lidded basket of woven green plastic. The crowded sea sipped at the stretched lines and hung its pale vestiges, briefly, briefly, on them. Had Virgil a phrase for such temporary water?

Gilbert's doze supplied what his ferreting mind could not: '*Stillantia*'. What should he do with it when he found it on the tip of his tongue? How many times did one not frown at the loss and feel triumph at the recovery of what, once repossessed, had no useful purpose? In his dream, it was she, skimpy as water, who gave him the word; and he woke, with a hot shiver, to that tritest of fantasies, reality. The fisherman was gone and in his place there lolled a Latin mother to whom her luridly sunglassed, yellow-bucketed boys were traipsing sloppy samples of salt-water. A man, cut off at the knees by splashing sand, lugged a wide basket along the holidaymakers: *Bombolini, gelati, aranciate!*'

The heat worked coldly on Gilbert. He went for the coffee from which Hotchkiss *frère* had deterred him. Although the only English newspaper in the bar was the D.T. he had had for breakfast the morning he left Surrey, he could not resist bending the pages for one more look at Tuesday. Then he bought *Paese Sera*.

The red sun was hanging like a low target over the long-shadowed promenaders as he drove back towards his evening meal. He passed the lit pumps where Mario had played his old trick; a small boy was pissing to steam the weeds by the roadside, but there was no sign of the peculating *pompista*. Was he turning white in honour of the kitchen? When someone cheated you, he took something of you with him and left something of himself behind: the personal touch.

Gilbert lay down on his bolstered bed, penitential in the cage of shadows from the shuttered side window. When he heard the summons of crockery, he went and looked down, as cautiously as if it were forbidden, and saw Mario, scrubbed up, with a knife in one hand, the other arm sleeved in a drooping silver fish as thick as a porpoise. What omens could be drawn from the guts which the cook unstrung and let fall, with a surprising rattle, into the zinc dustbin? Even at a very late stage in Roman life, when the *mos maiorum* had lost its solemn hold, the augurs could declare what the gods forbade more certainly than they could announce what they favoured. The last vestige of divinity was the existence of the negative, Gilbert wanted to say to someone (Percy Porritt, probably, who might have had the decency not to shrug).

It was still warm enough to eat under the flexed bulbs in the patio. Having leaned out to be sure that he would not be the first at table, Gilbert walked to his place, *Paese Sera* under his arm, like a regular. Would Hotchkiss have a fresh conundrum to offer as *hors d'oeuvres*? Revising conceivable snubs quite acclimatised Gilbert. However, before he was called upon to select his barb, a woman appeared; her evening heels made a little stir in the gravel. She stood for a moment under the rusty hoop between path and patio and then, with a winning rumple of her dark brow, she walked to Hotchkiss's table.

'Is this all right, do you know?'

'I'm sure it's fine.'

She had put a book on the table, next to her quiver of *grissini*: *Roman Holidays*.

Gilbert sipped his *minestrone* slowly, as if his appetite, which had been so strong, were now for something else entirely. Was she a girl or was she a woman? She had a kind of pleasantness which was more woman than girl; some remembered experience had marked, yet not creased, her nice forehead and lent a hint of amusement to the not quite symmetrical eyes (one unplucked brow was canted a little higher than the other). Gilbert finished his soup only a minute or two before she did. Others had come to dress the tables with their conversation and stopped to tell each other where they had been all afternoon. Hotchkiss, with a distant salute, joined a quartet who unfolded many maps and had trouble resuming the right creases when their *minestrone* came. Gilbert's neighbour cast no casual line to adjacent company; she sat with her neat knees together under the pierced metal table and waited for the next course. It pleased her, he thought (as it pleased him), not to advertise for conversation.

Mario knew how to make an entrance. He advanced with a sort of slow rush and had to duck his white hat under the metal arch over the path which had brought him from the kitchen. His gleaming forearms bracketed an oval dish domed with a silver lid. Too virile to stagger, he declared the succulent weight of the fish only by the rigidity of his muscles. Having signalled to the wall-eyed girl ('Angelina') to bring a side-table close to the quartet whose maps were so embarrassingly inflated, he revealed the size (and savour) of the next course with a clean lift and twist of the lid so that not a drop of its sweat fell back in the dish. The fish was chintzed with herbs and sliced tomatoes and fronds of greenery. Which emperor was it who had a Caprese fisherman's face scrubbed raw with the abrasive mullet which the guileless man had scaled the cliff to bring him as a gift?

Mario wiped the rim of the plate he set before Gilbert's neighbour and lingered to be generous with *un po' piu di salsa*. She returned him a portion of the humour which lodged her so nicely between girlishness and womanhood. Gilbert heard the murmur of her Italian and he winced, but

189

slightly, at the ingratiating modesty of the cook's reply. It was a seasoning which had been denied to the common dish. Mario stood, with his arms folded, and watched while she took her first taste. She liked it.

Gilbert's portion was wetter than he would have chosen and he did not finish the thick potatoes. She did, and opened Finlay's book and held it down there to read a few pages, without ever looking up, while the plates were cleared. After the *flan*, which was spooned in generously bent slices from another broad oval dish, Mario came from the kitchen and stood there, just shy of the metal arch, as people began to leave. Unhatted, he gave those who could rise to them a chance to drop him their Italian compliments.

Gilbert moved his chair as she did and said, 'I know him.'

'Excuse me?'

'Are you American?'

'Isn't that allowed? Who do you know?'

'Yardley. I taught him.'

'Yardley.'

'You're reading his book.'

'You taught him?'

'By no means everything he knows,' Gilbert said. 'He now knows more than I do. Was it Domitian who scrubbed the fisherman's face raw with the fish he brought him?'

'I think so. So did Tacitus, didn't he?'

'You must be a teacher.'

'An American who knows something everyone used to know. And a woman too. That's pretty rare, right?'

'Not at all. Not in the least.'

'And you – you're a teacher who *lies*?'

'They're not rare. If you're not a teacher, what are you? And will it go with a cup of coffee in the *caffè* in the square?'

'You want to get out of here? Did I say I wasn't a teacher?'

'My name is Gilbert Masterman.'

'Amanda Keller. I am a sort of teacher and also a sort of publisher. Nothing that won't go with a cup of coffee.'

She went ahead of him past where Mario was sentinel.

Gilbert waited like a husband while Amanda listened, with her favourite ear, to what the cook had to say. Gilbert's indifference seemed to burn the soles of his feet; looking up, he hopped with patient discretion and, like a procrastinating consul, gazed at the stars. '*Molto buono*,' he said to the cook, when his turn came. The words fell like reluctant buttons into the offertory plate after a dull sermon.

Amanda was a little shorter than he, even in her heels, but her stride was at least as long as his and she took him, without noticing it, more briskly across the *piazza* than his usual pace. He was not breathless when they sat under the awning of cheap music in the *Caffè Lombardo*, but he felt something unusual in his chest. It might only have been hope.

'What sort of teacher,' he said, while twisting for the waiter who was already on his way, 'and what sort of publisher?'

'A small university press. Very small. Have you ever heard of Arkansas? That small.'

'We've hardly met,' he said, 'and already you make it seem I've made a bad impression. That's very generous of you. I did geography. I've heard of Arkansas; I've heard that's where Arkansans come from.'

She said, 'Gilbert, huh?'

'*Espresso*? With a liqueur?'

'Liqueur?' she said. 'Maybe not tonight. And you? What university do you teach in? Oxford?'

'No such luck, no such qualifications. I'm a schoolmaster alas. That's where I taught young Yardley. All but middle-aged Yardley as he is now.'

'He does make a few mistakes,' she said.

'They're probably mine. For instance?'

'He says Ovid was in exile in the Crimea.'

'He's not *that* wrong, is he?'

'Wrong is wrong,' she said. 'Have I lost you?'

'I find I like you very much,' Gilbert said. 'I really do. Is that all right with you?'

She laughed and said, 'Damn right it is!' The waiter was

back with the coffee. 'I'll tell you what: *due Vecchia Romagna*. What the heck? Cross between a proof-reader and a scold, that's me.'

'You teach what?'

'This is where I plummet in your estimation. Classics. Wait for it: in translation. Can you possibly still like me?'

'Ovid, for instance.'

'Ovid. Virgil. Propertius is coming through on the rails.'

'I'm old-fashioned,' he said, 'I prefer Ovid to Propertius. Less of that damned sincerity. Are you an actress at all? There's something about the way you move your head, something . . . *practised*.'

'My mother was an actress,' she said.

'So she was,' he said.

'Listen, while there's still time to say it, I like you too. I always tell myself it's going to be great alone, after all that academic community stuff, but is it? Sure it is. But not that! Are you a widower by any chance?'

'I never got round to it,' he said.

'What? Killing your wife?'

'Marriage. I lacked the Ovidian facility.'

'He did it three times, didn't he? Marry, I mean. Or was it twice?'

'We must check with Yardley,' Gilbert said.

Amanda's laugh started and stopped, like a well-turned compliment. 'I'll tell you what I think about Ovid. I think he liked it out there on the Pontic shore. What do you say he sent the *Tristia* back to Rome, all wet with Euxine tears, in order to make Augustus feel good? He only ever wanted to please.'

'Yes,' Gilbert said, 'undisclosed sources may well indicate that the local people thought him a cheerful sort of cove. Didn't his landlady speak of his dreading a recall to Rome? How could an unaffected man like that want to live in a big city?'

'You're kidding,' she said. 'The straight face! I love it. But why not? The guy wrote *Metamorphoses*, didn't he? He knew about changes.'

'I like the way you leave out the article,' Gilbert said. 'That's neat.'

'You evidently know the jargon all right,' she said.

'But rarely use it out of school. If Juvenal wasn't a moralist, more a stylish trope-hound, as the latest research suggests, why shouldn't Ovid be one? A moralist, I mean. Changing places is all the rage these days.'

How easy and how sweet it was to prattle out there under the murmurous silence which replaced *Volare* and similar musical flights as midnight knocked twelve times on the city's clocks! They sat, Gilbert and Amanda, and nursed their new and quiet friendship. It was a baby which would certainly not wake them in the night.

He wanted the walk across to the *Pensione Tiberio* to be as long as Percy Porritt's Easter sermon, but it seemed as short as 'Jesus wept'. He said, 'Are you here tomorrow?'

She said, 'I didn't come all this way to leave right away.'

'The *Ponte di Diavolo*,' he said. 'They speak well of it. It's in the hinterland somewhere. I have a car. Will you come?'

She said, 'You don't have to do this.'

'Why else would I do it?'

'Ten o'clock.'

'We could take a picnic.'

'Gilbert, you know what you are?'

'I do, and as long as you don't . . .'

'You're a treat. A British treat. Quote me. Goodnight.'

He had the AA map on the bed in the morning before the sun had time to pitch its stripes across it and, remanded to feeling in his faded pyjamas, he sat there planning her surprises. When the wall-eyed Angelina brought him his breakfast, he looked at her in grateful reproach; her routine climb deprived him of the chance to sit in the patio and not expect to see what he was waiting for. How lucky he was, he told himself, that she was so much younger than he: Amanda! But how much?

'Do you mind shorts?'

'Shorts? They seem a wise idea. I wish I could join you in them.'

'Go put some on.'

'As Mr Kipps might say, I don't carry them,' he said. 'I'm quite accustomed to being hot and uncomfortable.'

'Kipps or Chips? We should buy you some.'

'You and who else?' he said. 'H. G. Wells' haberdasher: Kipps.'

'You slept well,' she said. 'I can see that.'

'*Vecchia Romagna*,' he said. 'I've checked the road and I think I can promise you that we're going to get lost.'

'Listen, a lot of people have told me to do that. But first, we have to go get that picnic. I stole a knife from my breakfast tray, and I hope you did too. Oh well, you can always share mine. This is strictly Dutch, OK? If we each put ten thousand in the kitty, we can shop till we pop.'

They pooled their funds and their vocabulary in the little *Supermercato* and then they drove out past the Shell station and turned northwards. Having lowered the canvas roof of the Renault, Gilbert was glad when shadows puddled the road into the hills. The ease of their conversation in the *caffè* made him less easy now; he did not dare to presume on it, but he was pained by her failure to be more fluent than he was. She appeared content simply to be his passenger; when she turned her head here and there, her sunglasses mirrored more images than he chose to see. He had the impression that she was photographing the landscape for people who were more important to her than he was. Who, after all, was not?

'Who's your favourite,' she said. 'Your *preferito*?'

'My favourite what?'

'Among the Romans. Who would you choose to be, if you had the chance?'

'Goodness!' he said.

'Not many of them you'd accuse of that, are there?'

'What kind of books do you publish?'

'Have you got a proposal? Propose! We have a small

budget; we pay lousy royalties; we do a few nice books for a few nice people. What have you always wanted to say?'

'Nothing a University Press would choose to print. Lepidus. I should like to ghost his memoirs for him. The Abbé Siéyès of the second set of triumvirs. One of the few Romans who found even third place a little too demanding and, I guess, was happy to accept the quiet life which Ovid had thrust upon him.'

'Lepidus! We can do better than that, surely? How about Gallus? He at least had some talent, didn't he?'

'He didn't know he had suicide waiting for him, but if I had to play the part, presumably I'd have to. Is there a Roman woman you'd like to have been?'

'How about Clodia?'

Gilbert said, 'A little racy, wasn't she?'

'Gilbert, you're not going to be a prude on me, are you?'

'I'm an English schoolmaster. Be warned, but don't be gone.'

'We are on holiday. Lighten up. We both could. Imagine being loved by Catullus. Then again, imagine treating him badly. The Genius and the Goddess, right? Imagine being the bitch of bitches.'

'I can't see you doing that. Huxley. I lent it to someone once. And never got it back. Half-calf.'

'Why go all the way back to ancient Rome and be myself? I don't know Huxley. OK, you think I should mother the Gracchi, don't you? Gilbert, give me a break: don't file me under G for Good before I even have a chance to have a good time.'

'Perhaps I don't like the idea of Cicero making a fool of you.'

'Gilbert, you truly needn't look after me. He was crazy about her. He just couldn't cut it. You seriously never married? Why?'

'*Ponte di Diavolo*,' he said. '*Giù in fondo!*'

She looked at him as if he had tripped some secret understanding between them. Glad to be practical, he parked the car on the verge and came round to open her door. Her eyebrows went up. 'Why are we getting out? Do we have something we have to do?'

'Walk over it,' he said. 'I wouldn't really want to be an ancient Roman. I'd sooner be a Housman, or Winckelmann. Winckelmann.'

'And know you were going to be murdered? Do you know why the chicken crossed the road?'

The inconvenient bridge had grass between its steep stones. Its high hoop rose in an arch too acute for regular use; no recent wheel had smudged the moss. Gilbert and Amanda trudged to the peak and looked down, as if it mattered, at the rocky river-bed beneath. With a shrug of agreement, they went on and descended, less steeply, to the sunless farther side.

'Why did it? Cross the road?'

'Because it wanted to leave Poland. Winckelmann! Today one of the great unread, or am I unright?'

'I've never been to Trieste,' he said.

'That reminds me of the one about Moshe Dayan.'

'I'm thinking of going. Would you like to come? Moshe Dayan?'

'I have a few weeks and I've never seen Ravenna. OK, these two women meet in the street in Tel Aviv. One says to the other, "I never slept with Moshe Dayan." "What do you know?" says the other one. "Neither did I. Small world!" ' She saw Gilbert not laughing. 'Forget it. After all, who goes to Trieste? Have I fallen with a bump in your estimation? I have. Bad timing; my speciality.'

'What can we do about that? Anything? Moshe Dayan was . . . OK, I'm sorry: I've blown it. My credibility. So, back to ancient Rome. Fast. Tell me something: why is the Adriatic a separate sea? Who gave it that kind of status, and why?'

'It's also masculine,' Gilbert said. 'Hadria. The only noun in Latin I can think of which is masculine and ends in "a".'

'How about Cinna?' she said. 'Or Cota. What about Cotta? And isn't there *poeta*! Cinna the *poeta*!'

196

'*Poeta* is common, like *incola*. And not proper. I know there's *something* unique about Hadria. But evidently not . . .'

'Why did he go there? Your friend Johann. Trieste. Why?'

'To be murdered perhaps. Did he find something intolerable in an aesthetic ideal which gave him so heightened a sense of life that, finally, he could not really live at all?'

'Gilbert, you're truly an education. Even your questions are answers. You don't need pupils; you need copyists.'

'A cook's knife in his guts. Did he know – because don't we always know? – it would all *tourne mal*? You're not cold, are you?'

'That's not my reputation,' she said. 'Why is it the Devil's Bridge, do we know?'

'It's a hunchback, isn't it? There's something . . . disturbing in its asymmetry. It seems to stand for something diabolical.'

'Gilbert, the trouble you take over things!' She clapped dry moss from her hands. 'I bet you write a lot in the margin when you mark student's work, don't you?'

'Only if they haven't made too many mistakes. We only seriously want to correct what's already pretty well all right.'

'You think he was gay?'

'But never skittish. No. That's something no one thinks himself when alone and I think of the great J. as sublimely alone.'

'Poor man.'

'Yes, he was also that. Most of his life. In fact, if he hadn't been, and hence obliged to the servitude which poverty entails, unless you're willing to live in a tub, he might never have been in Trieste at all. They say he was acting as a courier, perhaps on some secret mission for the authorities in Vienna. That could be why he had more cash on him than he knew how to hide. It doesn't matter whose money you have in your pocket, does it? Its presence gilds you. You know what is wonderful, and alarming?'

197

'Why else did I come to Europe?'

'The statue he admired most, the Laocoon (God knows entirely why), what was it about? The man who warned the Trojans against that bloody horse. He was right, and hence unforgivably wrong: never stand in the way of history and wave your arms. Apollo sent a couple of snakes to kill him, and his sons. Divine justice in the German style. Do I synopsise correctly?'

'Like a master.'

'You know what puzzles me?'

'Out with it, Gilbert.'

'How did three sculptors co-operate on the monstrous thing? Think how rare that kind of troika is in art history, and yet Johann – and he was not alone, was he? – thought almost as well of the Laocoon as of the Apollo Belvedere. Apollo, Apollo! No wonder Dionysus armed the cook!'

'Gilbert, you're making my trip. You're truly making my trip.'

'Be careful, Amanda; you'll encourage me to overreach myself.'

'I'll certainly try,' she said. 'Let's picnic in the hills. Maybe there'll be enough wind for us to throw caution to it. What do you say?'

Jesus wept! How fast the day went! Already, already by the time they reached San Gemignano, the sun was slipping down the far side of the sky which, like the hard bridge they had crossed, seemed asymmetrical: long in the morning, short in the afternoon. To Gilbert's apologetic relief, the tilted village had no towering lure, none of the tall rivalries which brought the videoed buses to its homologue, San Gimignano. He and Amanda were alone among the chickens, the roasting peppers, the strung maize, the sizzle of flies, the ratcheting cicadas. What was there on that bright hillside that Virgil could have not scanned?

Back in the car, she said, 'This has been so great.'

'Is it over then?'

198

'So far, so great. Gilbert, you're also a flirt.'

'Not my reputation.'

'You are also a flirt. It's truly thoughtful of you.'

'I've never thought about it.'

'You're strictly Silver Age really, aren't you? You'd be positively rococo if you dared. Is something wrong?'

'Something is not wrong exactly, but something is certainly . . . lacking. In a word, petrol.'

'Gas. You're out of gas?'

'I rather hoped you might be with me. I'm afraid so. I've been swindled. And what's more, I knew it, I *knew* it.'

'Johann comes again.'

'That damned cook. He gave me short measure.'

'The *cook* gave you gas?'

'He also doubles as a petrol-pump attendant.'

'Great-looking,' Amanda said. 'Don't you agree?'

'Reluctantly.'

'A silent star. Ramon Navarro. *The* Latin Lover! What do we do?'

'We roll,' Gilbert said. 'If we're lucky, and we seem to be.'

'Hills do use up a lot of gas,' Amanda said.

'Don't defend him,' Gilbert said. 'He's guilty. I saw him cheating me. Ramon Navarro was Mexican, wasn't he?'

They rolled through the hooked bends in a sequence of gravelly *rallentandi* and moaning accelerations. It was sweet to feel, in tandem, the suction of the earth as it towed them to the valley. They coasted down the last hard crest of the road into a petrol station.

'Do you want me to talk to him?' Amanda said. 'I'll talk to him. The cook. You want me to give him hell?'

'I do *not* want you to.' He watched the numbers on the new dial. 'It's too late anyway. And I'm not having you with a knife in your ribs.'

'Least of my fears! Sometimes a woman can do something a man can't.'

'Very often,' Gilbert said. 'If not invariably.'

As they drove past the Shell station and threaded the city

gate, Amanda looked at him with a smile which seemed, after all the things he had said, to appreciate what he had not. There was something delicate in her condescension, but his reticence also commissioned a certain boldness. 'You seriously live alone?'

'I have my moments of levity,' he said.

'Too many maybe.' The words were less kind than the lips which delivered them. 'You make light of yourself, but you're not too light really, are you?'

'You're cruel enough to be observant.'

'I'm not cruel at all,' she said. 'Not before I get to know people anyway.'

'And when they get to know you?'

'You've given up on women, Gilbert, is that how it is?'

'Not really,' he said. 'To give up something suggests having been its possessor.'

'Is "give up" what I said?'

'Here we are,' he said. 'It feels as if we were back at school. Thanks for the outing. Thanks for your company.'

'Gilbert,' she said, 'are you bidding me farewell? Are you afraid of being seen in my company? Is the evening, in a word, over? You know what you're like?'

'Similarity is a sorry condition,' he said. 'What?'

'Something out of Henry James.'

'Not one of his sentences, I hope. One of his sentences? Too long, too full of qualifications and dependent clauses? Do I thank you for that?'

'I don't know who you should thank, but don't try to be offended with me, because I really like you. You really want to turn and run, don't you?'

'I really want not to,' he said, 'but I'm a little old for schoolboy embarrassments. Blushing is a sad thing in a man over fifty. They put an L on my birthday cake.'

'Why did they do that?'

'You can guess,' he said.

'Roman fifty!'

'You've guessed. But you're wrong, of course. It was L for learner.'

'I've made you sorry for yourself. I apologise; I shouldn't have. We are going to have dinner together, aren't we? You don't truly want not to flaunt our relationship, do you? I can't believe it's gone far enough in your mind to require *discretion*. I dare not even suspect you of purposes that diabolical!'

Gilbert said, 'To an alarming degree you make me hate myself. I wish I were almost anyone but the large, bald person I am.'

'I never noticed you were that person,' she said. 'I promise you! Gilbert . . .'

He was making a more complicated procedure of locking the car than the manufacturers would have wanted to advertise. 'I once had an unfortunate experience,' he said. 'The unfortunate thing being that it meant little to me at the time and a great deal since.'

'We all have those,' she said. 'Bet you! Take what's unique to market and the guy always tells you they're a dime a dozen.'

'You're very kind,' he said.

'I'm thirty-seven years old, Gilbert. Are you afraid of me?'

'You? No.'

'It?'

'It?'

'Don't be innocent; you're not innocent. Are you afraid I want something from you that maybe you can't deliver? You'd like to be Catullus, but you're afraid you're Cicero, is that the problem?'

'I'm prose not poetry, that's true.'

'Gilbert, let's get something straight: no one has asked you to marry them, OK? I only want to have dinner and maybe some coffee afterwards. You owe me a *Vecchia Romagna*, you know. Pay up.'

'With pleasure.'

'If we can have some of that too, why not let's do it?'

'It's only because that is what I should like that I give every sign of not wanting it.'

'You're very chivalrous,' she said. 'Only you can't quite bring yourself to tell the truth, can you?'

'The truth is always what can't be told,' he said. 'Why else would people swear to tell it?'

He climbed to his room in eager reluctance, knowing that he would be waiting for himself there. Alone, he donned the double weight of himself, like an unnecessary coat, and gazed after the waning day through the rouged shutters. Memory was a suitcase in which one folded things for which, when it came to it, one would almost certainly never have a use. What did it matter how the shadows had lain across the *Ponte di Diavolo*? How many chickens were needed to give San Gemignano its clucking nervousness? Why *Poland*?

His volume of Tacitus did not contain the story about Domitian and the mullet. If he had found it there, what difference would it have made to what? He heard voices below and was frowning at their unintelligible fluency – the jumbled conjunctions and petty lacunae which plunged off again into chuckles and easy currency – before he began to attach her, and him, to any of the speeches. It was as if new batteries were needed to bring the play of dialogue cleanly to his ears. He did not want to hear what was being said; he wanted to hear that nothing was. The rustle of conversation was a gentle assault that caused him to look at his watch, to consider his wardrobe, to taste that cocktail of dry dread and sweet apprehension which the actor mouths before a first night: without its proleptic threat, he would dry on stage or be surprised by his costume. He took it as a hard kindness that the cook and Amanda should rehearse their lines under his window.

Would she be waiting for him? Or would she time her arrival in the *patio – che bella*! – with his own? What would she have decided about dinner before leaving the decision to him?

Gilbert put on a ruffled shirt and a black jacket over grey flannels. Were silver-buckled shoes too fancy for a *trattoria*?

He consented to find self-mockery in a measure of pre-
ciosity: he dressed up so that Amanda might have the
chance to be indulgent. How had the great Johann been
dressed, he had to speculate, when he made his fatal date,
if date there was, with the smiler who knifed him? He
might well have worn a ruffled shirt; it was unrewarding to
imagine his nether garments. Nankeen breeches? The
conversation two steep floors below came to a stretched
end; Gilbert did not need to look down in order to see that
the speakers had lengthened the line of chat between them
and that their final, louder courtesies, conducted at several
paces, also whispered of conceivable resumption. Where
had she gone now? Where had he? Where had Johann first
met the man who cooked his goose? When did he, the old
undergraduate dared to wonder, first goose his cook?

Gilbert took Horace's *Satires* as a priest might his Missal
and went downstairs. The *cittadini* were walking under the
trees which now garrisoned the ramparts. Gilbert was
standing by the *pensione* door, wondering whether there
was time (or inclination) to make a circuit, when he saw
Mario, in his whites, gazing at a BMW motorcycle which
had been wheeled onto the path leading to the kitchen.

'*Buona sera, dottore!*'

'You do me too much honour,' Gilbert said. '*Non sono
dottore.*'

'You had a good day, yes?'

'I had an excellent day.'

'I hear.'

'How long will it take me to walk round the walls, *far un
giro, quanto tempo?*'

'*Quarantacinque minuti?* It depends how fast you walk.
You not go before dinner, I don't think. After dinner,
maybe. Before you sleep.'

'You speak good English.'

'I speak bad English. In Birmingham. I work six months
in Birmingham. But I never walk round it. Take too long.
You have an English car?'

'No, I have a French car actually.'

'English cars no good. Why?'

'I don't necessarily admit the premiss.'

'Why no good?'

'Some are; I just don't happen to have one.'

'You are hungry? I have something good for you tonight. She is very nice.'

'I'm sorry?'

'*L'Americana. Molto gentile. Simpatica. La signora.*'

'Oh yes, yes; she's . . . very nice indeed.'

'You take her for a ride in your French car.'

'Yes, we had a very pleasant time. I think I'll take a stroll.'

'*Professore, no*? She tell me.'

'She is; I'm not. *Maestro, di scuola, niente di più, io.* How long will it take me, do you think, to get to Trieste, by car? Can I do it in a day?'

'You should stay here. Trieste, Trieste is not really Italy, you know, and the food . . . the food is not so good in Trieste. You stay here. You teach me English; I teach you Italian. You save money on the petrol too.'

Gilbert said, 'I save money on the petrol by going to another petrol station.'

Mario touched Gilbert on the arm with his clean hand. There was a gold ring on the little finger, with a gleam of dark hair spilling over it. 'The English sense of humour. I like it.'

'Do you just?'

'You want to walk around the town after dinner? I take you. I show you. I take you both, yes?'

'That depends. On . . .'

'On her? No! Men decide things. Women want them to. We decide; she comes. I bet you.'

'We'll see,' Gilbert said.

'*Le piace la musica?*'

'Some music.'

'She likes music.'

'If you say so.' Gilbert walked towards the *piazza*. 'I daresay you're right.'

'You are not married, *dottore*?'

'Not at the moment,' Gilbert said.

'Not at the moment! I am married at the moment. Three children. Three! First one cries, then the other. Then the third. Then my wife. That's why I work so hard. You walk; I work. You come back, it's all ready for you. You no go to Trieste, not a nice place. Not like this. *Impari l'italiano, Signore, con Mario; eccomi, Signore, il tuo maestro, e Lei il mio! Amici! Amici! Perchènon dobbiamo approfittare reciprocamente della nostra occasione? Sono sincero, Signore. Mi credi?* We talk about it, yes?'

'Later, possibly,' Gilbert said.

'*Ma dove va*? Why you run away?'

'I'm not running. This isn't running. This is walking, rather sedately in my view. I want to buy a postcard.'

Mario put his hands on his hips and shook his head in a parody of fondness. Gilbert walked away, a pedestrian Orpheus determined not to look back. He kept his resolve until he had touched the carousel of postcards as if it were a sanctuary. When he looked back, Mario was moving his head here and there in conversation with the BMW. He waved at Gilbert and did not disappear.

'Good evening.'

'Oh, good evening,' Gilbert said. 'I didn't know you were still here. We went to your bridge.'

'What bridge was that?'

'The *Ponte di Diavolo*. You mentioned it to me yesterday. Very unusual.'

'I've moved,' Hotchkiss said.

'Have you really? Why have you done that?'

'To tell you the truth, since we don't know each other, I've been invited to stay with a local archaeologist.'

'Oh how very nice!'

'Yes, it is, in his house. It's rather a stroke of luck.'

'It certainly sounds it,' Gilbert said. 'Remember me to your brother when you speak to him. Harry.'

'I shan't,' Hotchkiss said.

'You're not on speaking terms? I'm sorry. Why?'

'He's dead. He was murdered.'

'*Hotchkiss*? When?'

'Not so long ago. In Algeria. He went to look at some ruins. And ended up being one himself. Stabbed.'

'I'm most frightfully sorry. I never heard.'

'Probably mistaken identity.'

'That's true of most of us,' Gilbert said. 'I must write.'

Amanda came down the stairs to the checkered hall as Gilbert was re-closing the green gate of the *Pensione Tiberio*; when he turned, there she was about to step outside. She was wearing a rather stiff, pleated blue skirt with a white shirt and a blue silk waistcoat. A fluffy white stole was looped over her forearms and went behind her. She did look nice. 'Gilbert!' she said. 'What a glutton you are!'

'Glutton? Am I, Amanda? How so?'

'For sightseeing. You've been out. I imagined you in a hot bath.'

'Was that wise? Was it decent?'

'Oh Gilbert,' she said, 'you truly are the best value in town!' Her arm was through his and she was looking up at him; tact seemed to make her shorter. Presumably it was all a matter of shoes. 'Are you as hungry as I am?'

'That's the problem with hedonism, isn't it?'

'Remind me,' she said.

'We have no reliable measure for appetites. Hence we can never calculate what truly gives the greatest happiness to the greatest number.'

'Are you all right, Gilbert?'

'Flawed,' he said, 'but not fatally, I trust. They call damaged goods "seconds", don't they? They're almost certainly right.'

Amanda smiled and then she had to detach herself in order to walk down the narrow concrete, past the kitchen door, to the patio. The droop of white stole behind her back drew attention to her sharp elbows. It seemed to Gilbert that he had known her for a long time. There was a sturdy frailty about her; her back looked to be very trustworthy.

Angelina served them with *pastina in brodo*. There was little call for conversation when drinking soup, but Amanda looked at him keenly over her charged spoon and when she had swallowed the last of the soft pearls, she wiped her mouth and said, 'Gilbert, are you ready for this?'

'Almost certainly not,' he said. 'Am I ready for what?'

'I'd like to make you a proposition.'

'Pray do it slowly. I've waited all my life for one of those.'

'A serious proposition.'

'That sounds like a comedown.'

'You're being naughty. Ravenna. Can I tempt you? OK, you've been, but I'll happily pay my share of the gas. I wouldn't happily do anything else, in fact, and then – here's the pay-off, if pay-off it is – I thought we could go to Venice and catch a boat to Trieste, if there is one, and I bet there is.'

'You've been thinking,' Gilbert said.

'Scheming, you mean. OK, what do you say?' She put her elbows on the table and propped her face closer to his. 'So far so good; you'll grant me that, I hope? I'm hustling you, right? So how often do you get to be hustled? Can it seriously damage your health? What does the surgeon-general say? Have I handled it badly?' Angelina subtracted their used plates. 'Internal evidence says I've handled it badly. Your face. You can't see it.'

'My privilege! On the contrary. It sounded like a very . . .'

'Chose carefully! Adjectives have fire-power.'

'. . . *generous* idea.'

'But then again, you work all year to avoid having to accept the generosity of strangers. Don't shake your head just because I'm right. You'd sooner be alone.'

'I'd sooner not want to be.'

'Who chooses to understudy Garbo, after all, is that it?'

'I used to do Marlene. She was a speciality of mine.

Falling in Love Again/ Never wanted to/ Can't 'elp it! Something, something . . . *And if zey burn zair wings . . .* etcetera!'

'How about I'll be Jannings? A little role reversal, why not? Crack an egg on my head whenever you want to, professor.'

'I'm an old moth, Amanda, not a sacred flame. Don't be taken in. I think you should find another way of getting to Ravenna.'

'I'm not short of those. I just wanted your company. I can see the mosaics just as well in a book. Better, probably.'

'Better, but not so well.'

'Gilbert, I like you. A lot. Can you handle that or can't you? If you're afraid I'm going to ask more of you than you want to give, depend upon it, but what I am *not* going to do is judge you, not I. Every time you reassure somebody, it sounds like a threat, right? Only this isn't.'

Gilbert was looking at Mario, who had brought the silver dish once more into the centre of the *patio*. After Hotchkiss's defection and the departure of his companions, fewer diners were there to turn their heads to admire the cook's dexterity as he doffed its dome. Mario contrived to give the impression that he had prepared more particularly for Amanda, and Gilbert, than for the anonymous clients to whom Angelina administered their portions of roast pork and wet potatoes. The chef himself attended to the table where Gilbert and Amanda had slightly to move apart in order to admit him. He was at once solicitous and correct, in his many-buttoned, wide-lapelled whiteness. That unsmiling courtesy offered them the compliment of discretion. His silence promised the availability, to them, one day, or night, of something spicier than any public menu could spell out.

'He sure knows what he knows, doesn't he?' As Amanda spoke, Mario was coming back with a plate of caramelised *cipollini al forno* in one hand and buttered carrots, with green freckles of parsley, in the other. Amanda smiled at the onions, as if Mario had guessed her little weakness.

However, when Gilbert thumbed the dish politely towards her, she denied the appetite she had feigned. 'They're all yours, Gilbert. Be a pal and cover for me, will you? Don't tell me you don't eat them either. I'll have to put them in my bag, and I don't have a bag.'

'I'll be the bag,' he said.'

'My debt to you is mounting and mounting.'

'Don't worry,' Gilbert said. 'I'll make sure to pay you back. Is this how it's supposed to taste?'

'What? How?'

'The meat. It has a kind of vinegary tang to it, do you notice that?'

'It's . . . it's probably regional. If you want to justify something to yourself, in the culinary domain, try "regional". You want to go to Trieste by yourself, right? You're afraid Johann'll be a no-show if you hit town with a woman. You're not afraid of ghosts; it's people that make you shake.'

'What was the last book you had something to do with?'

'I edited? Do I have a stinging cheek or what? Is there a red patch? Because have you switched tracks! OK, the last book I had anything to do with, as if you really wanted to know, was an anthology of *odium academicum*. Why do people with a whole lot in common always end up knifing each other? Doctor Cain, Professor Abel. Do you have an answer? Gilbert, are you OK?'

'I discovered an old friend of mine was dead this evening.'

'Wait long enough, you'll discover the same about yourself. You think wanting something has to mean you don't deserve it. Well, maybe I don't either, but so what? Let's go on together, Gilberto, what do you say? Let's pretend being grown up can mean something other than too old. I don't ask anything more of you than your company. I can handle loneliness, but I can also do without it, can't you? Hell, look at what we have in common! Why does it have to come between us?'

'I don't deserve you,' he said.

'Damn right. So help yourself. Use both hands. *Carpe noctem*. It implies no just philosophy; nothing has to be radically revised. I'll unsplit that. Revised radically. We happened to find each other; it may not be treasure, but at least it's trove. I'll call you Ben.'

'You are a treasure,' he said. 'You shine.'

'Pretend I'm a bargain. Why not? Listen, in case you're worried; I'll never tell you the story of my life. How about that for a promise? We'll travel hopelessly and we'll arrive as often as we can. Gilbert?'

'It'll be all right.'

'Is it what I said?'

'It's what I ate. It's all coming back to me. I'm sorry.'

Mario came out of the kitchen as Amanda was retreating in a slow two-step with Gilbert along the path past the fuming kitchen door. '*Si sente male?*'

'It'll be all right,' Gilbert said. Mario might have been a medicine man; his appearance was a stimulant. 'Or I shall be, in a minute. As soon as I'm dead. Christopher Mortimer writes . . .'

'*Che cos'ha successo?*'

'I think he had too much sun.'

'*Non imparano mai niente – i professori!*'

'I need to get upstairs,' Gilbert said. 'But I can manage on my own. Truly. *Facilis ascensus*, I don't think.'

He was not sure that he wanted to be left alone, but it pleased him, in his clenched state, to convince her that he would be less embarrassed if he could have his symptoms to himself. When they had reached the checkered floor where Angelina made her daily puddles, he raised his hand in a dumb speech of reassurance and gratitude and then applied it, with drunken care, to the banister and drew himself upwards. 'Go and finish your dinner. Please.'

Amanda said, 'I've held a lot of heads in my time. I'm very willing to hold yours. *Nihil humanum* and stuff like that. No? So how about if I come up later and make sure you're OK?'

'No *Vecchia Romagna stasera!*' he said. 'I do apologise.'

'You do too, don't you? But I forgive you. Take care. And, Gilbert, forgive the indelicacy but . . . don't hesitate to throw up? It's better up than down, you know.'

In the room, alone, he could almost believe that he had blackened his evening for obituary reasons. *In memoriam Henrici Calidaechbasiationis.* Pain declined into polyglot games in him. His second self was there to watch, and not quite applaud, while he tried to imitate a successful impostor. Was it cool or was it hot? The high window was open in front of the shutters. A smell of fish, although there had been none for supper, seeped through the slanted slats. It seemed to require a long walk to close out the threat of another blast from the cook. No symptom was quite enough to determine how he felt; neither sick nor well, nor chilled nor feverish, he was the emptiness in the room.

Plumped on the wide bed, he slid off his silver-buckled shoes. His feet seemed to have put on weight and stood out in the air, bagged in their clocked socks. Did he want to be ill or did he want to take a deep breath and return to Amanda's company? He imagined homage to Johann in his queasy affectation of self-control. He stood up, on those soft feet, and waited, as if at sea, for the pitch or roll which would warn of further trouble. Bicephalous with pity and disdain (one head aching, the other not), he speculated on the durability of his digestion.

Mario's laughter came to him, despite that closed window, like yet another unpalatable recipe. Its carelessness was crueller than cruelty. Gilbert wished himself asleep; he would have jumped gladly, eyes shut, clean into the next day. He wanted to be waking to feeling better; if he could only digest his pain, he would welcome coffee and the rosy rolls on his breakfast tray. This nausea and his inability, for the moment, to attack so intricate a problem as his shirt-buttons were bilious interruptions to a smoother future. Rolling sideways, he tried, as if to amuse someone, to ease his trousers under his hips without lifting himself from the yawning bed. Had there been a spy-hole in the hard wall, he might have seen her and him walking together across the *piazza*. Did Johann double scholarship with espionage? It was an old ransom brains paid to brawn. Dead scholars were not so rare, or always so innocent: Archimedes, stranded on his beach, was done to death by Roman squaddies, under Sergeant Fell, who did not recognise his eminence or know that his calculated sand-castles could have taught them something. 'Touch not my equations,' he cried, when speared. The sergeant postponed solutions with a kick.

God, something hurt! In his dangling shirt, Gilbert wondered if he might not feel better for a walk. Was it Amanda for whom he felt bad or was it – ah speculation! – was it for Mario? Both! Or were both things one? A single knight could threaten two castles. They had put the knife between his shoulder-blades, could they not have spared him the fork? His mind was another stomach, churning with the indigestible; he tried in vain to distinguish the sweet and sour when all was one. *To hen*!

The last of all Greek myths and the most pernicious was Reason, with its orderly vanities. They were walking under the trees. He was admiring her; she him. *Quarantacinque minuti* to make the *giro*. How many hours was that? Would they speak of him or would they not? Gilbert longed for sleep: oh for oblivion! *Obliviscor* and the genitive: a poignant connection with a dagger's thrust. Hotchkiss dead? What was *her* name? *Tumtitty noster amor*. Had Johann wanted to go out that night? Was it desire or scruple that drew him to the disreputable? He was the kind of wise fool who kept his word. They were under the trees, under the trees, under the trees. And what did it matter to Gilbert? Why should Gilbert care? About what, about what? Why should love and fear have the same symptoms? Nature had a vile economy. What did he love? What did he fear? He feared love; he loved fear. Yes? No? The road up and the road down, were they really alike? Discuss.

He felt the knife but he could not see the assassin. It hurt; it hurt. He slumped and stumbled from the bed, with a Cheshire wince of a smile (the only hint of mastery he could muster). Groping in the lit room, he went on a wink – to save the other eye from the same lance – as far as the basin and bent to deliver his message. Assassinated and alone, he had not even the satisfaction of the Latin eyes which had done him down. He was wretchedly alone.

Empty, how had he got back to the bed? How was he there, so much later, to hear the tap on the door which he declined to hear? How, asleep, did he see the twist of the knob and hear the unheard footsteps that came across the marble? She was carrying her shoes like two hollow fish. How did he recognise the perfume she had not had before? In his dream, she had been adjacent, but never on him; his blurted ecstasy came like the flutter of the figures on Mario's pump, a fraudulent flurry and, immediately, blankness. Quintus Horatius Flaccus came and went (*Satires* 1, 5).

'Gilbert. Are you all right?'

'I was.' He wore one hand over an eye. It flattened her. 'What time is it? Am I supposed to ask?'

'I was worried about you. Pretty late. Did you throw up?'

He frowned at the breathing torso on the bed by his chest: *sans* head, *sans* feet. 'I smell something.'

'It's the darkness.'

'He did it on purpose. That damned meat. He knew what he was doing, and why.'

'No, he didn't. Gilbert, he didn't. He didn't.'

'You're smiling.'

'Am I? Let's not get into that.'

His fingers were stung by the freckled blood crumbling on her face. He shifted his body like a piece of furniture that stood between them, and winked at the light he had to turn on, a brass-stalked glass daffodil with a button he fumbled to find. He one-eyed her happy bruises. 'Italian lessons,' he said. 'You've had Italian lessons.'

'Gilbert,' she said, 'can I stay? Can I, with you, tonight? Please. If that helps. Only don't ask me what happened. You know.'

'Fish,' he said. 'You smell of fish. You and Transom.'

'I don't think so.' She stood up. Let her not take off her clothes. Let her, let her not step out of her clothes. Oh the uses of *utinam* and *ne*, both with the subjunctive! How long would it be before she did one thing or another? How long could she do neither and, sweet and sour, do them both?

'You don't want to stay here.'

Like someone taking an airline's advice, Amanda seemed to make sure that she had all her belongings. She even checked her brow with the tip of her forefinger. What was that on her hands? Where had she leaned, what had she grasped, oh, oh, oh, to give her those green bruises? He saw her humped, a-dangle, forked flesh and blood, *Ponte di Diavolo*. She looked at him, to be sure that he was not hers, and then she sniffed, as if to gather the vestige of some last, unseen possession, and said, 'As long as you're all right . . .'

As she disappeared, *ceu fumus in auras*, he raised a promising voice again. 'I'll kill that cook in the morning.'